When a hang-gliding stranger is found fatally injured in the cliffs above Monterey Bay, the investigation into his death becomes a cluttered mess. Professional organizer Maggie McDonald must sort the clues to catch a coastal killer before her family becomes a target . . .

Maggie has her work cut out for her helping Renée Alvarez organize her property management office. Though the condominium complex boasts a prime location on the shores of the Monterey Bay National Marine Sanctuary, aging buildings and the high-maintenance tenants have Renée run ragged. But Maggie's efforts are complicated when her sons attempt to rescue a badly injured man who crashed his ultralight on the coastal cliffs.

Despite their efforts to save him, the man dies. Maggie's family members become the prime suspects in a murder investigation and the target of a lawsuit. Her instincts say something's out of place, but solving a murder won't be easy. Maggie still needs to manage her business, the pushy press, and unwanted interest from criminal elements. Controlling chaos is her specialty, but with this killer's crime wave, Maggie may be left hanging . . .

The Maggie McDonald Mystery

Address to Die for
Scheduled to Death
Dead Storage
Disorderly Conduct
Cliff Hanger

Cliff Hanger

Maggie McDonald Mystery Series

Mary Feliz

LYRICAL UNDERGROUND
Kensington Publishing Corp.
www.kensingtonbooks.com

LYRICAL UNDERGROUND BOOKS are published by
Kensington Publishing Corp.
119 West 40th Street
New York, NY 10018

Copyright © 2019 by Mary Feliz

All Kensington titles, imprints, and distributed lines are available at special quantity discounts for bulk purchases for sales promotion, premiums, fundraising, educational, or institutional use.

Special book excerpts or customized printings can also be created to fit specific needs. For details, write or phone the office of the Kensington Sales Manager: Kensington Publishing Corp., 119 West 40th Street, New York, NY 10018. Attn. Sales Department. Phone: 1-800-221-2647.

Lyrical Underground and Lyrical Underground logo Reg. US Pat. & TM Off.

First Electronic Edition: July 2019
ISBN-13: 978-1-5161-0527-4 (ebook)
ISBN-10: 1-5161-0527-3 (ebook)

First Print Edition: July 2019
ISBN-13: 978-1-5161-0530-4
ISBN-10: 1-5161-0530-3

Printed in the United States of America

For George, without whom there would be no books. Thanks for keeping the mystery and the dreams alive, always.

Acknowledgments

Thanks, as always, to my editors Martin Biro, Rebecca Cremonese, and Jennifer Fisher. And to everyone at Kensington and Lyrical, including those I've not yet met, who have worked to put Maggie's stories into the hands of readers. And to everyone in Sisters in Crime and Mystery Writers of America, fantastic organizations of generous women and men who get it. And to my husband George, who, among all the many other wonders he brings to my life, holds everything together while I spend time with my imaginary friends in Orchard View.

As promised, I also need to thank Amanda Terry for her willingness to proofread nearly all the books in the series. Any errors that remain are mine and mine alone, but readers can thank Amanda for scouring out typos and keeping Maggie's friend Elaine from cleaning her gutters on a daily basis.

Thanks to Michael. His expertise helps me confidently write about my tech-savvy characters. But again, it's all on me when I veer from the possible by mistake or for the sake of the story.

For this book particularly, I'd like to thank the hardworking people of the resort that inspired Heron Beach. Their expertise, patience, and creativity assure the actual location is nothing like the fictional one, except in the unsurpassed setting they share on the shore of Monterey Bay National Marine Sanctuary (MBNMS). The team at the real Heron Beach do their best to keep residents and guests safe, comfortable, content, and able to spend as much time as possible experiencing one of the most amazing wildlife sanctuaries in the world.

I'd also like to thank those who work in all the federal, state, local, and private agencies that protect and explore the sanctuary and surrounding communities. Sometimes referred to as "The Serengeti of the Sea," MBNMS protects more than six thousand square miles of ocean. Designated by the National Oceanic and Atmospheric Administration in 1992, the sanctuary aids in understanding, utilizing, restoring, and maintaining the preserve as a center for research, education, recreation, tourism, commercial fishing, and resource protection.

The preserve offers unique research opportunities in the form of a submarine canyon whose depth rivals that of the Grand Canyon and offers deep-water exploration opportunities just offshore. As engineering breakthroughs make it possible for scientists to explore more of the ocean floor, new species of plants and animals are discovered along with new information that expands our understanding of biology, ecology, acoustics, oceanography, geology, evolution, and many other fields, including space exploration.

I hope it will remain a rich environment for discovery and recreation for many generations. For more information about supporting, visiting, and exploring this amazing resource, visit https://montereybay.noaa.gov.

And finally, if you can read this book, please thank a teacher. If you were able to find this book, please thank a teacher, librarian, or bookstore owner. Without the members of all these professions, I would not be able to do what I do.

I remind readers that this is a work of fiction. I've taken great liberties in creating unique characters who are nothing like the honest and hardworking farmers, agricultural workers, young people, and law enforcement officers of Watsonville and the counties of Santa Cruz and Monterey.

Chapter 1

Packing for a vacation on the central California coast means packing for weather extremes. While the average temperature in June ranges from a comfortable sixty-five to seventy-five degrees, summer daytime temperatures can plummet to fifty degrees or climb into triple digits—sometimes within a 24-hour period. On a typical summer day you're less likely to need your bikini than a warm coat.

From the Notebook of Maggie McDonald
Simplicity Itself Organizing Services

Monday, June 17, Late morning

"Mom, you sure those directions are right?" Fourteen-year-old Brian leaned over the back of the front seat. His sixteen-year-old white-knuckled brother David clutched the wheel and peered into the fog bank. "GPS says this road runs straight into the ocean."

David lifted his foot from the accelerator and hovered it over the brake. The car slowed to a creep. "Seriously?" he said with a hint of panic in his voice. "I can't see a thing. Let me know if your feet get wet and I'll start backing up."

"You're doing great, David," I said to my newly permitted driver. "Up here on the right, you'll turn and take a narrow road out to the condos."

"Narrower than this?" David's voice squeaked a tiny bit as he tried to keep an eye on his mirrors, his speed, the fog-obscured road ahead, and

the deep drainage ditches on either side of a road barely wide enough
for two cars. The speed limit was 40 mph. The speedometer hugged 25.
Luckily, there was no traffic on the rural road flanked by fields growing
strawberries, artichokes, lettuce, and Brussels sprouts.

As we approached the turn, the fog lifted. David easily navigated the
narrow bridge over the slough.

"Blue heron!" shouted Brian as one launched itself from a dead log
partially submerged in the slough. With a few pumps of its massive wings,
it disappeared behind the ridge separating the farmland from Monterey Bay.

I rolled down my window to appreciate the cool salt air. We'd left
oven-like temperatures behind us when we'd left the Bay Area less than
an hour earlier.

Our golden retriever Belle shoved her nose between the headrest and
the window frame for a sniff. Santa Cruz County was home to some
five hundred species of migratory and resident birds. She appeared to be
smelling and identifying each one.

"Ultralight!" shouted Brian again, pointing out the back window.

"That hang-glider thing?" I asked, locating a lime green and shocking
pink oversized kite that looked much like a committee had tried to reverse-
engineer a dragonfly. It roared above us.

"They're like hang gliders with engines," Brian explained. "You don't
need a pilot's license to operate them."

"Don't even think about it," I said in response to the note of anticipatory
glee in his voice. "Ultralight aviation is not included in our summer plans."

"It could be…" Brian began.

"Nope. Not while I'm your mother." I squinted at the aircraft. "Is it
supposed to fly like that? All wobbly?" A sharp explosive sound echoed
through the hills. "Or is there something wrong with the engine?"

David ended our discussion when he pulled the car onto the gravel
shoulder immediately after we drove over a second small bridge. Flexing his
hands and fingers, he turned to me. "Can you drive? That last bit was nuts."

As we changed seats, I shivered. The condominium resort complex
was only three miles from the nearby agricultural town of Watsonville,
but I heard no cars or other sounds of people or civilization. Water lapping
in the slough, the screech of a red-tailed hawk, and the crashing waves
of the still unseen Pacific were the only sounds I could identify. A brisk
wind coming from the ocean, refrigerated by the sixty-degree temperature
of Monterey Bay made my summer outfit of shorts and a T-shirt seem
ridiculous. I grabbed a sweatshirt off the back seat and put it on quickly
before taking a deep breath and restarting the car.

There was no going back and no way I wanted to. The boys were looking forward to their summer vacation at a beach resort, days filled with surfing, skimboarding, hiking, and doing odd jobs. I was committed to helping the condo association management through a contentious transition. The new manager, Renée Alvarez, was a cousin of my best friend, Tess Olmos, who had vouched for Renée's honesty and work ethic.

In exchange for the use of a condo and a small stipend, I would use my professional organizing superpowers to help. The plan was to organize office storage and files, and compile a history of the complex. If time allowed, we'd clear out a few neglected units whose owners had long since abandoned them, unable to sell them or keep up with the taxes, mortgages, and association fees following a market downturn.

It was an idyllic proposition, and I'd agreed to it readily. My husband Max planned to join us every weekend. During the week, he'd commute from our home in Orchard View to his engineering job in Santa Clara while juggling the supervision of several home-remodeling projects that would be easier for construction workers to tackle while the boys and I were out of town.

As we approached the visitor gate, the fog rolled back in, a gust of wind shook the car, and Belle growled. I shivered, but this time it was due to trepidation rather than the chill. I eased the car forward, fighting off the sudden sense that I was heading into unknown and possibly dangerous territory. I shook off the feeling. *Nonsense.* Just because a few of my recent jobs had led to serious trouble for my family and friends didn't mean I was the professional organizer's version of Typhoid Mary. Heebie-jeebies aside, I had every reason to believe we were starting our best family vacation ever.

"Good morning," said the guard, leaning through the drive-up window.

"I'm Maggie McDonald," I said. "Renée Alvarez is expecting us. She said she'd leave a key here in the office."

The guard smiled. "Are you an owner?"

"No, no. I'm working for Renée and the homeowner association this summer. She's giving us the use of a three-bedroom condo. She said she'd leave the key and information packet here for me."

"I'm afraid that only owners are allowed to bring dogs, though I can recommend several good local kennels."

Belle snorted, and I couldn't have agreed with her more. Part of the attraction of taking this underpaid job was the prospect of allowing our golden retriever the freedom of swimming in the ocean and chasing waves, tennis balls, and birds she'd never come close to catching.

"I think Renée said she'd asked the association to make an exception. Is she available at the moment? We can check with her."

A pickup truck pulled up behind me, and I became conscious of holding up traffic. The security guard must have felt the same way. "Tell you what. Pull your car around to the parking spaces. Maybe the boys can walk your dog while you and I straighten this out with Renée."

I followed the instructions. Brian and David took turns holding Belle on a leash outside the building while I sorted out our accommodations. The guard, who had introduced himself as Vik Peterson, handed me a dog biscuit bigger than my hand. "You've got a beautiful pup there," he said, nodding toward the door, outside which Belle sniffed bushes and barked at a rabbit. "Please give her this cookie with my apologies for the confusion. I'll give Renée a ring."

Again, I followed instructions, cheered by Vik's upbeat demeanor and attentive customer service.

"What's up, Mom?" Brian asked as I joined the boys outside. Belle snuffled my hand and took the biscuit. "Are they trying to cancel?"

"I don't think so. The guard is calling Renée right now."

"Should we phone Tess?" David asked. "She set this up, right?"

David was correct, as usual, but I wasn't worried. "Working with a new client can be a bumpy road. If they didn't have a few organizational problems, they wouldn't need me, would they?"

I glanced into the guard station, and Vik waved. When I opened the door, he held up a key.

"I've got the key to your unit," he said, looking triumphant. "I still haven't reached Renée, though." He glanced at his watch. "She's usually the first one here, well before seven o'clock. But her chief lieutenant and head of maintenance says you can go ahead and get settled in."

"Great! Thanks. And Belle?"

"Sorry, no. You wouldn't believe the number of complaints I'd get if I admitted a visiting dog without Renée's say-so."

"I guess we could get groceries and come back, but if Belle doesn't have access, it will sink the deal for me."

"Dogs are welcome at the state beach down the road. You passed it on the way in. You could hang out there while you wait to hear from Renée."

I thought for a moment, considering.

Vik barreled on as though I'd already approved the plan. "Do you have a cell number you can give me? I'll get in touch as soon as I hear from her. I hope she's okay. It isn't like her to be even a few minutes late."

"Do you know where she is? I was under the impression she spent more time on site here than she did at home."

Vik checked his watch and frowned. "Could be anything. There's a first time for everything." He pushed a notepad and pen toward me.

I handed Vik my business card and thanked him again. We all climbed back into the car and were about to set off when Vik opened the office door and called out.

"Your unit is in Building F. Fourth building from the north end of the complex. It's a short hike from the state beach if you want to check it out."

I saluted and put the car in reverse. After a small false start, it looked like the tide was starting to turn on our adventure.

* * * *

The boys had changed into their wetsuits in the picnic area of the state beach. Now they were boogie boarding while Belle chased them and tried to catch waves in her teeth. I checked my phone and my watch. If I didn't move I'd be lulled to sleep by the sound of the waves. I told the boys I'd walk down to the Heron Beach Resort property to check out our unit.

Brian and David had been thrilled when I told them they'd each have their own room for the summer. Our typical Spartan vacation budget meant they normally shared a tent or a room—with mixed results. When one wanted to sleep in, the other would be anticipating a dawn fishing trip. I'd enjoyed summers of overhearing laughter as they whispered to each other past lights-out. Rumbling older voices now conversed well into the night, replacing those early giggles. Mostly, they got along. But proximity also brought fights. Hurt feelings erupted regularly, particularly when they were tired. The three-bedroom condo was a luxury we'd all enjoy.

According to Tess, a third-floor ocean-view unit meant we'd wake up to share our breakfast with chance sightings of surfing dolphins, breaching whales, and playful seals and sea otters cavorting in the waves just steps from the building. It was my idea of paradise.

Wooden staircases over the dunes marked the beach-side entrance to each condo building, and I counted them off until I spotted the sign to Building F half-buried in the dune grass. I climbed the steps and looked for our unit. But when I took the stairs to the top level, the numbers were higher than I'd expected. I checked the key and the unit number again. There was no third-floor, ocean-view unit that matched the key Vik had given me.

I trudged down the stairs, discouraged. Had Vik handed me the wrong key? Had Renée misrepresented the promised accommodations? Had a problem developed that she'd neglected to warn me about? Until Renée surfaced, there was no way to know.

Still, while the third floor would have been a dream, all of the condos were steps from the beach and within earshot of the waves. Living on a lower level would make it easier to unload the car, bring groceries in and out, and keep up with Belle's bathroom needs. I tried to stay positive.

I hunted the shaded lower floors for the apartment number and found it on ground level, where the view would offer beach grass instead of open water. Disappointed, I quickly tried to adjust my attitude. Beach access was beach access. And most of the time we were indoors we'd be asleep. On the first floor, I wouldn't have to worry that the boys' clomping feet would disturb downstairs neighbors.

But as I unlocked the deadbolt and pushed open the door, I feared we'd have to contend with something far worse than a second-rate view. The smell alone had me gagging, and that wasn't the worst part.

Chapter 2

This tip is a bit of a stretch for a professional organizer, but as a mom, I celebrate the efficiency of wetsuits, pioneered locally to increase year-round ocean access. The Pacific in Northern California is bitingly cold. While wetsuits may seem pricey for vacationers, their value should be measured by the recreational time they allow. Rentals are sometimes available. One caveat: mashing small kids into wetsuits is a chore. For kids, buy wetsuits at least one size larger than what is likely to be suggested by surf-shop personnel.

From the Notebook of Maggie McDonald
Simplicity Itself Organizing Services

Monday, June 17, Early afternoon

A quick look round while holding my breath confirmed my initial impression. The now-empty condo had once housed a chain smoker and a slob. Flies circled plates half-filled with food. Untended garbage pails swarmed with maggots. The stench was overwhelming. Dust covered every surface. Piles of clothes or lengths of fabric lay jumbled at one end of a grubby sofa. Packages of fiber fill spilled from a cardboard box. Styrofoam balls and safety pins mingled with dust bunnies under the coffee table. Someone was a crafter, but this apartment was no vacation rental.

Based on the smell and my past experience, I hunted for a dead body. Relieved to discover that the flies were chowing down on a rotting hamburger, rather than a corpse, I left as quickly as I could. I sat on the steps facing the ocean, sucking in fresh salt air to clear my lungs and calm my breathing before phoning Renée.

Was this the last straw? It came close. The apartment didn't meet expectations in any way. Not in size, location, or basic standards of cleanliness. If this dreadful condo was any indication, the rental association needed to attend a customer-service boot camp. Renée was in way over her head and the organization's problems were more than I wanted to tackle.

I was surprised the neighbors hadn't complained about the stench from the apartment's rotting garbage. Or maybe other owners and visitors *had* protested and management had failed to respond. Renée still hadn't phoned me back. No part of this situation made any sense, and I wondered how hard I wanted to work to untangle the mess. I had plenty of customers at home I could be working with.

I looked up and down the beach for Belle and the boys, wondering how I'd break the news to them that our summer plans had tanked.

I couldn't spot them anywhere, but my cell phone chirped before I had a chance to wonder where they could have wandered.

"*Mom!*" Brian yelled when I answered the phone. "Call 9-1-1. We're okay, but this guy is in bad shape..." He wheezed, struggling for breath.

"Are you and David okay? Who's hurt?"

"Hurt doesn't cover it. We need an ambulance. Maybe a helicopter. It's that guy we saw with the ultralight. He crashed."

"Where are you?"

"I don't know. I don't know any of these landmarks. We're up in the cliffs where it's really steep, maybe half a mile north—towards Santa Cruz from the state park."

"Are you near a lifeguard station? What can you see?"

"Mostly ocean and strawberry fields."

"Did you try 9-1-1?"

"Of course," said Brian. "I had a terrible connection. You may need to call on a landline. I don't know if I got through. There was no voice response from their end. I told them everything I could anyway, in case they could hear me."

"I'll be right there."

"Call for help first, Mom. This guy"—His voice broke. "He may not make it."

Brian ended the call before I could ask more questions. I dialed 9-1-1 and waited, wishing I knew whether Santa Cruz County 9-1-1 connected locally. Early on in the history of cellular phone use, emergency calls from mobiles were answered by a centralized dispatch system in Sacramento—two or three hours distant. All law enforcement operations had realized the problem with that scenario immediately, but I didn't know whether changes had been made across the state.

"Santa Cruz County Sheriff," the dispatcher said. "What is your emergency?"

I gave the deputy my name and location and asked if he'd received a call from Brian McDonald about a severely injured ultralight pilot who'd crashed on the cliffs near Sunset State Beach.

"Units are responding."

"Is there anything else you need to know? My son asked me to call and follow up because he had a bad connection."

"Can you pinpoint the location?"

"I'm not with them," I explained. "My son said it's very steep and first responders might need a helicopter to reach the injured man in the cliffs about half a mile north of Heron Beach"—

The telltale beat of rotor blades and turbines made it impossible to hear the dispatcher. I shouted into the phone anyway. "A chopper is here. Is it yours?"

The aircraft moved further away, and my hearing recovered.

"Ma'am?" said the voice on the other end of the phone.

"Sorry. Was that your helicopter? Did it spot my kids? The ultralight?"

"We've found it. A search and rescue team is on scene. They can reach the injured man with their climbing ropes and bring him up using pulleys. An ambulance is en route."

"Thank you." I assured the dispatcher I would join my boys as soon as I could and started jogging down the beach as we finished the call.

After a few hundred yards, I slowed to a walk, my heart pounding less from fear than from skipping too many workouts. I rounded an outcropping and spotted the bright nylon fabric of the ultralight's wings caught in the sparse branches of a cypress tree that clung precariously to the steep hillside.

Belle spotted me and barked, then bounded toward me, occasionally losing her footing and somersaulting before regaining her balance and sliding a few more feet on her rear. How the boys in their stiff wetsuits had reached the pilot, I couldn't imagine. Climbers in orange vests and sturdy boots used ropes to guide a rescue basket from the top of the bluff toward the crash site.

I stepped up my pace to reach Belle and then the boys as quickly as possible, but had to stop several times to catch my breath, regain my footing, and grab hold of shrubbery I hoped wasn't poison oak. The boys had referred to the location as a cliff, and I decided that was probably the most accurate descriptive term. From the flat farmland at the top, there was a precipitous drop about 250 feet to the beach. Locals referred to the cliffs as sandstone. Geologists used the term mudstone. Either way, the terrain amounted to an overgrown sand dune, prone to sliding anywhere the soil wasn't held firm by vegetation.

Breathless, I scrambled to reach the boys. Belle, with four-footed stability, thought this was a fantastic game. She darted between the boys and me, barking encouragement.

As I drew closer, I could hear staccato statements of static-filled information passed between the search-and-rescue climbers and their unseen counterparts at the other end of their radio connections.

Brian and David perched on the hillside, out of the way of the rescue workers, their long legs braced against sliding, and their gaze glued to the scene. Perspiration coated their upper lips, though they'd unzipped their wetsuits, leaving their torsos and arms free. The top portions of their suits dangled from their waists.

I couldn't see much of what was happening, even as I drew closer. I wasn't sure I wanted to. Discarded wrappers for medical supplies fluttered in the wind. I grabbed a few and stashed them in my pocket to reduce the litter. I planted my feet firmly to keep from losing any of my hard-won ground. Brian sat and leaned into me. Belle licked his face. David remained standing, but his downhill leg slid until it was braced close enough for me to pat it in what I hoped was a reassuring gesture.

I felt his muscles tense, and I turned to glance over my shoulder when one of the EMT's shouted, "Get that chopper back here stat. He's a fighter, but we're losing him." One of his partners shook his head grimly. "What is he, twenty-something? A kid."

David groaned.

"Get those boys out of here," the EMT added.

The rest happened in a rush. If pressed, I wouldn't have been able to recite the order of events with any accuracy. A park ranger helped me stand and handed us each his card. I gave him one of my own, but not without sliding several feet further down the hill while I rummaged in my backpack. He stashed my card in his breast pocket. I read his: "Charlie Adams, Supervising Ranger, California State Park Peace Officers."

"I need to stay here for now, but I'll be in touch later," Adams said. "We'll want to know as much as you can tell us about what happened here." He looked back over his shoulder as a helicopter landed on the cliff top, stirring up sand and soil that made me squint against the gritty air.

"Thanks for calling it in. The victim's in good hands. Let's get you down the hill and out of this dust."

He offered me his hand. I waved him off, fearing I'd pull us both down. "We're fine. We're staying at Heron Beach"—I hesitated, as I wasn't sure exactly how long we'd stay. "For a few days, at least."

"For the summer," David corrected.

I slid further, and decided now was not the time to discuss the equally precarious nature of our summer plans.

"We'll talk later," Adams said. I nodded, and followed Belle as she bounded, rolled, and slid to the level sand of the beach. Before the boys and I joined her, the helicopter had taken off again. The *thup thup thup* of the rotors was a sound I felt as much as heard. Without thinking, I associated it with the beat of the injured pilot's heart. So much so that I had a moment of panic when the helicopter noise faded. I prayed or wished for his heart to continue at a steady pace.

"What now?" Brian asked as he pulled up the top of his wetsuit and struggled with the zipper. "Did you get into the condo? Is the view great? I want a hot shower, hot chocolate, and a grilled-cheese sandwich in that order. There's a Giants game tonight."

I half-smiled. Brian's plan sounded fantastic. And easy. But then I cringed, remembering the state of the condo I'd seen. No child of mine was going to shower or eat in that unsanitary pit.

"Do you think that guy's gonna make it?" David asked, his voice quavering.

"I hope so " I turned and eyed the cliff face where the nylon wings of the battered ultralight still fluttered in the strengthening wind. I was surprised the law-enforcement team hadn't already collected the aircraft, but then wondered if they needed special gear or a trailer to transport it. Or were the pilot and his family responsible for cleaning up the wreck? I didn't know. It wasn't important. I needed to focus on getting the boys settled.

"One thing's for sure," I said, giving David a quick hug. "Without you two, he didn't stand a chance. All the first responders confirmed that. I'm proud of you." I glanced at my cell. "My phone's almost out of charge. We'll call Dad as soon as I get it plugged in."

"Weak signal," said Brian. "The phone uses up battery as it hunts for a better connection."

I wasn't sure I understood how that worked, but I believed him. We'd have to be extra careful about charging up the phones this summer if I was going to give the boys the freedom I'd promised them. And if we were able to stay. But that was a concern for later.

"Let's head back to the car at the state beach," I said. "There's a great place for dinner about a half-hour south of here. With outdoor tables so Belle can sit with us."

"But showers. Hot chocolate. Cheese. And the Giants. The rookie's pitching." Brian's voice took on an uncharacteristic whiny tone—an outward sign of his internal exhaustion.

The wind whipped my hair in front of my face, giving me a fuzzy mouthful as I tried to answer. I gathered my hair into a ponytail and yelled into the increasingly howling wind. "I'll explain when we get to the car. It's too hard to hear. Let's hurry, though. I'm starving." I checked my watch. No wonder I was hungry. It was nearly six o'clock. We'd spent more time on the cliff face than I'd realized.

Belle's tongue drooped and she dogged my heels as we all trudged down the beach in the soft sand that remained safe from the incoming tide.

We picked up the boogie boards, towels, and beach blanket. Pure strength of will got us back up over the sand dunes to the changing area at the park where the boys shed their wetsuits. I urged them to forgo the chilly outdoor showers. "A little sand won't hurt anything. If we're going to be here all summer, the car will see more than that. Besides, no single shower will take care of all the sand that helicopter kicked up. My hair and ears are full of it."

We piled into the car with me driving. I sighed. "I know I told you about that great restaurant south of here, but let's save that for another night. A half hour suddenly seems like a long time to wait for dinner."

"There was that sandwich shop next to the gas station at the freeway exit," David said. "Will that do?"

"Perfect," I said, backing out of the parking spot.

I'd only just exited the state park and crossed the low bridge over the slough when Brian leaned forward and spoke over the seat back. "Why'd you tell the ranger we might be here only a few more days? What happened? Aren't we planning to be here all summer? Isn't Dad coming on the weekend? What's going on?"

I switched on the car's headlights. Not only had the sun set, but the thick marine layer of fog had rolled in, obliterating any moonlight. I steeled myself to give the boys the bad news.

Chapter 3

A rental with easy access to laundry facilities will simplify packing for your California coastal vacation. Choose layers adaptable to vacillating temperatures and conditions. Leave your dressy gear at home. As long as you're not accepting an Academy Award, you can get away without glitz almost everywhere.

From the Notebook of Maggie McDonald
Simplicity Itself Organizing Services

Monday, June 17, Early evening

The boys reacted better than I thought to the news that our vacation might be over before it had begun. But they were full of questions I wasn't sure I could answer about what would come next.

"As soon as we get some food," I began, stopping to get my chattering teeth under control, "and some hot drinks, we can figure out our next step. Ideally, Renée will have called to straighten all this out and the promised three-bedroom apartment will be ready for us. If not, we might be able to rent one."

"That guard said dogs aren't allowed," Brian said, putting his arm around the relentlessly upbeat retriever. She thumped her tail against the back of the seat.

"I'm sure there's a hotel in town that takes dogs. Particularly if we don't let them see how sandy she is. A hotel with hot showers, fluffy towels, and a TV we can tune into the Giants game."

The boys went into the sandwich shop, which was really just a corner of an overgrown gas station. While they ordered, I tried again to reach Renée in the management office and Vik in the guard house. Both calls went to voicemail. I was neither surprised nor disappointed. At the rate this working vacation was unfolding into an unmitigated disaster, I was about ready to pack it in and head for home. But not tonight. Tonight, I had an appointment with a hotel pillow. Regardless of why Vik and Renée weren't answering, I'd be much better prepared to deal with almost anything after a good night's sleep.

* * * *

We'd checked into the first chain hotel I came to. As soon as we reached the room, I hit speed dial on my phone to check in with my husband Max. I wanted to let him know how things were going, or rather, how they weren't, and give the boys time to bask in their father's praise for their heroics.

While the phone rang, I handed my cell to Brian. When Max answered, the boys took turns recounting their adventure and soaking up their dad's praise. Their young egos and energy were recharged by the time David handed the phone back to me.

"*Wow!*" said Max.

"I know. I'm so impressed. You've never seen such cool heads under pressure. All the first responders were saying the pilot wouldn't have stood a chance if the boys hadn't been right there on the scene."

"What happened?"

"I'm not sure. It was one of those ultralight aircraft things. Looks like a hang glider crossed with a lawn mower. A gigantic motorized dragonfly."

"Sounds like a steampunk monster, but I get what you mean. So, it was an accident?"

"I think so. The pilot was just a kid. Older than our guys, but still."

"You think he cut a few corners with maintenance and paid the price?"

"I'm sure there'll be an investigation, but I can see myself at twenty, wanting to get going rather than do a tedious safety check, can't you?"

"No way I'd ever go up in one of those things. Not in a million years. Not in two million."

"But if you did, you'd be lucky if two kids like ours were there to be your safety net, right?" I winked at the boys, who blushed. Then I told Max about the other hiccups in our plans, promising to check in when I knew more.

By the time I wrapped up the call, Belle was snoring in the middle of the boys' queen-sized bed, leaving little room for Brian and David. Determined, they crammed in on either side of her, as if she was a holster designed to keep them from kicking one another in their sleep. She perked up as they unwrapped their sandwiches, but I distracted her with filled dishes of kibble and water.

Dinner in bed proved an intriguing novelty. The boys wanted to watch television, but their eyelids drooped. In lieu of tucking them in, I straightened the covers on each side of the bed. As I smoothed the sheet folded over the blanket on David's side, he sighed. "Mom, I don't think it was an accident." He was asleep before I could delve further into his suspicions.

Shrugging, I chalked his concern up to the gloom that darkens everyone's perspective at the end of a long and stressful day. By morning, I was sure his outlook would be sunnier. After all, who'd want to tamper with the aircraft of some local kid?

* * * *

In the morning, other more immediate concerns shifted my attention from the mysteries surrounding the crash. Awakening stiff from our bluff-side scramble, I ached to dive back under the covers. But I was a mom, Belle needed a walk, and we all needed breakfast.

The boys stirred. "I'm going to walk Belle and check out," I told them. "Pack up your gear. I'll meet you at the car. We'll get breakfast and restart this adventure." With that rousing speech to instill enthusiasm, I leashed Belle and headed downstairs, hoping I hadn't waited too long to attend to her needs.

She made a beeline for a grassy patch as soon as we got outside. The day was cool, but the marine layer was starting to burn off. It would be another glorious day at the beach, if we ever got there.

No sooner than I had unlocked the car, the boys joined us.

"Where to?" David asked.

"Starbucks," Brian said. "If there is one in this little town."

"We can do better," I said. "Beach Street Café. The hotel desk clerk told me last night that it's a hometown favorite."

* * * *

It was. One part modern-foodie mecca and two parts hometown diner and information center, the place bustled when we arrived. A counter stretched across the one-room restaurant. It separated the kitchen from the dining area, which included an assortment of tables for two, four, and six that could be shoved together for larger groups. "Sit anywhere you like," said the waitress. "Coffee? Orange juice? Water?"

We seated ourselves while she poured my coffee and handed us each an extensive menu listing basic breakfasts and more elaborate brunch items. "Sandwiches are on the back if you're more in the mood for that. We get people in after the graveyard shift, so we serve breakfast and lunch all day."

I thanked her and glanced at the back of the menu. "How 'bout that, Brian? You can have your grilled-cheese sandwich and hot chocolate if you still want them."

"Nope. Cinnamon French toast."

"Buckwheat waffles for me." David said. The waitress, who introduced herself as Lucia, topped off my coffee and took our orders, including a veggie Eggs Benedict with avocado for me.

We settled in to wait, examining the table top. Under a layer of glass, a vast array of business cards advertised local shops and services. "Surf lessons," said Brian. "Can we do that this summer?" He flung out his arms simulating a surfer stance, and nearly cleared the table of sugar, ketchup, and salt and pepper shakers. David grabbed for the items, saving them from becoming shards on the spotless checkerboard floor.

"Breakfast is on us," said Lucia, plopping down the paper and pointing to a front-page story with the bold headline: **Local Researcher Rescued from Crash**. "Jake Peterson is a regular. Used to work here in high school. His grandma lives next door to me."

Below the fold was a photo of Brian, David, and Belle watching EMTs load a stretcher into the helicopter. Brian and David blushed, and I looked toward the kitchen, where the chef peered through the pass-through window, waved his spoon, and slapped the counter in applause. "Heroes eat free," he called out.

"Is everyone in town this cheerful?" I asked Lucia. "Where are the curmudgeons and the grumps?"

"We have our share, for sure, but as a rule we might be friendlier than the folks over the hill in Silicon Valley. Maybe we're just not quite as rushed. Or maybe it's our food that sweetens tempers." Lucia winked.

"Are you the owner?" I asked.

Lucia nodded. "Yup. Me and Sam, there on the grill. This place has been here for decades though. My mother worked here, summers, when she was a teenager. It's an institution. After work, before work, on the way home from fishing or the beach, everyone stops in here at one time or another. That guy at the corner table is Charlie Adams, the ranger at the state beach where you boys found Jake."

Adams looked up when Lucia mentioned his name. She waved and called to him. "Meet our local heroes," she said. He smiled, waved, and went back to reading his paper.

"Used to be, we were smack in the middle of the canning factories— Green Giant, Dole, California Giant, Martinelli's apples. Not too many of them left. We'll outlast them all."

Sam whistled from the window, and Lucia left to pick up our orders, then placed them in front of each of us, demonstrating a formidable memory for food and faces. "I'll leave you to enjoy your breakfast," she said. "Shout out if you need anything. Homemade salsa coming up for your eggs. Go easy if you don't like jalapeños."

The salsa was a perfect mix of freshness and a pinch of heat to balance with the smoother flavors of avocado, egg, and cheese.

"Thanks, boys," I said, wiping cheese from my mouth after a too-ambitious first bite. "For breakfast."

"That's not why we helped him," said David, sounding aggrieved.

"I know," I said softly. "Lucia and Sam know that, too, I'm sure. But it's making them feel great to say thank you. Your actions benefited their friend and the community, and they want to recognize that. It's generous to let them."

"'Kay," said David, taking a big bite of his waffle and closing his eyes. He opened them wide. "Okay!" He turned to Sam behind the counter and gave him a thumbs up. Brian nodded his appreciation without slowing his assault on his French toast. By the time they were finished, I was more than full.

"Do you want to order lunch to go?" Lucia asked, taking our plates.

I nodded. I'd been watching a series of customers pay for their breakfasts and pick up bagged lunches to go. If the regulars were all doing it, how could we go wrong? "But let me pay for those. Breakfast was excellent. Thank you."

She brought us lunch menus and we ordered, though I wasn't sure I'd ever be hungry again. When she delivered the bags of food to our table, along with the bill for lunch, she asked the boys to autograph the newspaper. "For our wall." Lucia pointed to a bulletin board at the far end of the restaurant that featured drawings by small children, photographs of young men and women in uniform, and framed articles touting the achievements of local teens. "You're one of us, now. Always. Please come back."

"We're staying for the summer," I said. "I'm helping out Renée Alvarez at Heron Beach."

Lucia laughed. "You're *that* Maggie? Renée told me all about her plan to reorganize the office out there. She's my best friend. She was married to my brother." Her cheerful expression darkened.

"I'm sorry," I said, though I wasn't sure why.

Lucia shook her head. "It was a long time ago. They weren't married long. Helicopter pilot. Iraq war."

On that somber note, she turned to address the caffeine needs of other patrons. "Haven't you had enough already?" she asked a man I was sure she'd called Oh-Oh. "Never," he answered. "I don't know why anyone turns to drugs when your coffee is available. Top off my little brother's cup, too." He pointed to a lanky teenager at the table across from him. "You've met Domingo, right?"

Lucia nodded and looked back at me over her shoulder, making me feel self-conscious about my eavesdropping. I'd never lived in a town that felt this small, where everyone was one or two introductions away from knowing all the other residents. I liked it.

I left a generous tip to cover both breakfast and lunch, and added my business card to the collection under the table top. Brian stopped to snap a photo of all the cards under the glass. I knew without being told that it was his way of noting the contact information for the surf school he'd expressed some interest in, along with a flight school that offered a free trip aloft to anyone under the age of fifteen. Rescuing a crashed pilot hadn't dimmed his love affair with altitude.

It wasn't until we were outside and I was tucking the lunch bags into the car that I realized Lucia had included a raw beef bone for Belle. "For the hero dog," she'd written on the bag, signing it with a heart.

I poked my head back in through the café door to say thanks. Lucia was busy, but mouthed the word "wait" as she handed out steaming plates of food at a table filled with beefy men wearing fishing gear.

"Thanks, on behalf of Belle," I said.

"So that's her name." Lucia laughed. "I fell in love the minute I saw that picture. She's gorgeous."

"And she knows it. But, I wanted to ask you if you've seen Renée. I've been trying to get in touch. She hasn't answered her phone or returned my call."

Lucia shook her head and patted her pockets, apparently searching for her phone. "That's not like her, but if you're calling from the beach, cell service can be sketchy. Have you tried texting her?"

"I'm sure she'll call soon. Everyone says she's reliable."

"She's got the kids," Sam called out from behind the counter. I was surprised he could hear us over the chattering customers and the other sounds of the busy diner.

He called out to a man in his late twenties or early thirties and held up a white paper bag. "Rivers, you can't pick strawberries on an empty stomach. Don't forget your lunch."

The man grabbed the paper sack and grumbled a thank you, making him the grumpiest person we'd encountered so far. He didn't wait to be introduced.

Lucia ignored him. "What's the hearing equivalent of x-ray vision?" she asked. "It's Sam's superpower. He's right though. I forgot. Something was going on with Renée's neighbor yesterday, and Renée's looking after her three little kids. Twin toddlers and an infant. She's got her hands full."

I tilted my head toward the waiting boys. "I remember those days. If you see her, please tell her that Maggie would appreciate a call when she gets a chance. If she's willing to give me access to the office, I can get started without her."

"Will do."

I ended our conversation and scurried back to the car.

"Can we stop at the hospital before we head to the beach?" asked Brian. "Check on the pilot?"

I thought for a moment. "Please?" asked David. "They might not let us see him, since we're not family or anything, but someone should be able to tell us how he's doing, right? He was in bad shape."

David had nailed one of my reasons for hesitating. The downed pilot had been in critical condition. What if he'd since died or was circling the drain? The kids would be devastated.

"It might not be good news," I said. "Even if he recovers, it might be a long road."

Brian and David nodded solemnly before climbing into the car, with David back in the driver's seat. I was in favor of giving teens as much supervised driving time as possible.

"Still…" I closed my door and fastened my seatbelt. "As long as you're prepared for anything, including the possibility that we won't learn much, what with privacy rules and all. Just remember that what you did yesterday was incredible. You did what you could to help and called in reinforcements. I'm proud of you."

David put the car in gear, pulling away from the curb and doing a U-turn to head back toward Highway 1. The community hospital was strategically positioned close to the next exit north off the freeway. The medical facility was near the airport too, for easy air transport of patients to Silicon Valley's world class trauma centers some fifty miles north.

Chapter 4

To reduce housekeeping chores on a beach vacation, set up a foot rinsing station outside your front door. Keep it simple. A plastic dishpan of water and a towel or soft brush will do the trick.

From the Notebook of Maggie McDonald
Simplicity Itself Organizing Services

Tuesday, June 18, Morning

"Main entrance or emergency?" David asked as he pulled into the hospital parking lot.

"Main entrance." I hoped the volunteers or staff in the front lobby would be less rushed than ER workers and more likely to entertain our non-standard request for information about a patient along with questions that probably broke all kinds of confidentiality rules.

David found parking easily, close to the door. There were distinct advantages to being outside Silicon Valley—namely, lower population, lighter traffic, and fewer SUVs crammed into compact spots.

The doors swished open automatically as we approached. Once inside, I introduced myself to the volunteer staffing the main desk and asked about the pilot who'd crashed. "Oh, you mean Jake Peterson," she said. Looking up, she spotted Brian and David, glanced at the newspaper on the desk in front of her, and her mouth gaped. "Oh! You're them!" She jabbed her finger toward the front-page photo. "He's in G-210, but let me see if I can get the nurse on the phone for you."

We waited while she dialed, though Brian and David found it hard to meet her enthralled gaze.

"Is this what it's like to be a rock star?" David whispered under his breath. "How do they get through the day?"

I smiled. "Are you boasting or complaining? Enjoy it while it lasts."

Before David or Brian could respond, the volunteer pushed a button to disconnect her call and looked up. "I couldn't reach the unit—oh wait." She waved to a white-coated man in his mid-fifties wearing a Mickey Mouse tie. "Dr. Bennett? Do you have a moment?"

He stopped mid-stride and looked us over with bushy eyebrows raised. "How can I help?"

The volunteer introduced us. "They're inquiring about Jake's status. What can we tell them?"

The doctor rubbed his chin and was silent for a moment. He sighed, and I feared we'd learn nothing, but then he spoke, his voice weary. "Thanks for being Good Samaritans yesterday. Your quick thinking made a big difference." He shook each boy's hand, then extended his arm, inviting us to sit in a nearby waiting area outfitted with dark green armchairs and sofas that made the room seem more like a hotel lobby than a medical facility.

"There are regulations that prevent me from sharing anyone's health information without their consent, but I can tell you that a patient transported here by helicopter yesterday is doing well. He's still in intensive care, but we hope to move him this afternoon. No promises, but thanks to you, he's stable."

The boys beamed.

Dr. Bennett stood. "I'll talk to my patient about allowing you to visit as soon as he's strong enough. I'm sure he'd love to thank you in person. Do you have a card or something I could give him?"

For a moment, I thought he meant a get-well card, but then I realized he was referring to our names and contact information. I rummaged in my backpack, pulled out my business card, and handed it to the doctor, repeating our names for him.

As we were leaving, a young man in a gray hoodie with a camera bag over one shoulder barreled through the door, nearly knocking Brian over. "Dr. Bennett!" he called, grabbing Brian's shoulders. "Sorry," he said quietly before shouting the doctor's name again. I glanced over my shoulder, but the doctor was gone, and the doors to the wing behind the volunteer desk were swinging closed.

The young man looked from Brian to David. "You're Brian and David McDonald, yes? Have a minute? I'm Roger Montero from the *Register*— local paper. Very local. But I work for the television station in Salinas too. We'd like to run a follow up."

The boys looked to me, and I nodded. *Why not?* It would be good experience for them, and I was certain the reporter was only looking for a photo and a brief quote in lieu of an interview with the hometown pilot. "I'll get the car and meet you back here," I said. David tossed me the keys. Characteristically, I whiffed the catch but scooped them up quickly after they clanked on the ground directly in front of me.

As I left, I heard the raspy static-filled voice of the public-address system: "Dr. Bennett to post-surgical, stat. Dr. Bennett." Even in a small town, the lives of trauma surgeons offered little downtime. I was grateful he'd spared a moment to talk to the boys. My upbeat thoughts were replaced by worry before I reached the car. Could the emergency that drew Dr. Bennett away have been a change in Jake's condition? I scanned the empty parking lot for anyone who might be able to give us an update. But there was no one.

I pulled the car to the curb in front of the portico, but before I could locate anyone, the boys climbed into the back seat. "How'd it go?" I asked.

"Fine," David said. "He just wanted a quote from us about the rescue. We said it was really the search and rescue team and the EMTs who deserved recognition. We just called in the cavalry."

"Good job."

David squared his shoulders. He might have been a teenage boy who wished his parents could be neither seen nor heard, but he wasn't beyond basking in his mother's praise.

"But enough of the spotlight," I said. "Let's find out what awaits us at Heron Beach."

"Hang on, Mom," Brian said in a low voice. "Look." He pointed toward the information desk inside the building where the volunteer wiped her eyes. The reporter stood in front of the counter with his shoulders drooped. He shook his head, then looked back toward us and frowned.

We didn't need anyone to spell it out. "Jake's dead," said David, sucking in a deep breath.

Ordinarily, I'd have advised the kids to avoid jumping to conclusions and to wait for more detailed and accurate information. But the body language was clear.

"I'm afraid you're right," I said. "I'm so sorry."

"What happens now, Mom?" Brian asked.

David spoke before I could answer. "This is messed up. It isn't right. How can he be dead?"

"It was a terrible accident. You said yourselves he was badly hurt. Sometimes internal injuries—"

David wiped at his eyes. "That's just it, Mom. I don't think it was an accident."

"Why do you say that?" I asked. "Are you saying Jake crashed deliberately?"

David closed his eyes and shook his head. "No. No. Not at all."

"Then what?"

Brian fiddled with the window control then looked from his brother's tortured face to mine. "He kept trying to tell us something. He was angry."

I wasn't sure how easy it would be to tell the difference between extreme emotion and the pain Jake must have surely been suffering, but I decided that listening would be the most useful skill to deploy at the moment.

David rested his head on the back of the seat in front of him, then sank back. "Brian's right. What did he say? Something like 'bad prop.'" He looked at Brian for confirmation.

"Or 'check prop' maybe?" Brian picked at a piece of loose rubber on his sneaker. "Like there was something wrong with the propeller."

I thought back to my first sight of the ultralight. "That might explain why the machine was so ungainly. For whatever reason, it sure looked like he was having trouble getting it under control."

"We need to tell someone," David said, his face still reflecting his emotional pain. "Like, right away. Someone tried to hurt Jake. Maybe kill him."

"*Whoa*," I said. "That's a leap. Isn't it more likely that you heard him berating himself for skimping on safety checks or something?" David's insistence on contacting the authorities surprised me and derailed my recollection of the oddly flying machine. I had the sense I was missing something, but it didn't matter. What mattered was the kids and their grief. We'd all grown attached to the idea that they'd saved the young man. They'd worked hard to do so. Beyond our empathetic sorrow over the tragedy of Jake's death, the news was a blow to their pride in their accomplishment. But our wounds were too fresh to allow for cogent thought.

"Let's think about this and talk later," I said, speaking quickly in an attempt to change the subject and distract the boys. "We'll call the sheriff but let's head out to the beach first. I need to know where we're all going to sleep tonight." I put the car in gear and pulled away from the curb. "If there's still no condo ready for us, and no word from Renée, I don't think we can stay. We wouldn't be able to have Belle with us, for one thing. For another, if Renée doesn't have time to return my phone calls and straighten out this misunderstanding, I don't think she'll have the time or commitment required to get her business organized. Working under those conditions would be a waste of everyone's time."

"Go home?" Brian asked. "But this place is so cool."

My heart sank. Instead of providing a practical distraction from the tragedy, I'd added to his grief.

"I agree. The ocean, the slough, the birds, the sea mammals…and the freedom. It feels like we're a million miles from Silicon Valley. Your dad would love it, too. If we need to ditch the plan to spend the summer here, we'll look for a week we can come down for vacation."

"But that would mean without Belle," David said. Belle wagged her tail, either artfully pleading her case or oblivious to the possibility that she'd be left out.

"'Fraid so." I said. "Let's wait and see though, before we panic." We passed the rest of the journey lost in our own thoughts.

I pulled into a parking space in front of the main office and guard station. The boys leashed Belle and walked her back toward the bridge to sniff for rabbits and birds, and take care of any hygienic needs she might have. I checked my phone for coverage. Three bars. "I'll text you when we're ready for step two," I called to Brian and David, then muttered to myself, "Whatever step two turns out to be."

I opened the door and stepped inside, pausing to allow my eyes to adjust to the dimmer light in the office.

"Morning, Maggie, I've got good news." Vik reached into a cabinet on the wall behind the desk that was filled with metal keys. He selected one and placed it on the counter. "I finally reached Renée. She asked me to tell you how sorry she is for yesterday's mix-up. She'll be here shortly to tell you herself, but in the meantime, if you give me your receipts from wherever you stayed last night, we'll reimburse you. And your condo is ready. It's freshly remodeled and cleaned, three bedrooms on the third floor with a great view of the ocean." He stepped back, shoulders squared as though he'd engineered the entire solution himself. Maybe he had.

I picked up the key with a sigh of relief. "Thank you. I'm thrilled."

"Turn right after you go through the gate. Then a left, right, left to reach the parking area for your building. Take the ramp to the second floor then the first set of stairs. Your unit is the first one on the south side of the building."

Vik rattled off the instructions quickly. I struggled to replay his words and visualize them.

"Never mind. You'll find it. It's not that complicated. Unit numbers are indicated at the entrance to each parking lot and there's a map for each building. If you have any trouble, just give me a call." He handed me his card. "That's the number for the guard shack here, not just for me. Pop it into the contacts on your phone and your boys' cells. Any questions, any emergencies, we'll be here. 24/7."

I thanked him again and left the building. I glanced at the card and groaned. I ducked back into the lobby. "Vik *Peterson?*" I asked, holding up the card.

He nodded, smiling.

"Any relation to Jake?"

"My cousin. More like my little brother. His parents raised me up, mostly."

A ringing phone stole Vik's attention and saved me from having to report the worst news possible. He didn't need to hear it from a stranger.

It was hard to focus on anything else in the face of such a dreadful tragedy, but what else could we do but trudge forward? I stepped outside and forged ahead, looking both ways as I crossed the small parking area searching for the boys.

Like Huck Finn and Tom Sawyer, prepped for an idyllic summer, Brian and David lacked only old-fashioned fishing poles as they leaned over the white-painted wood railing of the small bridge. I called out and waved the key in the air.

* * * *

I checked the number of the third-floor unit twice and opened the door slowly. I sniffed, testing the air in case this apartment was as bad as the first, but the condo smelled of new paint and freshly cut wood. Belle pushed past me, and the boys dogged my heels. David crossed the living room and flung open the shutters that blocked the view to the ocean. Without a word, he slid open the balcony door and stepped out. Belle and I joined him, as did Brian after proclaiming he had dibs on a bedroom with a balcony of its own.

David uttered no protest over his brother's preemptive strike to commandeer the larger bedroom. He seemed entranced by the view, which included breaching dolphins. He turned. "How soon can I invite my friends down?"

"Are those dolphins?" I asked. "There..." I pointed as they spouted then disappeared under the waves. "Did you see them? They'll be back up in a moment, watch."

"Friends, Mom." David repeated. "Can they come down this weekend?" His voice was full of teenaged nonchalance with a twist of impatience, but only for moment. "Whoa! Right there." He pointed and we all watched until the dolphins disappeared into the distance. Belle sniffed and her tail thumped against the railing.

"Friends?" David reminded me as though he feared I'd grown feeble-minded at my advanced age.

"Not until the car's unpacked, at least," I said, handing him the keys. "Once you're done, get started on a grocery list. I'll go shopping later this afternoon."

I dialed Renée's number. My spirits sank as the phone rang with no answer. I sighed and left a message, not bothering to keep the disappointment out of my voice. "Renée, it's Maggie McDonald. Please give me a call back as soon as you can." We needed to talk about commitment to this project. If now wasn't the right time to tackle it, rescheduling would make more sense than struggling with an overfull agenda. I ended the call and went to help the boys.

I'd ring Max tonight. We needed to let him know about the fate of the pilot. Talking to him about it would help us all. But I also needed to discuss plans for Renée's project and the rest of the summer. I didn't want to disappoint anyone unnecessarily, but more and more it seemed our original plan had no hope of working out. We could stay through the weekend when Max could join us. We'd enjoy the perk of having Belle with us in a resort that typically didn't allow dogs. But after that? I was nearly one hundred percent sure we'd be headed home.

Organizing is hard work, even for those who are wholly committed to the time investment required to revamp storage and time-management systems. I'd tried working on projects funded by relatives who thought their loved one would enjoy a more structured and organized life, but they seldom worked well. My jobs went smoothly only when clients were invested in both the process and the outcome.

In Renée's case, we'd talked on the phone earlier about her budget and expectations. Without considerable participation on her part, she'd never achieve her goal of creating an efficient, attractive office space, appropriately staffed to meet the needs of modern absentee homeowners, tourists, and an aging infrastructure.

I wasn't desperate for clients. I'd considered working with Renée only because my best friend Tess had asked me to. The deal was sweetened by the perks Renée had promised. But I had clients back in Orchard View who needed my help and with whom I was more likely to be successful.

I didn't know what the problem was with Renée, but it didn't much matter. She was making it clear that now was not the time for her to tackle revamping her business. It was going to break the boys' already wounded hearts.

Chapter 5

To manage sand in the car while at the beach, line passenger foot wells with old towels you can carefully lift and shake out when necessary. Keep a whisk broom handy for the driver's area, where a towel could get dangerously tangled among feet and pedals.

From the Notebook of Maggie McDonald
Simplicity Itself Organizing Services

Tuesday, June 18, Late morning

My phone rang again.

"Maggie? Maggie McDonald? It's Renée. I'm finally here in my office. I'm so sorry about the last couple of days. It's not like me. I have a good explanation. I promise you, I'll be much more reliable going forward."

Renée continued to breathlessly assure me that she was serious about her project and ready to begin. I asked for directions to her office. She described a building on the opposite side of the property a few hundred yards beyond the gatehouse. I didn't much feel like work and would have preferred a long walk on the beach talking to the boys, but I couldn't put Renée off—not after insisting that she either show up or reschedule. I sighed. Life was so much simpler when it marched forward in accordance with my plans. If only the world worked that way.

After letting the boys know where I was headed, I walked past the small pond where a mother mallard was attempting to get her eleven ducklings into line. I sympathized.

I followed a path to Renée's office in a building that looked as though it had started life as a clubhouse for the tennis courts it overlooked. I knocked on a metal screen door and, hearing no answer, entered at the corner of an expansive but dreary room. Fluorescent fixtures dangled precariously from rusted chains attached to beams that vanished in the darkness. On the floor were sagging cardboard boxes and dusty file cabinets topped with piles of stray cords. Three utilitarian steel desks topped with clunky desktop computers hugged the corners of the room, like heavyweight prizefighters waiting to square off. Tess had warned me before I took the job that the office had suffered through a series of inept managers who'd fostered a climate of back-biting and infighting. The room reflected its history.

What a mess. I sneezed. And sneezed again.

A woman emerged from a back room. She extended her arm toward a folding banquet table surrounded by collapsible metal chairs. "Maggie? Please, have a seat. Can I get you anything? Coffee? Water?"

"No, thanks," I said. I introduced myself, shook her hand, and made appropriate social conversation. But then it was time to get down to business. I pulled my computer from my backpack. Though I still personally preferred taking notes on a yellow-lined pad, I'd forced myself to use only my laptop or tablet for client meetings. Much of my approach to organization hinged on eliminating paper clutter, and there was no better way to do that than to avoid creating it in the first place. I found it easier to convince customers to curtail paper use when I set a good example.

Renée looked around the room and frowned. "I wouldn't blame you if you ran out of here at once and never looked back. I haven't given you the best first impression, and this mess of an office doesn't help."

"No one calls me unless they need help, Renée. I've seen worse."

Renée's shoulders relaxed. "I'm sure that's true, but..." She waved her hands toward the stacks of boxes and the remnants of abandoned projects covered with dust. She sank into her creaky desk chair. "My next-door neighbors got picked up by ICE last weekend. I'm looking after their three kids."

"Ice?"

"Immigration and...what's the rest? Customs Enforcement?"

"You're not kidding? The real ICE?"

She pushed back her hair and sighed. "They've been staking out day care and health care centers, food banks, and schools."

I shook my head, struggling to believe the words I understood individually but couldn't fathom once they were all grouped together. "What happens now?"

"I know the parents have worked on their citizenship papers, but I can't find them anywhere in the house."

"Can they stay with you? The kids I mean?"

"I'm not an official foster mom. But no one has come by to ask questions or check on the kids either."

"Does ICE or CPS know they're with you?" I asked, referring to Child Protective Services.

Renée stared at her hands. "They work hard, but money is tight. They've focused on raising the kids. Immigration details took a back seat."

I was sympathetic, but wasn't sure how to respond. Renée continued talking as my thoughts drifted. There was nothing I could do to help. The situation was a disaster for a small family and had upended Renée's life, but how did it measure up against the Peterson family's tragedy? I sighed, noting how my outlook had changed in the last 24 hours. My vision of an idyllic summer was becoming obscured with one catastrophe after another. I struggled to refocus on Renée's words.

"Do they need a lawyer?" I asked. "How does this work?"

"I've made a few contacts but now we're all in limbo, waiting to hear back. I don't know what I need, but I'm thinking diapers and baby food are probably both more important than a lawyer right now." Renée looked at her watch. "I'm hoping to get started on this job while I wait for them to return my calls."

"How can you even focus?"

Renée shook her head, then stood and dusted off her hands. "Let's see what we can make of all this in whatever time we have. I'm the fifth new manager in the last two years. The financial records are a mess. And—"

I held up my hand. "Let's not get ahead of ourselves. Or heaven forbid, scare ourselves. Before we get in too deep, I want to talk about what I can do and what I can't. And what your expectations are. I may not be the type of assistance you need right now, but I can help you figure that out pretty quickly."

"I'm still not sure an arsonist or a bulldozer isn't what I really need," Renée said. "My priorities—on this project at least—are to figure out what's here and prepare a board presentation that will secure vastly increased funding to address long-deferred maintenance."

"I can help with all of that," I said. "And get this paperwork condensed, sorted, and organized for off-site archival storage or more efficient retrieval.

Honestly, the way things look in here right now, it would take you so long to locate a document that you might as well shred your paperwork instead of filing it."

I typed some quick notes, telling Renée that I'd forward them to her later. "What I'd like to do first thing tomorrow is phone the resort's lawyer, accountant, and insurance company, and look over the homeowners' association by-laws. Many of your records may already be stored offsite. In that case, there's no need to save papers that the association is paying other professionals to archive. I also want to verify what each of those entities requires you to have on hand. Unless you already know?"

Renée shook her head and tapped a well-worn yellow pad. "I've just started taking notes on all of that," she said, running her hand through her hair. "I'm good at my job, and this is the third small-business office I've signed on to organize and turn around. But it's a daunting challenge."

"I can see that," I said. "How 'bout we say I'll stay for a week and we'll reassess? By then we both should know a great deal more about what we're working with, where you stand with the kids, and whether you want to dig in or run for the hills."

Renée smiled, looking at least five years younger, and held out her hand to shake mine, but then looked at her dusty fingers and drew them back. "I'm sorry. I've been here for fifteen minutes, and I'm already covered with dust. It's revolting."

But before I could summon a tactful response, the phone rang. Renée picked up the receiver. "Oh, Vik, I'm so sorry," she said. After listening for a moment, she added. "Of course. She's here with me now. We'll be right over. Do you need to take off?" She held the handset in front of her, stared at it, and shrugged. "He hung up."

I raised my eyebrows in question.

"It's the Petersons," Renée said. "Jake's parents. And Vik's, er, well, it's complicated. They're here with the sheriff and want to talk to us and your boys."

Sheriff? I froze. Two days ago, I wouldn't have thought anything of a visit from law enforcement, since we had good family friends at all levels of our local police force at home in Orchard View. But today, not twelve hours since the ultralight crash, my fears went straight to the direst of circumstances.

"Sheriff?" I said it aloud this time. "Are Brian and David okay? I need to text them." I pulled out my phone and tapped the screen. Beads of sweat prickled my scalp even as I shivered and the room started to sway. I'm not prone to panic attacks, but my reaction seemed over the top, even to me.

Apparently, the injury and death of a young person can be unsettling in far more ways that I had imagined.

"It's okay, Maggie. Everything is okay," said Renée.

The boys responded quickly.

"What's up?" David replied. I explained that the sheriff and Jake's parents were in the gatehouse, asking for us. The boys agreed to meet us there.

* * * *

Everyone looked up when our entourage entered. Belle bounded forward, wagging her tail, and knocked a pile of brochures off the coffee table. The tension in the room made the air seem to crackle. An ashen-faced couple in their late fifties sat on the edge of a worn sofa. They held thick pottery mugs, while a man in a sheriff's uniform stood splay-legged in front of them with a somber expression and his hat in his hand. His posture and position seemed to hold the couple in place. The woman glared at the mug in her hand, then scowled at the sheriff.

Vik Peterson came out from behind the desk. "Maggie, Brian, and David McDonald, these are my...parents. Dot and Bill Peterson. And the sheriff, Nathan Sanchez.

The couple stood and tried to smile. Bill Peterson held out his hand and David shook it. "Vik is my brother's son," the man said. "But emotionally, legally, and every which way, he's ours and we're his. Jake was his cousin, but they were like brothers."

Dot Peterson reached into her pocket for a tissue and dabbed at her eyes. She started to speak and then waved her hand in front of her face and left the room. Vik followed her.

"Have a seat," the sheriff said, then frowned at the lack of available seating.

Vik returned from a back room carrying a stack of metal banquet chairs. He put it down and, detaching one at a time, invited us all to sit. He cupped his fist and made a gesture as though he was drinking from a mug. "Tea, Maggie?"

I shook my head and turned to Mr. Peterson. "I'm sorry for your loss."

He nodded and cleared his throat. "We wanted to thank you and your boys for helping Jake yesterday. The sheriff here tells us that you did everything you could."

The boys nodded and looked uncomfortable, unsure how to respond in a situation that had few rules and no right answers. "We tried," Brian said. "Sorry..."

An extended awkward silence ensued and the sheriff stepped forward, rescuing everyone. "The Petersons wanted to know if Jake said anything to you boys when you were with him. I'm interested too."

"Like, a police interview?" David asked.

The sheriff brushed non-existent dust from his pant leg. "Not at all. The medical team says you both helped Jake. We just want to know more about what happened, and I thought you two could help."

Brian sat, and then reached out to grab the back of David's T-shirt and pull him into the chair next to him.

Mr. Peterson sat and leaned forward. "Our son was meticulous about maintenance and safety, so it's hard for us to understand how he crashed. Did you see it happen?"

David stared at the ground. "I don't know much about ultralights," he began. "It was super windy up on the cliff." He looked up and then lifted his palm, using it to demonstrate the unsteady movement of the aircraft. "It was wobbling, back and forth, up and down. Is that normal?"

Vik answered too quickly and too loudly, "Not for Jake. He was always in control." His face reddened and he looked away. When he spoke again his voice was lower, slower, and softer. "Something was wrong."

"Did my boy say anything?" asked Dot as she returned from the back, still clutching her tissue.

Brian and David stared at each other, each waiting for the other to speak. "Something like 'mays prop bad check,'" David finally said. "Does that mean anything?"

Brian cleared his throat. "It could have been 'prop bad check mays.' Or something else. He repeated it several times, but it wasn't clear, and then he passed out."

"Could something have been wrong with his propeller?" I asked. "Or a car payment for last month?" If Jake had known how badly injured he was, would he have wanted to get his finances in order? Was that something young adults thought about?

Dot and Bill looked stricken, and I realized I'd overstepped. "Sorry, your son's finances aren't any of my business."

"It's not that," Dot said. "Like Bill said, Jake is really careful with his safety checks. No aircraft he worked on has ever had a problem. If something was wrong with the propeller, he'd have discovered it before he took off. He wouldn't have flown until it was fixed."

"So you think something bad happened mid-flight to either the ultralight or to Jake that caused the crash?" I asked.

Bill reached for his wife's hand. "None of this makes much sense," he said. "We keep expecting him to walk in, apologizing for worrying us."

The sheriff held out his arm, like a theater usher, but I wasn't sure whether he was encouraging the Petersons to leave or excusing my family from further questions. "Let's wait for the experts to weigh in. The National Transportation Safety Board will be looking into it, and they'll be able to tell us more," he said. "Jake's ultralight is on its way to their lab at the San Jose airport." He turned to the boys. "If you two remember anything else Jake said or did, please let me know." He handed each of them a card. "Dot, Bill, I'll see you out. Let's allow these folks to get on with their day."

Bill Peterson shook the boys' hands again and thanked them. The boys and I nodded somberly, but said nothing.

As soon as the couple had gone, Brian and David sank onto the sofa. David summed up their feelings in two words. "That sucked," he said.

Brian's concern was more practical. "Did you know NTSB investigated little stuff? Are they really interested in tiny crashes? Is an ultralight even technically a plane?"

"Let's help Vik put these chairs away," I said, wanting to give the boys something physical to do to distract them from their pain. I gathered up the tea mugs while the boys stacked the chairs and moved them back into the storage room.

"That's weird, what the Petersons were saying," David said. "That Jake was such a good pilot and safety conscious and all. I mean, accidents happen when you don't know what you're doing, or you rush to get ready, right? Sounds like Jake really knew his stuff."

"Sometimes, accidents are just accidents," I said, grabbing Belle's leash to keep her from "helping" the boys.

"They're having a rough time," Vik said. "They want someone or something to blame. Me too. It's messed up Jake has cancelled flights before because conditions were bad or he wanted to fix the rig."

"Was he flying for fun?" I asked. "Was the ultralight a hobby?"

Vik shook his head. "It started out that way. He's had the flying bug his whole life, and built the ultralight as a project with Burt Mason, a machinist who's an old friend of my dad's. Growing up, Jake spent as much time at Burt's shop as he did at our house."

"Mason?" I asked. "You boys said one of the words Jake muttered was *May's*. Could Jake have been trying to say his name?"

Vik scratched the back of his neck and wrinkled his nose. "We'll probably never know," he said. "And it's going to drive my mother crazy."

She needs an answer for everything. Loose ends nag at her until she knows exactly what happened."

"I know the feeling." I wasn't sure I'd said it aloud, until I saw Brian and David nodding.

"We can figure this out, right, Mom?" Brian said. "I want to know what happened to Jake too. Why'd he have to die? That doctor said he was stable, and like, a few minutes later, he was dead. How does that happen? I mean, I'd get it if he was old or sick or weak, but he wasn't, was he?"

I turned to Vic. "Did your brother have some kind of underlying illness that would explain his sudden turn for the worse?"

"You were at the hospital?" Vik asked. "Talking to my brother's doctor? Why?" Before we could answer, Vik waved his hands as though he was erasing an imaginary white board. "Never mind. I wonder if something could have happened there. They've had staffing issues, trying to keep costs down and stay competitive. I wonder if they cut corners with his care?" He dashed back behind the desk and picked up the phone. "I got to call my mom. She has to look into this."

David looked gray and sick, and Brian shivered. "You mean you think the hospital killed him?" Brian asked, shaking his head in disbelief. "But why? Does that even happen in real life? It sounds like a bad TV doctor show."

Vik looked up from the phone console where he'd punched in numbers as though he were trying to put his fingers through the machine. His eyes blinked rapidly and he bit his lip. "They can't get away with this," he said.

Renée hustled us out of the office, but stayed behind to talk to Vik. Through the glass door panels, we could see her gesturing but we couldn't hear the words.

Vik slammed down the phone, firmed his jaw, grabbed his hoodie off the back of the desk chair, and stomped out the far door to the parking lot. He jumped into an ancient compact car with a bad muffler and roared off in a cloud of smoke.

Chapter 6

Having trouble removing sand from skin? Sprinkle baby powder over the sandy area. The powder absorbs moisture making it easier (and less abrasive) to brush the sand away.

From the Notebook of Maggie McDonald
Simplicity Itself Organizing Services

Tuesday, June 18, Late Morning

Before Renée could join us outside, Sheriff Nate entered the gatehouse through the door on the opposite side of the central hallway —the same door through which Vik had stormed off. Renée waved us back inside.

The phone rang and Renée rushed to answer it. "I'm going to have to staff the desk here until I can get someone in Vik's place," she said as soon as she'd wrapped up the call. "I was planning to do that anyway. There's no reason he needs to be here when his brother has just died. His parents need his support." The phone rang again. She picked up and answered in a soft voice. Taking a seat at the desk, she disappeared behind the high counter and her words were muffled.

"There are just a couple of things I want to talk over with you," Nate said. "Do you mind?"

"Not at all," I said. "We're happy to help. But we're at a bit of a loss. We were at the hospital this morning and Jake's doctor—" I reached into my pocket, pulled out a card, and read. "Dr. William Bennett." I handed the card to the sheriff, which he accepted, though I was sure he was already well aware of the doctor's name and his connection to Jake. In fact, based on what we'd experienced of life in Watsonville so far, *everyone* in town probably knew that Dr. Bennett had been Jake's doctor.

"The family is understandably emotional," Nate said, weaving the brim of his hat through his fingers. "Dot and Bill are planning to talk to the district attorney."

"They want answers," I said.

Nate rubbed his chin. "NTSB is pretty adept at finding answers. They have extensive resources. I've recommended that the parents leave this up to the experts..." He paused and shifted his weight from one foot to the other. "They've got other ideas. I've tried to talk them out of it."

"What are you getting at?" David asked. "Is something wrong?"

The sheriff wrung his hands. It was one of the few times in my life I'd actually seen someone perform the gesture that had become a cliché for anxious behavior. "They're convinced that Jake was either murdered or killed by those who didn't do their jobs properly."

"Like the hospital staff?" I asked. "Vik mentioned something about that."

The sheriff shook his head. "Like your boys."

My mouth dropped open and I pulled Brian and David toward me as if to protect them. "Seriously? Why would the boys have killed him? That's crazy. What are they thinking?"

"That's just it," Nate said. "They're *not* thinking. They're lashing out. I don't see the DA giving their ideas much credence, but she'll listen respectfully. And might well conduct an investigation. I wanted to give you a heads up in case you start getting calls for interviews from law enforcement or the news media."

"On what grounds?" I asked. "I mean, I get that the Petersons aren't necessarily rational, but you have to have some idea what they're thinking— as skewed as their thought processes might be." I'd always thought of 'crazed by grief' as a statement that was exaggerated for effect. But if what the sheriff was saying was true, the Petersons were loony tunes.

The sheriff scoffed. "They claim your boys were untrained and that they fatally injured Jake as they tried to rescue him."

"But we called 9-1-1," Brian protested. "And the rescue guys and that doctor at the hospital all said we did the right thing."

"Even Mr. Peterson thanked us," David added, his face flushed. "Who thanks someone and then takes them to court?"

The sheriff gestured for everyone to calm down. But I was outraged. "How dare they?" I said. "Their little visit here was just a pretext, wasn't it? Did they hope the boys would say something incriminating?"

The sheriff looked even more uncomfortable. "According to the Petersons, they already have."

"*What?*" David said. "How could we have said anything bad? You heard us." He turned to me, eyes pleading for me to back him up. I put my arm around his shoulder.

The sheriff checked his watch. "Apparently it's going to be on the local news station at noon," he said. "Renée?"

Renée stood to search the desk for a remote. She found it under a pile of papers I was itching to file away and pointed it toward a plasma television mounted on the wall behind the counter. David's image appeared on the screen. We'd caught the broadcast in the middle of the story.

"—no experts. We called in the EMTs and they worked on him. They're the heroes." Renée muted the rest of the program as a talking head appeared and the newscast moved on to a story about a warehouse fire in the neighboring town of Salinas.

I turned to the sheriff. "What's wrong with that?"

The sheriff shrugged. "I'm guessing it will all blow over quickly as the Petersons work through their grief. You might want to get some legal help for the time being though. Just in case."

"A lawyer?" I asked. "Why would we need a lawyer?"

Renée leaned on the counter. "California has a Good Samaritan law, doesn't it? Brian and David did the right thing. How can Dot and Bill bring charges against them?"

"Why do you keep calling them Dot and Bill?" I asked. "Are they cousins of yours too?"

"Neighbors. It's a small town. Get used to it." Renée smiled to take the sting from her words.

By sheer numbers, Watsonville was a little bit bigger than Orchard View. But my tiny hometown was surrounded by Silicon Valley, where megatropolis meets overcrowded suburb. My world on the other side of the Santa Cruz Mountains was close-knit, but nothing like life in the rural market town I was just getting to know.

Sheriff Nate wiped his forehead. "You done?" he asked Renée before turning to me. "How about you?"

He looked sternly at each of us and then carried on without waiting for an answer. "Good questions. Let me see if I can answer them in order of importance or something close to it. Maggie, yes. It never hurts to call a lawyer. California does have a Good Samaritan law that was intended to encourage people to help out in emergencies."

"So, the Petersons are blowing smoke?" I interrupted.

"Maybe. But test cases have shown that the law doesn't cover all the bases. There are some legal actions now moving through the appeals process that have revealed flaws in the wording."

"Why doesn't the legislature fix it?" Renée asked.

"If you ran the state, I'm sure the original act would have covered it," said the sheriff. "But the wheels of justice grind slowly..."

"It's *the mills of God*..." said Renée.

"You want to quibble?" Nate asked. "Or do you want me to go on?"

"Sorry," said Renée, though she didn't seem sorry at all. In fact, their conversation seemed to cover familiar ground, the kind that loving friends and family members return to again and again.

"Maggie's lawyer will know better than this simple country sheriff, but my guess is the law is meant to protect Brian and David. But that won't matter. At least not in the near term. It won't prevent Dot and Bill, in their grief, from making a mess of things. Let's let the DA handle it and see how it shakes out."

Renée opened her mouth to speak, but Nate quelled her with a look. "Let me finish with your last crop of questions before we start on a new batch. Do you have a sandwich or something around here?"

Renée looked at her watch. I glanced at my own as my stomach rumbled. It was 12:30. I was glad we'd grabbed sandwiches earlier.

"We picked up lunch at Beach Street this morning," I said. "Unless you're on specialized diets, we can split the sandwiches. They're huge."

Renée picked up the handset from the telephone console. "Let me get someone to cover the desk. I'll meet you at your place."

The sheriff added more detail as we crossed the complex to the oceanside condominium buildings. "The Petersons have already complained to the district attorney, who asked me to conduct a cursory investigation out of respect for their loss, though she's sure there's no case to answer." He shook his head and then stopped in the middle of the road. "This attack is out of character for them, Maggie. They're good people."

"Are we being arrested?" Brian asked.

"No one is being arrested," I said with all the firmness I could muster. "Sheriff Nate just explained that. All this is just a formality. So the sheriff and the district attorney can tell the Petersons they looked into it and found nothing." I looked up at the sheriff for confirmation.

He nodded. "That about sums it up."

We were nearly back to the condo when the sheriff's radio erupted in a series of static-filled code intelligible only to him. "I've got to go," he said. "Try not to worry. I'm sure this will all blow over." Brian ran up the stairs to our unit and quickly re-emerged with a sandwich wrapped in a napkin. He chased after the sheriff, and handed it to him.

How could anyone believe two children as thoughtful as my kids could have been criminally negligent? It was mind boggling, but that didn't mean we were off the hook. We might well need expert advice to navigate this situation with as little trauma as possible.

I needed to call Max, followed by our family friend and lawyer, Forrest Doucett. It wouldn't hurt to let Jason Mueller, chief of the Orchard View police department, know what was going on either. I sucked in a quick breath and held it. Maybe they'd already heard. On a slow summer news day, a volatile broadcast from even a small affiliate station was sure to be picked up by news outlets all over the Bay Area.

I tried to look at the situation objectively, through the lens of a media outlet trying to gain market share. A photogenic young graduate student was dead. His distraught parents were hurling accusations while local law enforcement struggled to keep up. It would make a great story. The kind that drove up ratings. My kids were smack dab in the cross-hairs of the blood-thirsty and highly competitive Bay Area news hounds.

I had no idea how to handle any of this—and zero experience talking to the media. I was all set to speed dial Stephen Laird, a retired Marine veteran with a wide variety of caped-crusader type skills and a solution for every disaster my family had landed in since we'd moved to Orchard View nearly two years earlier.

But then I took a deep breath and refocused my attention on my kids. We had plenty of time. I needed to comfort Brian and David, plan, and call Stephen later.

I missed the security of facing a potentially perilous situation with the support of my friends in Orchard View. Here in Watsonville, a town in which everyone was a stranger, I was working without a net.

Chapter 7

On vacation at the beach without sand toys? Check your rental kitchen for durable, unbreakable measuring cups or containers. Be sure to return them to the unit at the end of your stay.

From the Notebook of Maggie McDonald
Simplicity Itself Organizing Services

Tuesday, June 18, Afternoon

I curled up on the rental unit's monster of a sectional couch and dialed Forrest Doucett.

The receptionist put me through to Nell Bevans, a young associate at the firm whom I'd worked with before. I trusted her to relay the pertinent information to Forrest.

"Wow," Nell said after I'd recounted the events of the past few days. "You're in way over your head. I'm glad you called."

My spirits sank as she dashed my hope that phoning the lawyers was overkill. Nell reacted as though she'd heard my heart hit the floor. "Don't panic. This situation isn't that complicated from a legal perspective. The tricky part will be managing the news outlets and social media. Their attacks can be swifter, harsher, and more reactionary than the law. Lucky for you, we've just hired two people who are experts in that arena. We all need to become adept at fending off slings and arrows in cyberspace."

"I hadn't even thought to ask for help with the media."

"No problem. Forrest is in a meeting right now, but I'll catch him when he comes out. Is this number the best way for him to reach you?"

"Cell-phone coverage is a little sketchy out here in the boonies, but text messages seem to be reliable. If Forrest sends me a text, I can find a spot with a strong signal or a landline and phone him back."

"Perfect. Don't sweat it. You know we'll look after you."

I'd seen Nell eloquently argue legal precedents in a sharp black suit like the reincarnation of legendary attorney Clarence Darrow. In contrast, the informality of her phone conversation delighted and reassured me. I thanked her for restoring my confidence and ended the call. I winked at the boys and phoned Max.

"I saw the news and I'm on my way—about to leave the house," he said as soon as he answered. "Trying to beat the traffic backup after the fishhook."

Max referred to the exit from Highway 17 to Highway 1, a sweeping turn that jammed up rush-hour traffic for miles and for which no reasonable alternative routes existed. The warning sign for the curve looked like a fishhook, hence the local nickname for the notorious bottleneck.

"What about the cats?" I asked. Our two cats, Holmes and Watson, pretended to be independent but became anxious and unruly if they were left too long without humans to boss around. The last time we'd left them alone for more than twenty-four hours, we'd returned to find Watson perched precariously and uncomfortably atop our living room curtain rod. She had meowed plaintively through the night before returning to floor level.

"Paolo volunteered to housesit."

Paolo, the youngest member of the Orchard View police force, was a friend of every member of our family, but he was especially beloved by Holmes and Watson.

"Then they're in good hands."

"Yes, but what about you and the boys? How you holding up?"

"We'll be better when you get here. I'm not sure I've had a chance to process it all. I called Forrest and talked to Nell Bevans. She's the one who helped us out when Stephen was in jail last year."

"Good. I was about to suggest that. Did Nell have any action items for us?"

"Maybe after checking with Forrest. She wants us to meet their handlers for social media and the news outlets."

I heard a sharp intake of breath. "I hadn't thought about that, but Nell's right. The last thing we want is for the boys to be tried on social media, particularly with David's college applications in the offing."

Ugh. College applications. The bane of the existence of every high school junior or senior and their parents. I looked up to see if David and Brian had been able to hear Max's comments, but the boys seemed oblivious, thank goodness. I didn't want to bring the stress of essays and transcripts into an already dreadful situation. I sank further into the couch cushions, cupped my hands over the phone, and lowered my voice. "We've got enough to worry about without borrowing trouble. One thing at a time. Anyway, Nell seemed confident."

"That's what we need."

"Can I fill you in on the rest later over a glass of wine or a walk on the beach? I've got a few more calls to make."

"See you soon."

"Be safe." For someone driving over the steep, winding, narrow, and heavily traveled twenty-six miles between Los Gatos and Santa Cruz, the words took on added meaning. Tight curves, skinny shoulders, frequent mudslides, distracted drivers, and young people who mistook themselves for NASCAR racers all contributed to wrecks, casualties, and slowdowns. Deer and the occasional mountain lion dashing across the road compounded the problems. Though some people commuted twice daily over the deadly highway, no one I knew ever took it lightly.

"Dad will be here in an hour or two," I told the boys.

"Pizza?" asked Brian.

I chewed my lip in thought, remembering that our cupboards and fridge were bare. I ripped a clean sheet of paper from my notebook and handed it to my youngest son. "Start a list. We've got nothing, so think about what you want for breakfast and lunches too."

David frowned and started to protest.

"And when you're done," I told Brian. "Hand the paper to your brother. Include dinner ideas for later in the week if you want, and I'll get the ingredients."

From the boys' perspective, I hoped I seemed like an indulgent mom, fulfilling their every gastronomical whim. In my own mind, I'd neatly delegated meal planning and creating the shopping list. I wondered how much other help I could snag. "David, do you have charge left on your phone?" I asked.

He reached into his back pocket, pulled out his phone, glanced at the screen, and nodded.

"See if the local grocery has a delivery service. If so, enter your choices into the online order form directly."

David tapped and swiped. The apartment's wall phone rang. Brian answered, spoke briefly and ended the call. "That was Renée," he said. "She can't get anyone to cover the front desk, so she'll get in touch later."

"Safeway has Peapod delivery," David said. He sounded thrilled but quickly deflated. "But the first appointment slot is three days from now." "That's no good. Okay, a trip to the grocery store and office supply, then." I said. I made a quick call to Renée to ask if she needed anything in town. It was three miles to the nearest stores, and it seemed silly not to offer to pick up anything she needed while I was there. I thought for a moment and then added, "Unless you already have a good supply of packing boxes or you know a grocery that delivers. I'm all for hiring other people to complete chores that don't need our immediate and personal attention."

Renée shook her head and frowned. "Sorry. I'm going to put locating a delivery service on my list though. I'd like to have a business to recommend to renters and homeowners who are busy, ill, or pressed for time."

Depending upon your generation, grocery delivery might sound like an old-fashioned amenity, an essential, or an indulgence. In my grandmother's time, when not as many people owned cars, delivery by local businesses was a given. Nana could mail her list in the morning, and get all her essentials delivered in the afternoon. After years of thinking that kind of service was lost to the ages, it was making a comeback. It was particularly popular in the San Francisco Bay Area with busy families who had less time than money. Needing to make every moment count, they were reluctant to spend unnecessary time stuck in traffic or parking lots. Google Shopping offered free delivery from a variety of businesses in the heart of Silicon Valley. Amazon provided next-day and sometimes same-day service, while many local stores had drive-by pickup options and delivery services.

Because my work hours were flexible, I typically found it convenient to do my own shopping. But I wasn't shy about utilizing the free services on days like today when I had more to do than hours in which to accomplish it.

I couldn't delegate my chores today, though. Lack of delivery service was another reminder that Santa Cruz County was a vastly different place than its immediate neighbor, Santa Clara County, a.k.a. Silicon Valley. I glanced at my watch. Two o'clock. I needed to get moving if we were going to eat at home tonight. I drummed my fingers on the table as I sorted through the possibilities. I wanted the boys to come with me for my own comfort and sense of security. But dragging them to the grocery wouldn't protect them from the judgments of social media and might expose them unnecessarily to hungry news hounds or comments from strangers. They hadn't spent any time on the beach today either, though I knew that we'd go for a walk later when Max arrived. Belle, at least, would insist upon it.

My phone's text alert interrupted my train of thought

Turnip raid a vee, the message said. I frowned in confusion, then handed the phone to Brian, who was adept at interpreting words garbled by an automated voice-to-text conversion system combined with predictive text.

"Turn on radio or TV," Brian translated. "Dad must be in the car. Voice to text has trouble sifting out road noise." He typed something quickly into the phone with both thumbs, pressed send, and the phone chirped cheerfully in response.

Standing, he moved to the dusty television in the corner and pushed the power button.

A talking head appeared, speaking in Spanish. We all recognized the footage, which included shots of the cliffside rescue of Jake Peterson. Brian clicked through the channels until he found another news station broadcasting in English. David's image filled the screen.

"No, we don't have any special training," on-screen David said. "I hope we didn't hurt him."

My heart sank as the image shifted to a smug looking news anchor. "The victim's family filed suit today in Santa Cruz County saying that untrained thrill seekers may well have done more harm than good, hampering efforts of first-responders to save the life of local graduate student Jake Peterson. The sheriff's office had no comment when asked for an update. We'll follow this tragic story and update you as information becomes available."

My older son's charming self-deprecating personality might well have secured his doom.

Chapter 8

Use mesh laundry bags to transport sand toys. Shake to get rid of excess sand and rinse off in the ocean, with a hose, or under a faucet at the end of your trip.

From the Notebook of Maggie McDonald
Simplicity Itself Organizing Services

Tuesday, June 18, Afternoon

"Mom?" asked David, his voice trembling. "Are we in trouble?"

"How much trouble?" added Brian, ashen. Belle picked up the tension in the room, whined, and pressed against my legs.

"It will be okay," I said with as much confidence as I could muster. My words did little to reduce the overwhelming tension in the room. I tried again. "Remember what I said yesterday on this same topic?"

"That all the praise we were getting didn't matter?" David said.

"Exactly. You did the right thing. At the right time. That's all that mattered yesterday and all that matters today. The rest of it, especially all the media coverage, will find its own level. And almost certainly will be overshadowed quickly by some other big news story, probably before the nightly news comes on."

I stood up and gathered my things. "Let's talk about it in the car. We need those groceries."

* * * *

Max arrived just after we'd pulled back into the condo parking lot. My car was loaded with groceries, all of which needed to be lugged up the stairs to our third-floor condo. We had coffee, wine, cookies, and ice cream. All the essential food groups plus fresh produce and the makings of a dynamite spaghetti sauce that would come together in a flash.

But Max had thought ahead. He carried two cloth grocery sacks filled with thawing containers of his homemade soup, along with a loaf of fresh sourdough, a salad in a bag, and a box of gingerbread sandcastle cookies baked and decorated by our Orchard View neighbor Elaine Cumberfield.

Max poured wine, sliced bread, and put the soup on to heat while the boys filled him in on the latest news and I stashed the groceries in a fridge, freezer, and cabinets designed for smaller appetites.

"Beach before dinner?" David asked. I looked at Max and nodded.

Originally I'd envisioned a hearty hike, but the emotional strain of the day's events had left me exhausted. Max and I decided in favor of the beach. We also sheepishly defied the rule against glassware and alcohol on the beach. We spread out a vivid Mexican blanket woven in colors that could stand to fade and plopped ourselves down, wine glasses in hand, to watch the boys skimboard along the shoreline. Belle gleefully chased both boys and the waves.

"So…" Max touched my hand and lifted his eyebrows.

"We've only been here a couple of days. I'm already overwhelmed."

"Tell me about it," he said, as a gull approached slowly, hoping we were serving cheese and crackers. I scowled.

"No, really, I mean, *tell me about it.* I'm inviting you to unburden yourself, my dear. My statement was not an attempt to shift the conversational focus to me as I beg for sympathy and regale you with a list of the ways my life is so much worse than yours." He lifted his glass to mine. "Tonight is all about you. And maybe developing a plan to make things a little bit better tomorrow."

I felt my shoulders relax and I wiggled my butt in the sand to create a custom recliner. "Where do I start?"

"You okay? The boys?"

"Did I pass along the news that I contacted that lawyer, Nell Bevans? She took notes and will confer with Forrest. I can't remember who I've told what. The law firm is sending someone down soon with a plan for handling the media and the legal issues. I've got calls in to Jason, to see if he's got local contacts who could help out.

Max stroked his chin, which needed either a shave or a commitment to growing a full beard. "Good idea. We haven't run into a problem yet that the dynamic duo of Jason and Stephen couldn't help solve."

I nearly spit out my wine, laughing at Max's description of our friends. Stephen, whom Max referred to alternately as the caped crusader or the ninja marine, was a veteran who'd been injured in the line of duty. Now a VA hospital volunteer working with discharged service members both canine and human, he had contacts all over the Bay Area that would put any covert operation to shame. His husband, Jason, also a marine veteran, headed our local police force along with a volunteer team of officers and first responders who could be deployed to disaster areas to support local emergency personnel. Their commitments to serve hadn't ended when they left the armed services. They'd put their impressive protective net of experienced ex-soldiers at our disposal more than once.

"What?" said Max with fake innocence as he handed me a napkin. "You know it's true."

"But too on-the-nose for me to keep a straight face."

"We called out the cavalry. We're waiting to hear hoofbeats. What's next on the agenda?"

I thought for a moment, looking for wisdom in my wine glass and wishing we'd brought the cheese and crackers the gulls coveted. "In no particular order, I need to..." I settled my glass in the sand and counted off on my fingers. "*We* need to help the boys maintain their confidence and hold their heads up when they run into anyone who has heard and believed the Petersons' accusations. I need to help Renée get her office in order and develop a proposal to the board for the money she needs to make the plan succeed for all the stakeholders."

"A tall order."

"Especially since it may require resolving child care issues and other problems she's got managing three foster kids she's taken on."

"Taken on?"

"Long story. I don't think she was expecting them, or in any way prepared for fostering. Friends and family are chipping in to get her all the baby goods she needs to care for them."

"What happened to their mom, dad, granny, aunts, or other family members?"

"Some sort of immigration status glitch involving ICE. Renée hasn't had time to fill in the details. But if she wants me to work my magic on her offices, I'm going to need a lot more of her time than she was able to offer me today."

"What about daycare?"

I smiled. "How quickly you forget. Three kids. Twins under two and an infant. Renée could barely get out a syllable. Forget any follow-up questions I might have had."

"Can the boys help?"

"My thoughts exactly. I hope they see it the same way. Renée's got more than enough work to keep them busy in the office even if she doesn't need support looking after the children." ·

Belle ran up, tongue lolling and coat dripping. "Wait!" I ordered. She obeyed, but then shook her entire body as only the loose-skinned retrievers can, transferring most of the water and sand from her body to ours. Laughing, we stood, spit out sand, shook the blanket, and plucked up our wine glasses. If I couldn't tolerate a little sand in my adult beverages, I wouldn't have brought my golden retriever to the beach. But as any golden retriever lover knows, there is nothing on earth quite as contagious as the joy of a water-loving dog on an ocean beach with her family.

Max leashed Belle and trotted with her to a hose in the condo building's common area. I toted the rest of our belongings.

Max put his fingers to his lips and whistled to the boys. Words would have been lost in the wind billowing off the waves, but the shrill tone cut through the beach sounds, and he pointed toward the condo. "I'll whistle them up again when Belle's clean. They may lose track of time."

I turned away and reached for the door between the beach and the building's inner courtyard.

"Did you see that?" Max called in a voice mixed with excitement, alarm, and disbelief. "Right there. Did you see?" He pointed toward the beach, and I was almost afraid to look. The boys were there. Yesterday, the unexpected had resulted in a young man's death.

I heard the boys call out in tones echoing Max's. Max grabbed Belle's leash and sprinted toward the boys. I followed, visualizing the worst.

"What is it? Max. Just tell me. What's happening?" Nearly a foot shorter than Max, my field of view was smaller than his, particularly when it came to seeing whatever was going on just beyond the dunes.

"Blue!" said Brian. "A *blue* whale. Do you know how rare they are? Who's got a phone?"

I squinted into the glare from the setting sun, seeing nothing but the bay's mirror-flat surface beyond the breakers. But then what looked like a small island emerged from the sea and slowly disappeared. I gasped, overwhelmed with reverence and awe. Nothing in life or imagination had prepared me for this moment. I took Max's hand and felt the boys and Belle press close to me. We watched the sea for several minutes more, saying nothing, then all breathed out as one when the whale spouted a plume of condensation that dissipated into the mist.

Chapter 9

On one vacation, we met a family with an inexpensive inflatable beach toy. They were about to fly home and passed the toy along to us for the rest of our stay. We passed it to another family when we left. It was a great way to foster friendships, teach the kids about generosity, and save luggage space.

From the Notebook of Maggie McDonald
Simplicity Itself Organizing Services

Wednesday, June 19, Morning

We began the day with the hike we'd skipped the night before, hoping to spot more whales and other marine wildlife. Max wanted to inspect the spot where Jake Peterson's aircraft had gone down—where the boys had struggled to save him.

Tiny shorebirds, rare snowy plovers, dotted the beach, moving between waves and sand like a troupe of dancers or ping-pong balls blown in the wind. Day-trippers hadn't yet arrived, and most of the campers at Sunset Beach were still waking up. A few families with early rising small children built sand castles or roads for tiny construction trucks.

Dunes hid tents and campers from view, but we could smell the cozy scent of wood fires and bacon as we walked by. Just beyond the camping area, the headland rose abruptly to a couple of hundred feet. I'd been sure the spot of the dramatic rescue would be obvious to all of us, but I couldn't pinpoint it. Brian and David each thought they knew exactly where the events had played out, but they disagreed on the location.

"Let's take the stairs this time." I pointed to a rough series of railroad ties that formed steps in a path that zigzagged up the cliff. The beams reduced trail erosion and restored vegetation, but they also created a navigable staircase. And I was all for selecting the most straightforward path. Or at least one that was less grueling than our earlier mad scramble. Without the aid of adrenaline, even the gentle risers took my breath away. But so did the view from the top.

The entire Monterey Bay stretched before us, from Santa Cruz to Pacific Grove. If the bay was a backward "C," we stood at its apex. Sailboats and fishing craft with draped nets dotted the ocean surface. The blue whales must have moved beyond the horizon in search of krill. If they'd been within the confines of the bay, we'd have seen them. It's difficult to hide when you're the largest mammal on the planet.

Behind us, the view of the inland valley was nearly as mesmerizing. Santa Cruz and Monterey counties are home to some of the richest farmland in the nation. From our hilltop we spotted fields of strawberries, lettuce, artichokes, each being harvested by hunched farmworkers.

The slough system of wetland habitat snaked between the fields and Highway One.

Max was more interested in the ground underfoot as he walked through the sandy soil and scrub brush on the ridgeline. Every few moments he'd stop to scuff his feet through the dust.

"Here, boys?" he asked, then pointed out landmarks Brian and David had mentioned in their retelling of the tragic adventure. "There's the road out to the highway. And the parking lot and barn."

The boys looked at each other and nodded in agreement. To the right, a chain-link fence separated us from the farmland. Through the mesh, we could see furrowed plastic-covered rows of strawberries, a decrepit barn, and metal tanks marked with insignia that we couldn't identify from this distance.

"Do you know who owns this property?" Max asked. "I'd love to get in there and check it out a little more closely. Could Jake have seen something no one wanted him to report to the appropriate authorities? Could the barn be hiding something he shouldn't have witnessed?"

"Like what? Those look like ordinary propane tanks to me," I said.

"But why would they need propane way out here?" Max asked. He was right. Other than the small development of mostly vacation homes to the north and the state park below us, there were no dwellings that would have required heat, light, or hot water. Strawberries don't require much processing.

"Unlicensed housing?" I asked. The kids then shouted out a series of colorful suggestions.

"Meth lab?"

"Pesticides?"

"Sex trafficking?"

"Sweat shop?"

"Gang headquarters?"

"Secret government lab?" said Brian, finishing up the list that could have been ripped straight from the pages of a graphic novel. I reached out to ruffle his hair and then pulled my hand back, knowing he hated the gesture because it felt demeaning to him. Though it was a habit I'd developed out of love and affection for his unruly curls, I tried hard to respect his wishes and dominion over his own person.

"Enough wild speculation. We're way off in the weeds," I said. "I wonder if Renée would know who owns this land." I pulled out my phone, took a photo, and sent it to her with a brief text. Max turned toward the farm. "And what about that one?" he asked, pointing to a field south of the barn. While the strawberry furrows looked similar, they were covered with a different color of plastic. "Are they owned by different farmers? Does the plastic tint indicate one is organic and the other isn't?"

I had no idea, but it was a good question that led to several more. How would a farmer keep his organic crops pesticide-free if his fields butted up against a traditionally managed farm? "I'll call Renée later and see if we can get a tour 'round here tomorrow."

Max's stomach growled, and he glanced at his phone. "If we head home we'll be back in time for lunch."

"Home home or condo home?" asked David.

"Condo home." I zipped up my sweatshirt against the freshening breeze. Whitecaps marked the previously mirror-flat surface of the bay. Breakers crashed against the sand.

David grinned at Brian. "Race you?"

They were off.

Max and I descended the cliff more gingerly, choosing our steps. Belle dashed between the boys and us, barking. From headland to sand took one hundred and twenty steps. I counted. But descending via the staircase was still easier than sliding through the prickly scrub on my rear as I had last time.

As soon as the sand leveled out and I felt it was safe to take my eyes from my feet, I looked up to see Belle wagging her tail, standing over Brian, who sat hunched on the sand, within sight but out of earshot. I ached to turn down the volume on the waves so I could hear Belle and the kids. Max and I picked up our pace as David leaned down as if to help Brian up. Brian half rose and then sank back onto the sand. David looked back, spotted us, and stood, waving both hands frantically. *Not again.* What had happened now? Now, when we were almost back in our condo. Almost safe.

By the time we reached the boys, David had helped Brian hop down to the ocean to wash sand and blood from a gaping slash on his shin. I glared at the wound as if it would obey a stern parental look and heal itself on the spot.

"Aw, come on, Mom," Brian said. "It's not that bad. A few Band-Aids should fix it, right?"

I glanced warily back toward the dry sand without answering. If you'd asked me what I searched for, I wouldn't have been be able to tell you. Perhaps I had some idea that my kids had been attacked and I was ready to defend my offspring from any threat. But there were no sword-wielding ninjas or other enemies anywhere in sight. "What happened?" I asked.

David shook his head. "Wasn't me. I heard him yell. I looked back, and Brian was on the ground."

"I didn't yell. I tripped. It wasn't until I took a few steps that I realized it hurt. I must have hit a broken bottle or something."

Max combed the beach, examining the sand for whatever hazard had removed most of the skin from Brian's left shin. He looked up, shaking his head. "There's a giant steel spike pounded into the sand. Could have been there a day, a year, or more than a century. I can't tell."

"There used to be a shipping pier and a dance pavilion out here back in the Victorian era," I said. "Maybe it's part of the old structure? Part of the foundation or a tie-down for a boat?"

"Who knows? But that slash needs a doctor's attention, a tetanus shot, and a good cleaning." Max peered at the wound, pushing the sides of it together as Brian winced. "Maybe some stitches. Shins take forever to heal." He reached out a hand to help Brian up. "Come on, tough guy."

Brian sighed and stood. Slinging one arm over his father's shoulder and the other over his brother's, he limped over the soft sand toward the condo, where I stopped just long enough to pick up a dish towel and ice pack. My family never goes anywhere without a good supply of icepacks. When we weren't using them for sprains, strains, bruises, or burns, we employed them to fight the migraines that Max and David often endured.

The kids teased Max all the time about his flashlight collection, though it was an obsession that had helped us all on more than one occasion. My thing was ice packs.

* * * *

At the hospital, I dropped my guys off and drove the few miles to downtown Freedom to pick up take-out sandwiches, coffee, and water for the boys. Cookies and fruit rounded out our impromptu picnic. I had no idea how long we'd wait in the emergency room, but I was prepared for a major siege. At the checkout, I grabbed a year's supply of disinfectant gel to help me get over my heebie-jeebies related to eating in a hospital. I wasn't really a germophobe but, despite efforts to sanitize everything, I knew medical facilities to be among the grungiest places on earth.

Back at the emergency room, David was alone in the waiting room with his phone. He barely looked up when I plopped in the chair next to his.

"Doing research?" I asked. "Has Brian been seen?"

"He's getting stitched now, I think. Dad's with him. At first, they hustled Brian off into a room all his own to make sure Dad hadn't been trying to kneecap him with a lead pipe. Brian must have convinced them things were okay, but then they took Dad off alone to make sure Brian wasn't hurting himself. Then they interviewed me."

"I'm glad you all passed the test. Think I should risk running the gauntlet?"

"Only if your conscience is clear," he said in a dour tone. He couldn't hold his face straight for long, though.

"Sandwich?" I waved it in front of him. He set down the phone.

"I was checking out who owns the farms on the top of the ridge, and whether they're organic." He tilted his screen so I could see the Google Maps satellite display of the area. "Kevin Rivers owns this property. It's organic. You were right. He's some kind of relative of Renée's. I found a picture of them both at a birthday party for Renée's grandmother." He took a bite of his sandwich before continuing.

"*Hmm*. Good. Thanks, Mom," he mumbled as he chewed. "This farm here," he pointed at the screen to a property adjoining the one owned by Rivers. "It belongs to Diego Baker, and it's not organic. Not certified organic by the state, anyway. They could be working the farm organically and awaiting certification, but they could also be using traditional pesticides."

"Can you tell whose property the barn sits on?" I asked, squinting at the screen.

David shook his head. "The resolution isn't that great, and the farm roads cut through there. There aren't any fences or anything on either side of the barn. It's in a kind of triangle patch between the farms. It could belong to either one."

I thought for a moment. "So Kevin Rivers." I belatedly lowered my voice, suddenly aware that anyone within earshot could be a friend of Kevin's, and I wouldn't want them to think we were gossiping about him. "Kevin Rivers," I repeated softly. "He needs to keep chemicals from coming in contact with his crops, yet Diego would want to maximize his yields by using every pesticide or fertilizer that's allowed."

David nodded. "So if Kevin discovered that Diego had filled the barn with nasty pesticides or fertilizers, he'd be angry. Probably livid. It takes years to secure an organic certification, but seconds to lose it."

"But would that anger extend as far as murder? Assuming the Petersons are right about it not being an accident, that is."

"Follow the money. Organic strawberries go for at least a dollar a pound more than regular stuff. Growing the certified berries is way more expensive and time-consuming."

"So, if you grew fruit conventionally, but sold it as organic, your profit margins would increase."

"Right. Big time. And if someone sprayed pesticides on your organic fruit, you'd lose a bundle. Not just on that crop, but for years to come."

"But could you pull it off? Those fields are out in the open. Anyone could spy on your operation."

"Government agencies don't test every berry. Just random samples maybe once a year. So if you had *both* organic and standard fields, and could submit organic samples in place of your ordinary fruit, and then claim all your fields were organic, you'd make a mint."

"So what happens if you get caught?"

"I don't know what the legal penalties would be, or what might happen if your friends, neighbors, competitors, and employees discovered what you were up to—"

"If you were caught, could you still sell your fruit?"

David continued to squint at the screen. I wondered if he needed glasses. "The least that would happen is that the California Department of Food and Agriculture would yank your organic certification. You'd probably end up in civil court with tons of legal expenses..." His voice trailed off before he spoke again. "This says there are federal penalties as well as state ones. But the real liability is that, in California at least, people can sue anyone who passes off non-organic food as organic. You or I could do that. There was a test case a few years ago..." David's voice trailed off again as he continued reading, but then he looked up. "It turns out that government enforcement is sketchy and slow. I expect any jerk who got caught mislabeling would be a target for, let's say, more informal and direct forms of justice."

"Like what?"

"I dunno. Picketing? Boycotts? Shunning. Maybe a crooked farmer would find himself face down in a vat of pesticide or scarfing down burgers laced with rat poison."

"And maybe someone who wanted to keep their crooked practices a secret would threaten a guy who flew over his fields every day?"

David and I stared at each other. I still didn't fully buy the argument that someone had deliberately caused Jake's ultralight to crash. But David's research suggested there could be something going on behind the scenes. Something worth hiding. If his theories proved true, someone might have had a motive for silencing Jake. It would be difficult for anyone, especially the DA, to blame Brian and David for harming him when alternative explanations were at hand. But we still needed proof.

Chapter 10

In the terrifying event that a child goes missing at the beach, don't panic.
Look downwind. Beach lifeguards report that children generally take the
path of least resistance when wandering. (Just in case, always make note
of what your child is wearing. Bright colors are cheerful and easiest to
spot at a distance.)

From the Notebook of Maggie McDonald
Simplicity Itself Organizing Services

Luckily, David didn't seem bothered by the dark places our imaginations
were taking us. He took another bite of his sandwich without looking at it.
"I'm going to check on Brian," I said. "You okay here, or do
you want to come?"
David shuddered. "And watch someone stitch through my brother's skin?
No, thanks. Besides, I want to look up suspicious agriculture-related deaths."
"Enjoy."
"Wait." He handed me the bag of sandwiches and a bottle of water. "Don't
forget these. They're stitching his leg, not his hands. He's probably starving."
In the language of brothers, David's gesture meant *I love the little
guy*. I was touched.
I made my way past the gatekeepers who required me to show
identification yet still looked at me skeptically. Inside an emergency room
cubicle, I found a white-coated young man plucking debris from Brian's
leg with tweezers. My younger son's skin had gray-green undertones. Food
was the last thing on his mind.

"How ya doin', bud?" I asked, not able to resist ruffling his hair this time. When your kid is hurting, it's difficult not to revert to the mother-toddler relationship.

"Great!" he said, in what I suspected was a drug-induced haze.

I glanced at Max, who nodded. "High as a kite. They wanted to do a deep clean, so they numbed him up well. But there's so little flesh there on the shin, it was difficult and excruciating to anesthetize, so they gave him a tranquilizer, too. He's a little woozy, but he looks much better than he did a few minutes ago."

"A lot of happy juice," said Brian. "Can you tell?"

"Oh, yup, I can tell," I said.

"David okay?" Max asked.

"He's out there researching gruesome agricultural deaths and making a list of motives for murder."

"Cool," answered Brian, turning to the medical professional working on his leg, who didn't look that much older than either of my kids. Part of that was his pallor, which nearly matched Brian's. Clearly, this kid worked long hours and studied more. In any case, he didn't get out to the beach much.

"Dr. Eddie Singh, this is my wife and Brian's mom, Maggie McDonald," Max said

The doctor looked up, smiled, and nodded. "I won't stand up or shake hands, under the circumstances," he said, and went back to fishing for debris in Brian's wounds.

"Were you here when Jake Peterson came in?" Brian asked the doctor. "What do you think happened? Why did he die? He was badly hurt, but when we checked the next morning, we were told he was doing fine."

Dr. Singh looked up from Brian's wound. "You're *that* kid," he said. "The guy who rescued Jake?"

Brian nodded. "Me and my brother. You knew him? Are you from here?"

The young doctor shook his head. "I knew him, but not from here. I grew up in Santa Clara. But I live in Watsonville now. My roommate went to high school with Jake." He looked around the exam room as if hunting for spies who might arrest him for conveying too much information about another patient.

"Jake was an ultralight pilot," the doctor said. "Ultralight pilots tend to be into other active sports like mountain biking, skiing, and kite-surfing. When you add in trouble with bagel knives, abalone shells, and attack-trained garden tools, folks around here were considering giving him a special deal. Ten emergency-room visits and you get a free surgery."

Brian grinned. "My mom says the same thing to my brother and me."

The doctor patted the uninjured side of Brian's calf. "Frequent flyer, eh? I'm about ready to stitch you up. Just need to grab a suture pack. No dangerous gymnastics while I'm gone, got it?"

He winked at Brian who bobbed his head in slow, solemn agreement, then promptly nodded off.

"How much medication did they give him?" I asked Max.

"Enough. It was grim, but he was a trooper."

"That's our boy."

"I meant the doctor. Brian was tough, but I thought the doctor was going to vomit. I wasn't much better. I kept watching those tweezers disappear into his leg and pull out what looked like boulders of debris."

I shuddered. "Enough of that. Did he get a tetanus shot?"

"And an update on his pneumonia vaccine for good measure. I figure that if he has a reaction to any of that, it might help slow him down a bit and give the leg more time to heal."

"How are we going to keep him out of the water?"

"We may need to invest in a case of plastic wrap and duct tape to protect it. Short of leg irons and chains, I'm just not seeing him sitting on the beach."

Brian must not have been as deeply asleep as he appeared. "I've got a plan," he said.

But before could fill us in, Dr. Singh reappeared carrying a blue paper-wrapped suture kit. He closed Brian's gaping wound with twenty-one sutures. Later, he handed me a thick volume of discharge papers and went over what to watch for in the coming days, when to check in with our regular doctor, and when to be concerned. "Brian, I want you to rest and avoid putting any weight on that leg. We can't have it swelling up. Ice and Netflix are your new best friends." He handed me a prescription for antibiotics.

"Wow, Mom," said Brian, rolling his eyes. "When you said this summer was going to be an adventure, you kinda undersold it."

"Smart aleck," I said. "This wasn't exactly what I had in mind." I counted off our encounters so far on my fingers: "Helicopter, search and rescue, state park rangers, sheriff, emergency room…what's next?"

"Zombie apocalypse?" offered Brian.

I glanced at the doctor, who fought to avoid snorting and failed. "How 'bout it?" I asked. "Will these antibiotics protect us in the event of a zombie attack?"

Dr. Singh frowned and tapped his chin, then said, with exaggerated seriousness. "I think you'd need anti-viral medication, given my reading to date, but the research isn't really complete. If antibiotics were indicated, a broad-spectrum medication like this one would be just what you'd need."

"Good to know."

"I've prescribed an antibiotic that should help Brian's body fight against infection in the tissue and bone that was damaged in his fall."

"Bone?" I grabbed again for the edge of the gurney and felt Max take my other hand.

The doctor's gaze shifted from Brian to me. He pushed a chair in my direction and guided me into it.

"Sorry! You came in after we discussed that. We took an X-ray. Brian has a hairline fracture of the tibia. We'll keep him in a boot and on crutches until the wound heels. The splint will need to be replaced with a cast as soon as the swelling and chance of infection abates. Long term, the injury shouldn't pose a problem. He's young, strong, and will heal quickly. But the bone is at increased risk for osteomyelitis, which is just a fancy name for a bone infection. It's serious business. It can occur whenever someone has an infection, from pneumonia to an abscessed tooth, but we're particularly wary when we see an open wound that exposes a bone to bacteria. Has he had cancer, a transplant, or immunosuppressant?"

"Like prednisone for asthma?"

The doctor frowned. "How recently?"

I looked at Brian. He shrugged. I turned to Max. "I've got his medical records at home," I said. "Do you remember?

"Our ski trip, I think, was the last time," Max said. "Three months ago, or thereabouts. I can get you more precise dates if you need them." He reached for his phone.

Dr. Singh shook his head. "Like I said. He's young, strong, and a fast healer. I'll give you some more information about what to watch for, and you'll want to check in with an orthopedist. Let us or your doctor know if he develops any signs of infection over the next few days." My skin went clammy.

The doctor scooted his rolling stool closer to me and took my hands in his. "Look. It's pretty much our job to scare the heck out of moms. It gives us a chance to rattle off all the obscure symptoms and contraindications we're learning for our boards. But honestly, I'm guessing this will be a minor blip in Brian's health history. It's a big deal today, and it will cramp his style for a few weeks, but the other events of your family vacation will make this incident fade into the background quickly, I'm sure."

Dr. Singh had no way of knowing how accurate his prediction would turn out to be.

Chapter 11

Rolling instead of folding clothing reduces wrinkles and conserves luggage space.

From the Notebook of Maggie McDonald
Simplicity Itself Organizing Services

Wednesday, June 19, Late night

Brian's leg hurt, making it difficult for him to sleep. Hyperaware of his restlessness, I poked my head into his room in the middle of the night and invited him to join me in a snack of warm tea and hot toast, after which we could top off his pain meds. We iced his leg while we chatted. I tried to distract him from his discomfort.

"Would it help to have something to look forward to? Something that doesn't involve running or exposing the wound to water?"

"I had an idea." Brian reached into the pocket of the hoodie he wore to stave off the chill from the ice pack. He pulled out his phone and showed it to me. "I took this picture at the diner. When we had breakfast. It's a free ride up in one of those little planes at the airport. Free. I make the cut, age-wise." He grinned. "David doesn't."

I took the phone from him, squinted at it, and read aloud. "Founded in 1992, the Young Eagles program has dedicated twenty-five years to giving youth their first free ride in an airplane. It's the only program of its kind, with the sole mission to introduce and inspire kids in the world of aviation."

"I looked online. They offer rides by appointment through the summer. Every Sunday in the winter."

"You want to do this?"

"You kidding? Besides, if you take me, you can grill the ground crew and everyone else there about Jake Peterson, ultralight maintenance, flight conditions, and bad guys. David might be able to take that hunk of metal he's been carrying around and see if it's an important part of an ultralight."

"Hunk of metal?"

"Just something he picked up on the cliff. Probably nothing. It's not important." He took a sip of his tea. "Dad will undoubtedly find someone to schmooze. Knowing him, he'll find some fighter pilot who saved the free world."

I smiled. Brian was right. Max could charm the socks off almost anyone and learn their life history within about ten minutes of meeting them. We teased him about it, but it was nearly a superpower. In a different man, his ability to disarm might be used as a weapon to subdue or seduce. But Max was generally interested, fascinated in fact, by other people's dreams, barriers to them, and the things that drove them to bust through brick walls and make their aspirations a reality.

"Sounds like a plan," I told Brian. "Let's talk it over with Dad in the morning." I was a little nervous about the idea of sending my youngest up in the sky with a stranger in a small machine, particularly after what had happened to Jake. But I couldn't think of a rational reason to say no.

"There's a restaurant at the airport that's got great reviews, and it's not too far from the grocery store." Brian said. "We could combine several trips."

"You've been thorough."

"Sleeplessly surfing."

"Any other ideas?"

"Maybe the boardwalk? I'm supposed to keep the leg elevated. Most of the Typhoon ride is upside down."

I nearly spit out my tea. "Yeah, you know, I'm not sure that's what Dr. Singh had in mind when he said you should be resting. What about a whale watching tour?"

"Sure. But, you know, I could also help Renée in the office. I might not be able to run after the toddlers, but I could certainly play on the floor with them. And trip them with my crutches if they tried to wander off." He sighed heavily, and his shoulders drooped, in a posture perfected by unhappy teenagers and angry cats. Every cell in his body seemed dejected and limp, telling me that, for all his joking, the pain and the prospect of a protracted recovery had thrown him for a loop.

Without replying, I jumped up to bring him more ibuprofen, along with a banana and a cookie. If this kid ever got to sleep tonight, I wanted to be sure he had enough fuel in his body to sleep as late as possible. "How are you fixed for books?" I asked. "You can download stuff to your reader if you want."

"I'm rereading Harry Potter."

By now, I was sure both boys knew most of the series by heart, in English and Spanish. High school language teachers gave kids extra credit for reading translations and watching dubbed versions of their favorite movies and books. If there was a reading version of comfort food, Harry Potter had to be it.

He yawned. "Ready to go back to bed?" I asked. "I'll check online tomorrow and see if there's a good place to spot wildlife with the binoculars. Rumor has it there's a pair of bald eagles somewhere in the slough."

* * * *

Brian slept until nearly eleven. While he snoozed, Max called the airport and snagged a flight early in the afternoon. He had a late breakfast, the rest of us an early lunch, and we all trooped to the airport. David had snuck into Brian's room earlier to charge up his cell phone, prepping it to take tons of reconnaissance pictures of the farms on the ridge. The trip had captured the imagination of both boys as though they were planning a secret spy mission.

After the idyllic and unspoiled vastness of the marine sanctuary, the glare from the airport's windswept expanse of concrete and the pervasive odor of jet fuel was an assault on our eyes, noses, and sense of aesthetics. We pulled up close to the door of the office and restaurant to minimize steps for Brian, who was still mastering the art of walking with crutches.

We pushed open the door to a lobby filled with furniture fashioned from aircraft aluminum and leather-covered cockpit seats.

"Here for the Young Eagles flight? You'll have a blast," said the young woman behind the counter. Her ginger-colored long hair was nearly a match for Belle's golden-red fur. I held up Belle's leash and was about to ask if it was okay to bring her inside when the woman rose on tiptoes to peer over the top of the reception desk. "Bring her on in," she said, waving enthusiastically. "As long as she's well behaved, she's welcome." Belle thumped her tail.

In a similar gesture, the desk clerk flipped her long braid over her shoulder. She handed me a pen with a tiny propeller on one end, and a clipboard with permission slips and liability waivers. "Got sunglasses?"

Max pulled his sunglasses off his forehead and passed them to Brian, along with his favorite Giants baseball cap.

"I'll call over to Susie," said the ginger-haired woman who'd introduced herself as Kelly. "She's your pilot. Should be ready to go in a few minutes." Kelly smiled at Brian and then glanced at Max and me. "Susie will take you and your nervous parents through her safety checks."

Brian lowered the sunglasses and squinted at me. "Is it safe to let you near the plane, or do I need to make you stay here?" he asked. "Are you going to change your mind?"

Belle's tail swished tentatively against my leg. It was a hopeful and nervous tail wag. She was having trouble reading my mood and was expressing her hope that any fear I experienced was nothing serious.

"Doesn't matter," said Kelly. "Your mom already signed the paperwork. I'll give it to you to keep safe. Susie will need it. You can head out as soon as you're ready. It's the red and white Piper..." She glanced out the window and pointed as she counted softly. "It's the one, two, fourth one in that row just outside the gate. Follow the yellow line for safety."

Brian's hand shot out to grab the proffered document, rolled it in a tube, then stuffed it inside his hoodie, zipping it for extra security.

Together, we trooped outside toward the windy taxiway. "Hold up," said Max as Brian reached for the latch on the gate in the chain-link fence that served as the only barrier between the parking lot and the tie-down area for small planes. "If you two are okay here, David wants to check out the flight school and maintenance shed." He pointed to a sign and hangar on the far side of the parking lot. "I thought I'd go with him."

I nodded. Brian tapped at my foot with his crutch. "Mom, come on. Susie's waiting."

"See what you can find out about what happened to Jake's ultralight," I called after Max and David, unsure they'd be able to hear me over the rush of the wind. "See if they have any theories." I searched my jacket pocket for a scrunchie and brushed the hair from my face with my hand as I hurried to catch up with my youngest. I was both proud and apprehensive. On one hand, he seemed to be coping well with the wrench thrown into his summer plans. He'd spotted this opportunity and put a plan in motion to pursue it, all on his own. On the other, I couldn't protect him from unseen dangers while my feet were on the ground and his were hundreds of feet in the air and out of sight. I frowned. I'd better get used to the mixed feelings this stage of motherhood engendered. This trip represented only one brief stop on our high-speed journey into the future as both boys became independent young men beyond our direct influence. Bittersweet didn't begin to describe my mood.

After dealing with the bureaucratic details and supervising the safety check, I waved to the red and white plane as it taxied the short distance to the runway and took off in a northeasterly direction toward the mountains. It banked left and headed out over the ocean. I shielded my eyes from the glare with my hand and watched as the tiny aircraft disappeared into the distance. Susie had said they'd be back in twenty minutes, so Belle and I walked back inside and I ordered a latte at the bar.

"My son's up with Susie," I told the bartender. "On a Young Eagles flight."

"Lucky kid. It's a great program. Most of the pilots out here caught the flying bug on one of those flights."

"That's what I'm afraid of." I took the steaming mug he placed on the counter.

"Do you need something stronger?" he asked, waving to the array of alcoholic beverages behind the bar.

"Sorry to be so grumpy. My fledglings are making ready to fly." I straightened my back and shoulders when I realized how much my posture reflected my dejected mood.

"I get it. I've got four kids of my own. All in their twenties. Much as I love the fact that they're all independently pursuing their dreams, my heart still hurts a bit when they set off without a backward glance." He reached out his hand "Lindstrom. Mace. This gig is my retirement job. Keeps me out of trouble and out in the world, meeting new people." His name tickled a memory, but I couldn't retrieve it. My brain was too busy trying not to worry about Brian.

I shook his hand. "Maggie McDonald." I admired the artwork on the surface of the foam. An airplane. "Cute."

"Thanks. I had to take a three-week class to learn how to operate that beast," he said, pointing to the gleaming steel espresso machine, which squatted, hissed, and sighed on the back counter. "I learned to make those airplane designs, but don't ask for anything else. It's amazing how many ways a simple attempt to make a heart or a flower can turn pornographic in the wrong hands." He shuddered.

Either Mace didn't recognize me or he didn't consume local print or broadcast media or maybe he was just being polite. In any case, he avoided mentioning Jake Peterson and his parents. I was grateful.

"You're distracting me," I said, turning to peer through the windows at the runway.

"Not to worry. I'll let you know when they land."

"Do you work here every day?"

"Afternoons, weekends. I let the college kids take the later shifts and the bigger tips. I can't take that pace."

"How long have you worked here?"

"Yo, Zeke." He waved his towel in the air like a fan at a sporting match. "If you wait a sec you can take the lunch orders over to the gearheads in the shed." Mace disappeared through the doors to the kitchen.

I turned and spotted a young man leaning on the front counter chatting with Kelly, who twirled her braid and blushed. He loped into the bar and hopped onto a nearby stool, spinning it one way and then another in a way that made me queasy. In an effort to stop him, I held out my hand. "Maggie McDonald."

"Zeke Havers." As he reached toward me to shake my hand, the sleeve of his hoodie rode up, revealing a heavily tattooed arm. I winced involuntarily, empathizing with the pain involved in covering so much skin with ink. But the boy didn't look old enough to be tattooed. I was sure that you needed to be at least eighteen, though I wasn't up on all the details.

Zeke reddened, looked away, and covered the tattoos. I reached for my latte.

Mace saved us from our awkwardness as he burst back though the swinging doors holding several white paper sacks. "Lunch is ready, Zeke. Thanks for delivering it."

"No prob, Mr. L." He grabbed hold of the bags, but Mace didn't let go. He spoke softly but sternly to the boy. "You stay away from Kelly. She's too young. You can tell Joe I kept you here to deliver the sandwiches, but this is the last time I'll cover for you. If you want to keep that job, be on time."

Zeke took the bags and nodded. He turned toward me, made eye contact, and said, "Nice to meet you, Mrs. McDonald." Then he raced out the door without a backward glance.

Mace watched him, then shook his head, picked up a glass, and polished it with a flour-sack towel, like the bartenders in every movie I'd ever seen. "The energy of the young. Wish I could harness it for myself."

"Troublemaker?" I asked. "Ladies man?"

"Zeke? No, he's okay. A good kid, mostly. Needs a little sheepdogging from time to time. Joe, the manager over at the machine shed, and I are keeping an eye on him. Too smart for his own good. Gets bored, you know."

"I know the type," I said. "I have four older brothers. Seems like they all went through that phase. Them, and all their friends."

Mace polished the already clean glass. "Four years I've worked here. Almost everyone in the area comes through at one time or another, whether they're pilots, passengers, or just here for the food, which is pretty good, by the way. Our new chef moved here from Silicon Valley so he could afford a house, but his résumé includes some of the trendiest restaurants in the Bay Area. He put down the glass and folded the towel. "Sorry. Lost in my thoughts. A lot of kids work here. Most turn out okay, eventually. Some seem to have to learn their lessons the hardest ways possible."

"Did you know Jake Peterson?" I tried to sip my drink and watch his face at the same time, succeeding only in spilling coffee down the front of my once-white T-shirt. Mace passed me a clean towel.

"Friend of my kids. The younger ones, anyway."

"Terrible thing."

Mace didn't have anything to add, so after a moment I prompted him. "Do ultralights fly out of here? Do they need airports?"

He polished the bar top. "Here they do, I think. A complicated combination of state, local, and federal regulations covers ultralights. Officially, you don't need a pilot's license to fly one for recreational purposes. The exception is if you're flying in a congested area."

I looked out the window, past the runway to strawberry fields that extended as far as I could see.

Mace must have read my thoughts.

"Oh, there's lots of debate over what constitutes a congested area, but the club here requires at least a safety certification for the pilot and the machine."

"So I couldn't buy myself an ultralight tomorrow and fling myself into the wind off the nearest cliff?"

"You're thinking of hang gliders. No motors."

"Jake had a license?"

Mace nodded. "As far as I know. A mechanic's license too." He shook his head. "Took a course at Cabrillo College. He and Zeke might have been in the same program, though Zeke is several years younger."

"Cabrillo?" I asked, repeating the name of a local community college. "I thought Jake was in a graduate program at UC Santa Cruz."

"He's doing something academic in environmental science now. I mean, he was, before…"

"But he knew his way around aircraft, sounds like." I spoke quickly to relieve Mace's obvious discomfort over getting tangled up in the verb tenses he was using to refer to the recently deceased young man.

"Absolutely. Jake was out here all the time since he was a freshman in high school. Watching the planes, doing an internship, picking up hours to pay for tuition. Then he bought that used ultralight, fixed it up, and was out here even more. First for fun and then he figured out a way to use it in his research."

"Do you know what he was studying?"

Mace tilted his head and stared into the distance as if searching the past. "Someone must have told me, but I can't remember."

"But he took maintenance seriously? You don't think he would have skimped on safety checks, for example?"

"No way. His boss, Joe Fowler, used to tease him about how painstaking he was. Said it cost him money."

"Would Joe have encouraged Jake to cut corners?"

"I don't think so. That whole group eats here most Fridays. They get a little rowdy, but no one minds. Least of all me. They'd rag on each other. Teasing. But, no matter how sharp Joe's criticisms were, Jake would lift his chin, straighten his back, and speak clearly and very slowly: 'Not one of my planes has ever had an equipment-related malfunction. Not one.'" Mace had adopted the posture he described and looked like an aging Captain America. He rapped his knuckles on the wooden bar top.

I glanced over my shoulder, squinting into the sky above the airport. I wondered who was responsible for the maintenance on Susie's plane. I hoped it had been Jake.

"That's them coming back in now," Mace said, pointing his towel toward the runway. "Give 'em a few minutes. Susie likes to talk to the kids about taking more lessons and joining Civil Air Patrol."

It sounded much like a drug pushing scheme. The first flight was free to plant the seed, then came gentle pressure for a second trip, fanning the flames into a full-fledged addiction. My clichés and metaphors were hopelessly muddled, but I didn't care. I thanked Mace, left him a generous tip, and struggled to pull on my jacket without threading Belle's leash through the sleeve. I headed for the door. Brian burst through before I could open it.

Chapter 12

If you're flying to a vacation resort where you'll be grocery shopping, pack easily compactable fabric tote bags. They'll be handy for transporting purchases, picnics, and other items.

From the Notebook of Maggie McDonald
Simplicity Itself Organizing Services

Thursday, June 20, Afternoon

"How was it?" I asked.

"Awesome," Brian said, shifting his weight from one crutch to the other as though he were expending all available energy trying to be still. Trying and failing. "Were you bored waiting?"

"Not at all. I made a friend and learned a lot." I waved to Mace. "Tell me all about it while we look for Dad and David." How had I missed Brian's enthusiasm for aircraft? Why had we not done this years before? I bit the inside of my lip and struggled to stay in the moment rather than berate myself for a past I had no power to change.

"Oh my god! It's so beautiful. Incredible. Awesome. Like, the whole valley is laid out. Hay bales look like croutons, scattered across the fields. And the ocean? We saw whales. Whales! From a plane. The waves, they're like this lacy edge, and the water is so many different colors." Brian blushed and stopped to catch his breath and reorganize his crutches. All it took to turn my youngest son into a poet was one trip in a small plane. *Who knew?*

He traced an arc in the sky with the tip of his right crutch. "At take-off, the engine is so loud, but once you get up there..." He gazed at the horizon, awestruck. "For a moment, Susie shut the engine off—"

"Off? She shut the engine *off*?"

"Only for a minute. It started right up again. But that's not the point."

I thought it was *exactly* the point, but Brian chattered on. "It was so quiet. I don't think I've ever heard anything so completely silent. No wind noise. No people sounds like traffic or construction or radios. Just... silence. And me, breathing. Almost like I was breathing in the world, and I was just one cell within it, but part of it, all at the same time. Susie says that's what it's like to be in a glider, lifted by a thermal." He stared at me, waiting for a comment, desperate to hear what I thought.

"Wow," was as eloquent a word as I could summon. Brian's face fell.

"What? You expected me to turn around and buy a plane this afternoon?"

Brian smiled and nearly tripped. "Of course not. But...I wouldn't say no to going up again with you and Dad and David," he said, after regaining his balance. "These crutches are trickier than they look. I get my rhythm, and then I get going too fast and have to stop and start over." He glared at the crutches and the bandage-wrapped splint on his foot. "You'd think I could figure out how to just slow down."

"We'll see," I said, referring to the suggested family trip into the wild blue yonder. He rolled his eyes.

"No, seriously. Sounds like fun. But I need to talk to Dad and work it into our schedule. And check the weather forecast. Wouldn't do to plan an excursion and then discover the airport was socked in." It wasn't an idle deflection on my part. Early summer on the coast of Northern California had its own moniker: *June Gloom.* The bluebird sky people tended to associate with the surf cities was more common in September and January than it was at the height of vacation season.

Movement on the far side of the parking lot near a group of industrial buildings and hangars caught my attention. Max and David waved and walked toward us. Brian and I moved into the shadow of a parched and scraggly tree.

"Susie told me some other stuff," Brian said. "Like about the strawberry workers and Jake."

"Did Susie have any idea what could have happened with Jake and his ultralight?" I asked.

"Not really. She took Jake up on his first flight."

"Did Susie feel bad about it?"

"About Jake dying? Why wouldn't she? She knew the guy."

I stopped in my tracks, horrified that Brian would think I could be so insensitive. "No, of course not. Certainly she'd be saddened by Jake's death. I meant, did she feel responsible because she'd introduced Jake to the sport that killed him?"

Brian chewed his lip, frowned, and his face took on a vacant expression. I knew he was replaying, like a movie, the scene inside the cockpit when Susie had talked about taking Jake up for the first time. "No way. Susie's proud of what she does. Says some huge percentage of pilots were in the cockpit for the first time on an Eagle flight. Cool, huh?"

I wasn't too sure about that, but I didn't respond. Apparently, I didn't have to. Brian had heard my thoughts as though I'd shouted them from the rooftops.

"*Mo-om*," he protested. "Come on. It's safe. Twenty times safer than in a car, Susie says."

Tell that to Jake's mom.

"Do you want to hear what Susie told me about Jake or not?" Brian said, stopping to adjust his grip on his recalcitrant crutches. "She says Jake was a great mechanic. He heard changes in engine sounds that helped him diagnose problems."

"Interesting." Brian's mention of sound led me to thinking about the way my kids listened to music on their phones. The thought of hand-held devices segued into contemplating the research that might be locked in Jake's cell phone.

"I wonder if the police looked at Jake's phone?" I said aloud. "They had to have looked at the GPS, right?"

"*Whoa*, Mom. Slow down. Or at least signal when you're going to change the subject." Brian was breathing heavily due to the unaccustomed effort of talking while maneuvering on the ungainly crutches. "My point is that there probably wasn't anything wrong with Jake's ultralight. He would have heard a change in the engine sounds and identified anything that was wrong before he left the ground. Susie thought Jake's crash could have been caused by a problem with the gas. Or even, get this: Susie wondered if someone shot Jake down."

"Shot him down? Who would do that? This is real life, not Road Runner and Wile E. Coyote trying to blow each other up." I felt an itch at the back of my brain, as it struggled to remind me of something I'd recently forgotten. I ignored it.

"Susie couldn't think of a reason for anyone to have done it either," Brian said. "She figured a kid could've been using an airsoft gun, pretending to shoot him down, not knowing how far the pellets could shoot. That probably couldn't have hurt Jake, but it might have distracted him enough for something to go wrong. Or maybe someone with a real gun could have been random and stupid, just firing into the sky. There was a headline in the local paper we saw in the café about bald eagles and some idiots shooting at them."

"Huh?" I was having trouble keeping up with the plot jumps as Brian shifted gears from planes to guns to birds to newspapers. *And he'd teased me about changing subjects without signaling. Humph.* I decided to forgo a temper tantrum and waited for Brian to elaborate instead.

"Bald eagles. It was the headline. Birders have seen a bunch of them in the slough, but no one's sayin' where they are because they're afraid some idiot will kill them."

"There's no imagining the level of stupidity in the world, is there? Those poor birds! Wouldn't it be great to see them? I've never seen one in except on TV."

"Mom, focus. My point is it's possible someone hurt Jake, either accidentally or on purpose."

"But why?"

Max and David caught up with us near the car before Brian had a chance to explain. By then, the wind had shifted and increased. Max's curls were effectively straightened by the wind blowing them back off his forehead, making him nearly unrecognizable, even to me.

"Good flight?" he asked Brian.

"The best."

"Let's get you off those crutches and into the car. This wind will blow you off balance and you'll hurt the other leg."

A brotherly tiff nearly broke out in the back seat when Brian accidentally bopped his brother on the forehead with a crutch. Belle added to the confusion by taking the stem of one crutch in her teeth and tugging it, like a toy, evening the score when the armpit end bopped Brian on the bridge of his nose.

"We need padding for the crutches," Brian said, rubbing his nose "Some kids at school have those lamb's wool ones. Can we stop somewhere? My pits are killing me."

Max peered over the back seat. "It's probably not so much the chafing as it is using your muscles differently. We'll get you some ibuprofen before bed."

"But...blisters" Brian whined, uncharacteristically. Between the excitement of the afternoon, the energy output required to build new skin and bone, and the lingering pain, he was exhausted. It showed in his slightly gray and clammy face, and the circles under his eyes.

I nodded to Max. "Swing by the drug store and I'll run in. If they don't have them, we can check later online for a medical supply place and order them."

Max reached over the seat to pat Brian's knee, and we set off.

Max ended up running into the store, and in the short while he was gone, David filled us in on what they'd learned in the maintenance shed and at the flight school.

"One of the guys in the maintenance shed was there when NTSB took possession of the ultralight."

"I still can't believe NTSB is involved in this," I said. "I thought they investigated big airline disasters—rebuilding planes from the ground up to figure out what went wrong."

"We asked the mechanic. The T is for Transportation. That means NTSB investigates all sorts of accidents—trains, highway, ships, and ultralights. At least they do when there's a death or it's not obvious what happened. They have to, to keep statistics on safety and make recommendations for new rules to reduce fatalities and enhance air safety." David sounded as though he was parroting words someone had recited to him.

"Interesting," I said. "But isn't it all hush-hush? On television, NTSB swoops in as if there were aliens aboard and make the plane disappear to some secret lab in Washington."

"Hollywood over-dramatization," said David, repeating a term I used frequently to separate real life from the silver screen. Did we still say silver screen in the modern age, or was that an anachronism dating back to the days of black and white movies? I wasn't sure. I wrenched my attention back to the matter at hand.

"San José," said David.

"San José?"

"Keep up, Mom. Joe Fowler, who manages the machine shop and maintenance shed, said the NTSB packed the ultralight into a semi-trailer and transported it to a federal hangar at San José airport."

I thought for a moment, tracing the route as if I had a GPS system in my head. "That's not that far from here. It's what, under an hour in light traffic?"

Brian tapped his phone to confirm. "Siri says it's fifty minutes right now. Roads are clear."

Traffic on Highway 17 was highly variable. In rush hour, bad weather, or when a driver misjudged a turn or ran into a deer or mountain lion, travel slowed to a glacial pace. But during slack periods, it provided a swift connection between the beach and the bustle of Silicon Valley.

"But why wouldn't the NTSB use a plane?" I asked. "They were already at an airport. Surely it would have been easier to put it all on a cargo plane?"

"I asked the same thing, but Joe didn't know. He just threw up his hands and said, '"Government? Policy? Who knows? Who cares?"'

"Well, I'm not sure it matters, anyway. Did Joe pick up any other leads when the feds packed up the ultralight?"

"One of the agents asked whether all the pieces had been found and whether anyone had done a sweep of the crash area for debris."

"Had they?"

"Joe didn't say. But Mom, I was thinking. There's no reason we can't go back to the crash site and do our own sweep, is there? It sounds like the federal investigators thought there was some essential part missing from the machine. Wouldn't it be cool if we found the key that broke their investigation wide open and nailed the bad guys?"

As a mom, I felt it was my job to throw ice water on his enthusiasm. "Everyone I've talked to around here so far has made it sound like Jake's death was a rare and unusual accident."

"But Susie said there might be good reason for someone to want Jake dead," Brian said, sleepily stroking Belle's velvety soft ears. The golden was fast asleep, and Brian didn't seem far off.

Max returned to the car and tossed a small white bag to Brian. "Last pair. You lucked out."

Brian struggled with the overzealous anti-tamper packaging, slicing his thumb on the hard plastic. Occupied by dealing with the blood, we didn't return to the matter of Jake's death until much later.

Chapter 13

Forgot your charger? Check with your hotel's main desk or concierge. They may have a stash of chargers left by previous guests.

From the Notebook of Maggie McDonald
Simplicity Itself Organizing Services

Thursday, June 20 Afternoon

As soon as we got home, I made a few calls, and Max headed out to meet Kevin Rivers at his organic farm. He was itching to get a look inside the creepy barn that shared a border with Diego Baker's neighboring operation. Though I ached to join Max and continue our investigation, I had to delegate. I sensed that the kids were still reeling from the events of the past few days and needed a parent nearby.

I phoned Nell to see where she was with our legal plans. The fact that we were supposed to be meeting with the media people had totally slipped my mind. I hoped they hadn't come by while we'd been at the airport. Nell apologized, said there had been a scheduling glitch, and that she was now expecting them to arrive Friday. I checked my call log and told her I hadn't missed any calls from journalists. Nell promised to call when she knew more.

I was finishing up the laundry when Max returned. Before I could debrief him, the kids roped him into watching the Giants trounce their archrivals in what should have been a fiercely contested pitching duel. Between innings,

I heard a *clank clank clank* from the clothes dryer. It was a tell-tale sign that in my scrupulous checking of pockets, I'd missed something. I only hoped it was something that hadn't been damaged by soap and water and that, conversely, hadn't stained or ruined the entire load.

I rushed to pull out the clothes, but was unable to locate the noise maker. I dumped the laundry onto the coffee table and announced "social laundry folding"—a family tradition I'd recently created.

"Be careful," I warned them. "There's something in there that was clanking around in the dryer. Could be sharp."

David winced. "My fault. I picked up something at the crash site." He dug through the pile and pulled out a metal crescent with a nasty jagged edge that had to be disentangled from the inevitable hanging threads of bath towels. "Sorry. Did I ruin them?"

"The towels?" I held one up to the light and examined it. "Looks okay to me."

Max pawed through the pile, which, thankfully, was devoid of easily snagged Lycra exercise clothes. "We were lucky. But let me look at that thing."

David handed over the metal chunk, which fit neatly into the palm of Max's hand. Max squinted at it, removing his glasses and putting them back on. "Do we have a magnifying glass?" he asked.

"At home. Far right drawer in the kitchen," I said. Brian was more inclined to be helpful. He rummaged around in the condo's kitchen drawers, and pulled out a scratched and cloudy magnifier with the bold logo of a local car repair shop. He peered through it at the grain of the granite countertop. "I can't see anything."

"Right." Max ran his hand over one side of the object, and then scraped the edge with his fingernail.

He held the metal crescent up to the light and tilted it first one way, then the other.

"What is it?" I asked.

"I'm not sure...but...no..."

"Words, Dad. Use your words." David said. "What are you seeing?"

"Maybe nothing." Max tossed the piece up in the air and caught it again. "But I want to have a materials engineer take a look at this." He leaned over and pointed to one edge that was bumpier than the others. "It's an aluminum alloy. It looks like it could have broken off the end of a propeller."

"But I found it right where Jake's ultralight came down," David said. "I don't even know why I picked it up. If you're thinking it broke off and caused an accident—"

"Good hypothesis," Max said, though I had no idea what they were talking about. "You're right. If a part broke off mid-flight, which it would have to have done if it caused the crash, it would be anywhere except near the plane. It would have broken before the crash and been flung far from the flight path. But still..."

"What?" Brian asked.

"Something's not right," Max said, scratching his head and glaring at the metal shard.

"Shouldn't we hand it over to the NTSB investigators?" I asked. "If you really think it's part of the engine or propeller or whatever?"

Max tilted his head. "Let me have my friend check it out. If he thinks the feds need to see it, we'll make sure they get it."

"Could it still have fingerprints?" I asked. "From someone who tampered with it?"

Brian looked at me as though I'd gone nuts. "It just went through the washer, Mom."

Max was more tactful. "I doubt it. You picked this up in the sand, David?"

"That sandy soil on the hillside. Right near the crash. And the first thing I did was rub off the dirt so I could see it better. Habit. Sorry."

"Not your fault. I'll take it to Howard. He likes a good mystery." Max put the metal lump on a shelf of the hall tree, next to his keys, wallet, and sunglasses. "First thing tomorrow. I'll call and let you know what he says." He stepped back and brushed his hands on his jeans. "So, do we have time for another walk before dinner? The paper said the blue whales were coming in closer to the beach. They're after the krill."

"Crutches," said Brian. "You guys go."

The disappointment in his voice echoed in the silence that followed. "Never mind," said Max. "I'll bet we can spot them from the balcony. "

"No," I told Max. "If you're really going back to the Bay Area so that your pal Howard will get a look at that part first thing in the morning, you'll need a walk before you spend another hour in the car. Are you leaving tonight or in the morning?"

"Tomorrow morning, before the sun's up and the traffic gets bad. Howard's an early bird, and I want to catch him before he gets involved in anything else."

"You and David head out. I'll take the binoculars out on the deck while Brian ices his leg."

David and Max were on their way out the door before I had a chance to remind Max that he still hadn't reported on what he'd learned from his visit to the farm.

Brian perched in a chair on a balcony that made me nostalgic for the days when the boys were little and we would have pretended we were in the crow's nest of a Victorian whaling vessel, or perhaps a pirate ship.

We spotted no whales, and between the ice pack and the marine layer, Brian grew chilled. We retreated inside. He offered to help with supper preparations, but his crutches took up too much room in the tiny galley kitchen.

"I'm putting you to work tomorrow," I told him. "Sorting papers for Renée."

Brian kept me company as I cut up onions for spaghetti sauce. When David and Max returned, David told us more about what Joe Fowler, the mechanic shop manager, had said about Jake. "He confirmed that Jake was a gearhead, and would have spotted anything wrong with the ultralight before taking off. In his own words, Jake was meticulous."

"Did Jake have a regular schedule for taking his photos?" I asked.

"What difference would that make?" David spoke the words gently, making them sound like a polite inquiry instead of a challenge to his mother's intelligence.

I thought for a moment, unsure how to answer. Max jumped in to help. "Are you thinking that, if he had a predictable schedule, and someone else knew that schedule, and had it out for him, they'd know when the ultralight would be left unattended?"

I nodded. "Or…Jake could have been keeping an eye on some activity that happened on a regular schedule, but that someone didn't want him to document with his camera. If we knew that Jake always went up at the same time, we could narrow down what he might have seen on his flights."

David was skeptical. "Wouldn't he just go whenever he had a break in his work and school schedule? Or when conditions were good?"

"If he were basing his observations on the tides, he'd fly at different times every day," I said, thinking out loud, still unsure exactly where my brain was flitting. I handed my oldest son a stack of plates and pointed to the table.

"In that case, his movements would still be predictable to anyone with a tide table," David said. He placed each plate quickly, but then spun the dish so that the bottom of the blue willow pattern would be closest to the table edge. My mother had the same pattern on her china. As a toddler, David had found it upsetting when the birds flew upside down. I wondered if it still bothered him, or if he positioned the plates out of habit.

"Mom?" Brian's question brought me back to the present.

"Sorry, what was the question?"

"Hand me the stuff to make the garlic bread or give me something to cut up for the salad. I can do it while we talk."

"Easy on the garlic," I said, handing him the tools and ingredients. Brian's idea of enough garlic usually involved everything we had in the house. Enough to repel vampires and every other paranormal creature for miles around. As we worked, the homey scents of Italian spices filled the air.

"Backing up to brainstorming what trouble Jake might have stumbled into," Brian began. "When we flew over the spot where the plane went down, Susie said there'd been some conflict between the organic berry farmers and the traditional growers."

"What kind of conflict?" Max asked, frowning. "Should I warn you boys to stay away from those cliffs?"

Brian wrapped the garlic-butter-slathered bread in aluminum foil and carried on with his story. It contained far more detail than the bare facts he'd recounted to me when he was still enthralled by the excitement of the plane ride. "The organic farmers sell their crops for more money and claim the traditional growers are passing off their berries as organic when they're not. And the traditional growers claim the organic guys are poaching their workers."

I tapped my fingernails on the table, thinking. "If I were a farm worker, I'd feel safer on an organic farm than I would among some of those anti-fungal chemicals the traditional outfits use. Strawberry farming involves some particularly noxious materials."

"There's something wrong when we call farming with pesticides and chemicals 'traditional,'" David said.

"That's what organic guys say, according to Susie," Brian said. "And they don't poach workers. They just offer safer and more desirable working conditions. Susie flew over that barn we saw yesterday, and some other farm buildings up on the hill. They've got those tanks we saw next to them. Susie said that didn't look right. Either they're propane for people who may be living and cooking in the barn, or..."

"Or?" I asked.

Brian seemed star-struck, judging by the number of times in the last minute he'd quoted the pilot. He tapped a pencil on the edge of the table. "It sounded kind of like paranoid conspiracy theories to me."

"What? Pirates? Smugglers? Zombie viruses?" David taunted his brother, but Brian didn't react.

"A surprisingly accurate assessment," Brian said with professorial pomp. "She said it could be anything from a place to receive and process drugs brought in at night from the ocean to unsanctioned housing for workers. Or from an unlicensed pot farm to storage for pesticides."

"Pesticides?" I asked. "I thought that farm was organic." I turned to Max. "Did you learn anything from Kevin Rivers?"

"Lots," Max said. "Including the fact that natural doesn't necessarily mean organic and organic doesn't necessarily mean free of dangerous substances. Kevin's farm has been organic for twenty years and yet he uses..." Max pulled a crumpled piece of paper from his jeans pocket. "Stuff like copper sulfate, hydrogen peroxide, peracetic acid, and sodium carbonate peroxyhydrate." He passed the list to David. "None of the stuff used on organic farms is as dangerous as what Kevin says his dad and grandfather used to use. He seemed really honest and forthcoming in explaining what an organic farm is and what it's not."

"That doesn't sound like a guy who's hiding anything," I said.

David waggled his eyebrows and spoke in a conspiratorial whisper. "It could be a secret plot." I threw a baby carrot at him.

Max ignored us and continued his report. "Kevin said that the chemicals used by law-abiding traditional farmers aren't so bad, especially if the farmers put in time as strawberry pickers themselves and are sympathetic to their situation. Most people want agricultural workers to be safe. The worst stuff is outlawed here in the States, but is readily available in Central America. It's almost as lucrative for unscrupulous farmers to smuggle those chemicals in as it is to bring drugs. And no one, so far, has trained dogs to sniff them out. Besides that, crop testing is expensive and infrequent."

David picked up the carrot I'd tossed his way and drew invisible circles with it on the counter. "So, even if the chemicals aren't quite as lucrative as drugs, if you could get them in with less chance of getting caught, and if you could use them to increase your yields, the payoff could be huge."

"That sounds like the kind of guy who'd want to keep Jake from flying over his operation," I said.

"Exactly," Max said. "And Kevin's body language told me he might well suspect his neighbor Diego Baker of running that kind of farm."

"Did you figure out who owns that barn and those tanks?" I asked.

Max shook his head. "I suspect it's Diego. Let's think about this. If Diego used the barn to house workers, and the other buildings to school their kids, and provided food that he cooked with the propane from those tanks, he wouldn't have to worry about his strawberry pickers randomly encountering ICE agents as they went about their day-to-day activities."

"It sounds like slavery," I said.

"It kind of is, Mom," Brian said. "But it happens all the time. If people aren't documented, it's easy to take advantage of them. Easy for bad people, that is."

David scoffed. "Dad's plan is logical but complicated. Wouldn't it be simpler and more lucrative to cook meth in that barn?"

I shuddered, both in fear of the tales I'd heard of exploding methamphetamine labs and in sympathy for the people for whom near-slavery in the United States meant a better life than staying in the countries in which they'd been born. My skin prickled as my thoughts traveled from the desperate to those who preyed upon them. "If something like that is happening in his barn, Diego Baker is neck-deep in criminal activity. He'd be super motivated to keep someone like Jake from taking photographs."

Max finished my thought for me. "Or resorting to violence to keep any other prying eyes away."

"Like ours?" asked David.

"Like yours," confirmed Max.

I stared at my husband as my panic grew. Should we leave the area altogether and forget about helping out Renée? Did we need to develop new family rules about safety and monitoring the kids' whereabouts?

The kids, like teens everywhere, had no trouble hearing my unspoken thoughts.

"No way," protested David. "We're here this summer to be at the beach. You said we could invite our friends down. No way is that beach off limits."

Max and I exchanged expressions that included raised eyebrows, head tilts, and shrugs. Then he spoke for both of us. "No trespassing on the farms," he said, ticking off the rules on his fingers. "Make sure Mom knows where you are and who you're with. No loopholes. No freelancing. If you wonder if something's allowed, it isn't. If you start to question whether you're safe, you aren't. Get out. Your phones will always be fully charged before you leave the condo. If the low battery signal comes on, you come home."

Silence weighed heavily on all of us. I stared at the boys until they nodded and agreed. "Got it," David said.

"Shouldn't be much of a problem for me," Brian said, lifting one crutch. David snorted, but nudged his brother with what looked like sympathy for his predicament.

Max put his hand on mine. "Those rules go for you, too," he reminded me, to the boys' delight. "We call them family rules for a reason. They apply to all of us."

"Got it," I repeated the words in the same tone and cadence David had used.

"And Dad..." said David.

"Yup, me too," Max said. The boys retreated to the video game system David had set up in his room, followed closely by Belle and her wagging banner of a tail. But not before Max called after them, "And Brian?

Remember that retreat from any dicey situation is going to take you longer on crutches than it did when you could run. Factor that into all of your judgments when you're evaluating your safety and exit strategy."

I should have felt comforted and satisfied with our review of family rules and protections. Instead, I couldn't shake the nagging feeling that there was a vital piece of the puzzle that we were missing. Something that could pose as much of a danger to my family as it had to Jake.

Chapter 14

Traveling with kids inclined to roll out of bed? A rolled up beach towel or pool noodle tucked under the sheet can create a handy bolster or barrier.

From the Notebook of Maggie McDonald
Simplicity Itself Organizing Services

Friday, June 21, Morning

The next morning, Max set off at five o'clock to beat the brutal commute traffic over Highway 17 into Silicon Valley. I went back to bed, but couldn't sleep. Instead, I scribbled a note for the boys and drove into town to grocery shop and grab a latte at the local Starbucks.

In Silicon Valley, a predawn stop at any local coffee shop would mean taking your spot behind a short line of construction workers, parents of tiny children, and a few hardy souls who exercised themselves or their dogs before work. In Watsonville, it meant a long queue of impatient commuters eager to get on the road before the traffic over the hill grew unmanageable. At home, the coffee-shop lines also served as impromptu town meeting places where friends caught each other up on their news, bragged about their kids, and complained about their kitchen remodels. Here, half the conversations were in Spanish, but I eavesdropped as best I could. It turned out my best wasn't nearly good enough to keep up, so I zoned out and watched the people until a tap on my shoulder jolted me out of my thoughts so abruptly that I nearly upended a display of coffee mugs stacked precariously close to the line of caffeine addicts.

"Sorry. *Lo siento.*" I apologized to the coffee mugs before I looked up to address the young woman who helped me return the wobbly stacks of cups to positions of safety. "Thanks." I blushed and felt the eyes of everyone in the store on me, whether they actually were or not.

"I didn't mean to startle you," said the twenty-something young woman. "But..."

I stopped stacking and stood up straight, clutching my backpack to keep it from lashing out unbidden at the other breakables.

The woman took a deep breath and squared her shoulders. "We haven't met. I'm Jen Amesti. You're Maggie McDonald, right? Your boys found... helped..." Her voice broke, but she carried on. "I'm Jake's..." She shook her head in the same way Belle shakes off water after a swim. "This is so hard. Jake Peterson was my boyfriend."

I took her hands in both of mine. "Can I buy you a coffee? Do you have time? I'd love to hear more about him." I was telling the truth, but I had ulterior motives. Besides, the girl seemed suddenly fragile.

She sighed as if life itself had become overwhelming—as though accepting an informal coffee invitation might be more than she could handle. Just when I was sure she would decline my offer, she relented. "I'll get a table. Outside okay? Small drip."

"Seriously? I'm buying, and all you want is a coffee in a tiny size they don't even have a fancy name for? I'm getting a medium latte."

She smiled. "Same here, if you're sure you don't mind."

I shooed her out the door to snag a table. It was chilly in the predawn hours but quieter outside under the propane heat lamps than it was within the bustling coffee shop.

By the time the barista had filled my order, to which I had added several cookies, Jen looked like she'd fallen asleep in one of the cold and uncomfortable metal outdoor chairs. I set the coffees down as quietly as I could but bumped the metal table as I did so. I winced as it screeched across the uneven concrete with a sound that hurt my teeth and once again made anyone in the vicinity turn our way.

Jen opened her eyes.

"This is why I never pursued a career in covert intelligence," I told her.

Jen smiled, acknowledging my attempt at a joke. But her eyes didn't crinkle or light up, and smiling looked like hard work for her. She took a big gulp of her coffee. It must have scorched her lips, but she gave no sign of discomfort. On the contrary, she let out a contented sigh that made me think I'd inadvertently ordered coffee with a shot of Kahlúa.

"I needed this," she said. "I haven't been sleeping well since..."

"Of course not," I reassured her. "It takes time. Lots of time."

"This fancy coffee is ridiculous. Five years ago, there was nowhere in town where you could get anything other than black coffee from a giant urn. If you were lucky, you could get real milk or cream to add to it. Now, we're like everywhere else, with a population that fills up on espresso more often than we top off our cars with unleaded."

"I think they must put crack in it."

Jen snorted. "That would explain it. One sip and plain drip is no longer good enough. Soon you find yourself taking out a loan to buy a souped-up machine to make specialty brews in your own kitchen. It's a slippery slope."

The worry lines in Jen's young face eased for a moment, but quickly returned as her shoulders hunched. She grasped her coffee in two hands and drew it close to her as if aching to absorb its warmth and comfort.

"So, tell me about Jake," I said. She looked away from me toward the horizon so fast that I amended my tone and said softly, "Or tell me about you, if Jake is too difficult."

She wiped her eyes with one hand. "It's good to talk. And it's hard to tell you anything about myself without mentioning Jake. We've been friends since kindergarten. He was always the man for me. Always. Even when all the other boys had cooties."

"He seems to have been well-liked. You must miss him terribly."

"I don't," she said, blushing. "Not yet. I haven't been able to convince myself Jake's actually gone."

"Maybe when you love someone as long as you've loved Jake, they never truly leave you."

"You think?" She raised her head hopefully. "I've been kicking myself for not being able to move on or accept it. I feel like I'm going crazy, but it's still darn near impossible to even understand the words. You know... that he's de—" Her voice broke, and she rummaged in her pockets as tears spilled. I handed her a napkin. It was too rough for her tender skin, heart, and emotions, but it was at hand.

"Give yourself time. This is all still very new."

Jen stared into the distance. I hated to bring her back into the real world, but I needed to get back to the kids and my job, eventually. "Will there be a service? The boys and I would like to go."

"I'm so grateful to them for all they did for him. I feel so much better knowing he wasn't alone and scared."

I took her hand. Partly for her comfort and partly for mine. I couldn't think of anything soothing to say, and let personal contact do the talking.

"I'm sure you're a big help to his parents, sharing their grief," I said. "You've known him almost as long as they have." I should have stuck with the personal contact. Her nostrils flared, and I heard her quick intake of breath as though I'd struck her.

"They've told me it's all my fault," she said, with tears streaming. "They told his roommates not to let me in the house. Not even to pick up my own stuff, or a picture or anything. He lives way up in the hills. I drove all the way up there and then..."

Her voice trailed off and she tugged her hoodie tightly around her as she struggled to pull herself together. I sensed it wasn't the wasted trip that had upset her. Nor were Jake's parents the target of her anger. She was grieving, that was all. And grieving was messy.

"Sorry." She swallowed hard, then took a sip of coffee and started over. "First, they suggested that I drove Jake to suicide, and now they're saying he was so distracted by an argument we'd had that he must not have done all his safety checks." She pressed her lips together before speaking again. "There was nothing I did or could ever have done that would have made him skimp on his safety checks or take his own life."

"I've heard how careful he was," I said.

"It was one of the things about him that could drive me nuts." She sniffed. "It took him forever to get ready to go anywhere. When we were little, he had to pump up the tires on my bike and check the brakes before we went for a ride. Later, the car windows and headlights needed to be spotless, and he'd check the oil before we could take a drive, even if it were just into town or to school. There's absolutely no way he would have ever cut a safety check short. And even if he were planning to kill himself, which he wouldn't, he couldn't have done it in a machine he was responsible for maintaining. It would have killed him to have people think he'd messed up and caused an accident." She was silent for a moment, her lips moving slightly as though she were replaying her own words in her head.

"Oh, my god. My thinking is so convoluted. Did I really just say he wouldn't have committed suicide because it would have killed him? How crazy is that?"

"You're entitled to a little crazy. Sounds like Jake's parents have, at least temporarily, gone off the deep end. I believe you though. Everything I've heard about Jake makes him sound like a perpetually upbeat guy who liked doing things for other people and was excited about a lot of things in his life—all the portions of his life—school, career, hobbies, community, love, and family." I paused for a moment before adding, "He sounds almost too perfect."

She took a long sip of her coffee and licked foam from her lips. "Look, I know what you're saying." She put down her drink and lifted her hands with the first two fingers extended in an air quotes gesture. "Public reports of tragic deaths aren't always reliable. Jake and I have had friends who overdosed or had terrible car crashes. The deaths were ruled accidents, but you've got to wonder sometimes whether they were more than that. Were they going too fast or driving under the influence because something was bothering them? Were they thrill seekers who taunted death too many times? Did they take too many pills because they no longer cared?" She frowned and looked close to tears. "But I swear, in Jake's case, there was nothing. *Nothing* that would suggest suicide, reckless behavior, or self-medicating."

"So what's with the parents?"

"Grief. Grief and well…Jake and I kinda had a little breakup." Jen looked up and wrinkled her nose. "We knew we'd get back together. I just needed to get his attention. He was working too hard. Drinking triple espressos five times a day so he wouldn't fall asleep. It was easy for him to do since he worked part-time as a barista just off campus at the Jumping Bean."

"How many jobs did he have?" I asked, trying to decide whether the behavior Jen described was more reckless than she appeared to believe, or if it was just what was now required of young adults struggling to get ahead in the gig economy. If Jake had been exhausted, it might explain how the normally careful mechanic could have missed something in a safety check.

Jen answered the question I hadn't asked. "All our friends are doing that, the responsible ones at least. Anyone who's going to school and doesn't want to be buried by student loans their whole lives." She scoffed. "Turns out that lifelong debt wasn't something Jake needed to worry about."

"But seriously." I began listing his jobs. "The airport maintenance work, his academic research, classes, barista—"

"He did volunteer work too, with at-risk teens. Kids whose families had no money and who had no hope of a future…the ones who saw nothing but the easy money that comes with criminal activity and drug running for the gangs."

"What kinds of things did Jake do with them?"

"Made sure their families had all the services they needed, helped them get scholarships, tutored them, took them surfing, flying, had them help him in the shop—whatever they needed. It took time, but not as much as you'd think because he mostly just gathered them up and hauled them along with him."

"Did it work?"

"Sometimes. Better with some kids than others," Jen said. "But it didn't hurt."

"Did it tick off the gang leaders?" I asked. "Could they have wanted him out of the way?"

Jen laughed, but her face reflected a darker mood. "Are you kidding? Of course not. If there's one thing we're not short of in this area, it's poor kids with little hope. The gangs have no trouble recruiting kids, even when you take the ones Jake was helping out of the mix."

I winced, thinking about the pressures on the life of the county's poor and of Jake, already burdened with jobs, school, and volunteer work, plunging into political activism. Dozens of thoughts swirled in my head, but I picked the lamest of them to say aloud. "Picking berries doesn't offer much job growth. Takes its toll, too."

"It can, but there's stuff that makes the work easier. The university has a joint project between the sports medicine, agriculture, and mechanical engineering departments to design new tools like wheeled carts that make the berry picking jobs a little easier."

"Farms that update their procedures would have an easier time hiring and have more efficient workers. Sounds like a no-brainer."

"Ya think?" She wiped crumbs off the table so vigorously I feared for the table's enamel. "Jake was working on smoothing the road toward low-cost changes that could benefit everyone."

I registered everything Jen was saying and wished I'd had a chance to meet Jake. But I wanted to revisit the beginning of our conversation. "So, you've said there's no way Jake committed suicide or contributed to a mechanical failure through misuse or neglect of his machine. What do you think happened?"

Jen fiddled with her coffee mug. She looked at her phone, her wrist, and the clock in the tower at the center of the shopping plaza. But just when I was sure she was going to say she had an appointment elsewhere, she squared her shoulders and looked me in the eye. "I don't know, but…"

Silence followed her remarks, and I became aware of the bustle around us as the commuters left and parents began to arrive with toddlers in tow. I leaned forward. "That's the problem, isn't it," I said in a low voice. "As soon as you start to think about what happened, the world becomes a scary place. Did Jake see something he wasn't supposed to?"

Jen pushed her chair away from the table. The metal legs screeched as they scraped against the concrete. But then she leaned forward. "Something was bothering him. Like I said, he'd been hard to reach in the last few weeks. He was working longer hours and not returning my calls. We'd worked together at the Jumping Bean for a long time, but I found a job with better pay and more flexible hours—helping a professor analyze data from a marketing survey. I wanted to recommend Jake for an opening in the department so that he could reduce his hours, and we could spend more time together, but he only wanted to do what he called *real* work. He said marketing didn't fit that definition for him. It made me feel bad, like he thought my work was less important than his. That was probably the start of our fight."

Her eyes teared up, and I passed her another napkin. A bouncy group of high school students pushed two tables together and asked for our permission to drag extra chairs from our table to theirs. While they loudly got themselves and their seating arrangements settled, Jen pulled herself together.

"Jake and I were soulmates and would have gotten back together. The breakup was meant to be a kick in the pants. I've been accepted at a business school in Southern California for graduate work. I wanted Jake to go with me." She leaned back in her chair and scoffed. "Jake wasn't sure he wanted to move, but it's not like there aren't poor people, non-government agencies, and shoreline studies in Southern California that would have interested Jake. I didn't see much difference between living here and moving there. I even offered to apply to schools in San Francisco and wait until next year, but he was distracted. I couldn't get him to make a decision." She looked away before shaking off her grief and surging on. "So I told him to figure out what he wanted and let me know. Until then, I didn't want to see him or talk to him. If I'd known what would happen... as it is, I missed two weeks with him."

"It sounds like it was more than just the time crunch of his work that was bothering him," I offered, hoping she'd speculate more about what Jake's real problem could have been. Could he have sensed he was in danger and pushed Jen away to protect her? "Was someone threatening him?"

"I just don't know anymore. Have you talked to his parents? Or the people he worked with? They may have seen something or heard something Jake didn't want to worry me about."

I frowned. "My chats with the Petersons haven't been productive." My voice held far more anger than I'd intended, and I must have scared Jen. She gathered up her belongings and stood, shook my hand, thanked me for talking to her, and strode away. But she'd only taken a few steps before she stopped and turned around.

"There's one thing I can be sure of," she said. "If Jake thought someone was threatening him or that his safety was at risk, he would have distanced himself from me, to protect me. He was over protective and was never any good at sharing a burden."

"Look, Jen," I said, handing her my card. "If you think of anything else, or just want to talk, please call me. I'm a good listener. And, like I said, the Petersons are hell-bent on accusing my kids of killing Jake. They didn't, and I may need help to prove that."

Jen had had enough talk for the day. She took the card and stuffed it in her jeans pocket. Her shoulders shook as she walked away.

I scribbled a list of the places and people Jen had mentioned. They might be useful sources to mine for alternative theories regarding Jake's death. On television, cops learned as much as they could about murder victims' lives hoping some tiny detail would lead them to the killer. I needed to emulate them.

Jen had referred to Jake's department at the university, the Jumping Bean, his parents, the political organizers from Santa Clara County, and whatever the name was of the organization that helped the at-risk kids in the community. I needed to talk his co-workers. I'd have been happy if I never saw Jake's parents again, and doubted they'd share any information with me anyway. But maybe the sheriff or Forrest Doucett could help. The Petersons might have revealed information in their meetings that, added to what Jen had told me, could provide a more detailed picture of what had happened to Jake.

My phone rang, and I struggled to locate it in my backpack. By the time I found it, the call had gone to voicemail. I worked some cell phone magic and listened. It was Nell, asking me to phone her. I did, but thanks to sparse cell coverage in the south county, the call didn't go through.

Chapter 15

If you're traveling with family for a wedding, graduation, or funeral, it may make sense to pack everyone's event clothing in one bag. This trick is particularly useful if you're making a multi-day car trip. It means you'll only need to pack/unpack the special event bag on the day you'll need it.

From the Notebook of Maggie McDonald
Simplicity Itself Organizing Services

Friday, June 21, Morning

"Mom, you've got to hear this," David said before I had a chance to unload the groceries. "Brian remembered something. It's gold."

"Gold?"

"Well, not gold, exactly, but it changes the picture of what could have happened to Jake."

I looked at Brian, whose hair was flat on one side from sleep. He sat at the counter with his leg settled regally on a pillow perched on the stool next to him.

"So, spill, kiddo. Do you guys want hot chocolate or anything with those cookies?"

"Cookies for breakfast? Who are you and what have you done with our mother?"

"*Vacation.* You're on vacation. I ran into Jake's girlfriend at the coffee shop. She looked like she needed a boatload of carbs and about a year of sleep. I helped her out with the carbs, but she's on her own when it comes to the sleep. I wasn't going to buy *her* a cookie without having one myself. Then I felt guilty not buying them for you, too." Belle nudged my hand and thumped her tail on the floor. "You get a dog biscuit," I added. "My brain is not completely addled."

"Never mind that," said David. "Brian, tell her."

Brian broke his cookie into four even pieces. "Remember when I told you that Susie turned off the engine on the plane, and you freaked?"

I nodded. Of course I remembered.

"I didn't have a chance to explain. Susie wanted to demonstrate how quiet the plane was without the engine noise. But she also wanted to show me that the plane didn't need the engine to be aerodynamic. She said that even novice pilots can and do land planes when the engines have gone out."

I paused in the middle of unpacking the groceries and looked up. "Help me out. What's the significance of this tidbit?"

David started to answer, but Brian shushed him. "Ultralight pilots must practice engine failures, too. They're basically gas-powered hang gliders, right? So why would they need an engine to fly properly? Even if someone sabotaged the engine, or Jake ran out of gas, or something else went wrong, he could have landed the plane safely."

"Could Jake have been aiming for that strawberry farm on the cliff and, I don't know, hit some turbulent air?" I asked.

"Unlikely," David said. "Have you watched the hawks? They catch thermals on the edge of those cliffs that lift them up. Jake ended up nose down in the side of the cliff. If he didn't think he'd make the farm at the top, he could have landed on the beach. It was low tide. Plenty of nice flat beach to land on."

"So, where does that leave us?"

"Something bad happened to Jake, or the ultralight," Brian said. "Something that made it impossible for him to fly safely."

"Or something distracted him," David went on. "Or maybe startled him so badly that he jerked the controls, making the ultralight unstable. He could have been too close to the ground to correct the problem."

I considered the possibilities. "Jerked the controls? Like you'd do if someone shot at you?" My skin grew cold and I felt woozy. I sank into a chair, my hands braced on the table for support. That's what I'd been forgetting. The gunshot. That sharp sound I'd heard on our first day, when we'd watched Jake's aircraft wobble over our heads. I forced myself to stop my silent musing and say the words out loud. "Do either of you remember hearing a gunshot that first day? I thought it was a car backfiring or there was something wrong with Jake's engine."

There seemed to be no question in their minds about having heard a gunshot, because they both leaped ahead without directly answering my question. "Or maybe someone was shooting at something else and the bullet got too close to Jake?" David asked.

"Exactly," Brian said.

"On the other hand..." I began, unsure how to turn my fledgling thought into a fully viable theory.

"What?" David asked.

"Susie said the plane and ultralights were aerodynamic without the engine, right?"

The boys nodded.

"Well, what if the plane *wasn't* aerodynamic? What if there was a tear in the wing fabric, or something broke off?" I looked frantically around the room for the piece of metal David had found, before remembering that Max had taken it to the materials engineer at work.

"I took a picture of it," Brian said, scrolling through the photo library on his phone as if he'd read my thoughts. "There."

David and I peered at the picture. I tilted my head and squinted. "Could it be part of a propeller? If part of one blade broke off, would that create turbulence? Or worse?"

David pulled the phone close, picked it up, and tapped and swiped, making the photo bigger. "It's hard to be sure, but could that rounded edge be a propeller blade tip?"

"Has your dad called?" I asked. "We need to find out what Howard thinks about that piece of metal." I put the milk in the fridge and struggled to gather my thoughts. Thinking about the possibility that someone had tampered with Jake's ultralight made me retroactively terrified for Brian's safety during his Eagle flight. What had Max and I been thinking? I took a deep breath in an attempt to regain my sanity and equilibrium, then sank into a chair at the breakfast table.

"Text your dad," I said to Brian. "David, give your brother his phone. Bri, send him the picture. Ask him what he and the metal expert think. Could it be part of the propeller? Do they think it shows signs of tampering? Could a propeller missing a chunk of metal have caused the plane to crash? And if it did, how could David have found it next to the ultralight?"

"Yeah," said David. "Good idea. I think all that is a little beyond my introductory physics class. When in doubt, call an engineer."

Brian sent off the photo and the message. While we waited for Max to call or text back, I phoned Nell to return her earlier message. The call went to voicemail. After a quick tidying of the tiny condo, which had a propensity to become cluttered quickly but was equally swiftly put to rights, the boys and I trooped over to the rental office.

Brian clumped up the ramp to Renée's office and struggled to open the door. David and I refrained from helping him. Upon waking this morning, he declared he was going to be as independent as possible and wanted no one, *no one* to help him with *anything*.

I'd solemnly promised to hold back on my motherly nurturing.

David, who'd suffered a broken ankle almost a year earlier, was surprisingly supportive. "Whatever you want, dude," he said. "You're tougher than I was and your leg is worse. No shame in throwing in the towel, though, okay?"

Managing the crutches and the heavy door to the rental office wasn't easy. With determination, stubbornness, strength, and willpower, Brian conquered the challenge and then held the door for David and me.

"*Ay yi yi!* What happened to you? Are you okay?" asked Renée, looking up from behind the stack of papers and boxes on her desk.

Brian sank gratefully into a chair his brother pulled from the conference room. "It was on the beach. A post. Like a big metal stake." He held his arms far apart to indicate the size. "Smack in the middle of the beach like it was put there deliberately for someone to trip over." He glanced at each of us, his eyes pleading with us to believe him.

Renée was skeptical. "One of those old wharf pilings, you mean? The ones that are uncovered at low tide?"

"What *are* those things?" David asked. "My mom said there used to be a pier there."

"Not for almost a hundred years," Renée said. "There was a railroad track that ended there years ago in a shipping pier. Passenger steamers used to stop here on their way to San Francisco, too. There was a dance pavilion, race track—all sorts of entertainment."

"I'm surprised the pilings are still there," I said.

"After every big storm, I expect to find them gone. They knew how to build stuff back then."

"Uh, can we get back to the stake?" Brian said. "It was *metal*. Rusty metal. The doctor had a hard time cleaning fragments out of the wound. It wasn't wood. And it was high tide when we were walking, remember?"

"Definitely not the old piers then," said Renée. "They only show up at the lowest of low tides."

"But why is there a metal stake there?" I asked. "Surely that can't be safe. Brian can't be the only person who ever tripped on it. It wasn't even all that dark when we were out there. Twilight, at the most."

Renée shook her head. "I'll have to look. Something like that could be a liability for the association and for the state park, which manages everything beyond the high tide mark. If there were any permanently-placed dangerous obstacles, our risk-management committee would have addressed them. I've never seen anything like what you describe."

"We'll go for a walk later," David said. "I'll take a picture of it for you."

Renée thanked him for saving her a trip. She'd set up a babysitter for the children, but said that she might have to stop work in the middle of the morning to answer the phone or head back into town. Child Protective Services had contacted her, and she'd consulted an organization for help keeping the kids in her care rather than having them placed with strangers.

"What a nightmare," I said. "For everyone."

Renée nodded. "It is. *Pobrecitos.* I'm worried about their parents, too. But the Immigration Law Center is on it. They're trying to make sure none of the family members get lost in the system. The best thing for me is distraction."

"I may need to take a break at some point, too. Our family lawyer and some of his staff are going to help us deal with the media attention following Jake's death, and what we hope will turn out to be a nuisance lawsuit that the Petersons filed."

Renée shuddered. "I know most of the local reporters and it still makes me nervous to talk to them."

"Let's see what we can accomplish before our phone calls interrupt us," I said, changing the subject. "Have you had a chance to check with your lawyers and insurance to find out what records you absolutely need to save?"

Renée shook her head. "Not yet. All my time has been focused on the kids."

I handed her my phone, so that she could make the work calls without tying up her own line. "Give them a call now."

I handed an empty cardboard box to each boy. "You're on recycling duty. All catalogs and magazines go in the bin."

Renée's eyes widened. "*All* of them? What if I need to order office stuff?"

"Don't you do that online?"

"What about articles in the magazines? Those professional journals have great pointers for setting up offices like this."

"Find them online. If you can't, I'll pay to have the magazines send us new issues. When did you last read one of those helpful articles?"

Renée looked sheepish. "I always mean to."

I nodded. "Everyone does. But ninety-nine percent of the time we don't get to it. I'm going to keep you busy here for the next few weeks. You won't have time to look at catalogs and magazines anyway. And they'll all keep coming. I'll set you up with a phone app to help you reduce the size of the daily onslaught. But anything that's here now can go."

"Really?"

"*Really*. Dig in, guys. David, you can shuttle the cartons to the recycling dumpster. Brian, no break for you. Got your inhaler?" Dust wasn't the worst of Brian's allergy and asthma triggers, but we watched his exposure. "If it gets too bad, I'll get you another job. Keep me posted, okay?"

Brian nodded.

We worked steadily for an hour, filling up more boxes than David could take in one trip, even using the handcart Renée discovered behind a stash of cartons and a broken vacuum cleaner.

"Mom, I need to take a load out to the recycling bin," David said. "Would you mind if I took a run after that? I need to keep up my training for cross-country. And I told Renée I'd take a picture of that stake Brian tripped over."

I'd been separating a jumble of insurance records and tax receipts, and it took me a moment to shift my attention to my oldest son. I glanced up. "Huh?"

"Hang on there, mom, you've got a spider in your hair." I jumped back from the desk, as though that would separate me from my own hair and the spider within in it.

"Get it off me! Get it. David. Get it." I bent at the waist and batted at my hair, already mortified by my shrieks and my behavior, but desperate to separate the spider from me, the room, and perhaps, life itself.

David was more tender-hearted. Grabbing a Styrofoam cup, he coaxed the errant arachnid into it and escorted it outdoors, wishing it well in its web ventures.

He returned, looking smug, accomplished, and as though he'd defeated a six-ton Godzilla for me. I owed him. "Sure. Go for that run. Good idea." I eyed the pile of dusty papers cautiously, fearing a fraternity of attack-trained spiders lurked in its depths. *Ugh!*

"I'll watch out for violent spiders, snakes, and other dangers," David said, not making much of an attempt to keep the laughter out of his voice.

"Okay, okay," I said, waving him off. "I'm not proud of my behavior at all, but I can't help it. And I am proud of you both for not teasing me."

David glanced at his brother, who was rocking his head to the music on his phone as he sorted stacks of old mail and catalogs. Brian must have sensed us staring. He looked up and pulled the microphone buds from his ears. "Huh?"

"He doesn't get any points for not laughing," David said. "He was oblivious."

Brian waved an envelope in the air. "What do you want me to do with real mail?" He asked, stifling a sneeze and rubbing his nose. "This one looks like a check."

"Want anything from the condo, Bri?" David asked. "I'm on my way out for a run. Sorry dude, I don't mean to rub it in."

"Run for me, too. And bring back snacks and drinks. Please."

David nodded and was nearly out the door with the handcart full of boxes when Brian had an afterthought, "Run north on the beach and look for that stake I ran into. Take a picture of it for Renée."

David tactfully refrained from telling his little brother that we'd already discussed that plan.

"Good idea," said Renée.

"It's probably something you've seen a million times. You'll recognize it as soon as you see it, I'm sure." Brian said.

"I doubt it has a romantic history like those pilings, but taking a picture of it's a good idea," I said.

"Maybe pirates or smugglers turn up at night," said Brian, waggling his eyebrows and twirling an imaginary mustache.

Chapter 16

Pack zip lock bags. You'll use them for garbage, damp or messy clothing and sandy or drippy items. They're handy for creating individual snack packets and unforeseen emergencies.

From the Notebook of Maggie McDonald
Simplicity Itself Organizing Services

Friday, June 21, Midday

By the time David returned, the rest of us had settled down to a deli lunch Renée had ordered from town. I'd had to wash my hands twice to get rid of the grime and dust. Many organizers ask clients to have their homes or offices professionally cleaned before tackling a project. I felt that Renée had needed to do a first round of purging before a cleaning would do any good. But we were stirring up so much dust that she had already phoned the association's cleaning service.

"Grab a sandwich," I told David, as he plopped a bag of apples and a carton of water bottles on the table. "I was just going over what we're doing this afternoon."

Renée jumped in. "I'm letting us all out at two o'clock, but we need to work full tilt until then. I want you to stash the boxes of garbage and recycling on the deck for now, instead of all the way off to the recycling bins. Housekeeping is coming in as soon as we're out of here. I've asked them to do a thorough cleaning to try to keep the dust down."

"That should make our jobs much easier tomorrow, Renée. Thanks," I said. She pushed a stray piece of lettuce into the corner of her mouth with one hand, and in the process left a blob of mayonnaise on the tip of her nose. It was adorable. Before any of us had a chance to tell her about it, though, she pushed a yellow pad of paper toward me. "I got a list of what records we need to keep on hand for the legal department and the insurance," she said. "Are you sure everything else can go?"

"Probably even the legal and insurance records, if you have them duplicated on the computer. Do you have an automated backup system? With off-site or cloud-based storage?

She stared at me blankly, then her face reddened.

I pretended not to notice her embarrassment. "Never mind. Would it help if we roughed out a budget for a new system? I've secured bids for updating other small businesses. Those numbers might help you develop a proposal for the board."

"I've got some budget leeway," said Renée. "Go ahead and write up an order for what you think will work. Do we need new computers before we move ahead?"

I glanced at the closest desk and the spaghetti mass of wires and power bricks under it.

"You should be fine for now," I said. "I've got a computer guy who can come in and assess your needs…and the state of your current systems. We can get you budget numbers for new computers, cables, printers, and routers. I wouldn't wait too long, though. Electronics and home appliances tend to blow up as soon as you think about replacing them."

Renée folded up her sandwich wrappings and started packing up the remains of our lunch and stashing it in the fridge. "Guess what I'm having for dinner?" she said. "Do you want any of this?"

I glanced at the boys, who nodded eagerly.

I picked up the deli menu that had come with the lunch. "Let me buy lunch tomorrow. I'll order us dinner at the same time. Clearing out a backlog of junk like this is exhausting. Neither one of us will have any energy to cook or even think about a shopping list when we get home."

Renée pushed her hair back and sighed. "Thanks, Maggie. Tess was right. She said you take care of your clients."

I smiled. "I have to. This is hard work. Physically and emotionally. It's tempting for clients to throw in the towel after the first day. If I want to stay in business, I have to be adept at keeping you all going."

I put the tops on containers of potato and carrot salad and handed them to Renée. After that, we were all back at work, with Brian cracking the whip. He set up a timer on his phone and allowed us a brief break every twenty-five minutes, but other than that, we worked at a rapid clip.

I'd set Brian a new, slightly less dusty task—photographing the return addresses on all the magazines and catalogs, and entering them into a nifty app that would then contact all the senders and remove the condo association from their mailing lists. There were other less expensive ways to tackle the task of reducing junk mail, but I didn't know of any that were simpler.

We were making progress. The expansive entryway deck was covered with bulging plastic garbage bags and recycling bins. Renée said she hoped one day to set up the deck as a place for renters to relax as they waited for their condos to be ready. And as an informal meeting space for the whole community. At first, she'd offer complimentary coffee and snacks but hoped to eventually set up a small deli and gift shop to bring in extra income, particularly in the busy summer months. "The more people I can draw in here to browse," she said, "the more impulse buys of resort wear they'll make. If I can get some inexpensive refrigerated display units, I can be their source for the emergency carton of milk they forgot to get in town, ice cream treats for kids, and a whole lot of other small items with big margins. It will help take the pressure off the rest of the budget."

It was a great idea, and I applauded her vision. But right now the deck was a perfect staging area. We set aside several boxes of office supplies to donate to the local schools. Renée toyed with the idea of saving them, but I convinced her that it would be better in the long run to buy new items after she'd cleaned, repaired, and remodeled the office with purpose-built storage. If she kept every rubber band and paperclip, she'd waste a good part of her valuable time, energy, and talent moving her office supplies from place to place.

There was something ultimately satisfying about literally clearing the decks, and getting all the discards stashed in their respective disposal, recycling, or donation bins.

It wasn't until we were walking back to the condo that I remembered to ask David about the stake that had injured Brian.

"What stake?" David said. "I looked all over the beach, in both directions, and couldn't find it. I checked the tide charts to make sure it couldn't be under water. There was no stake. Not anywhere on the beach."

"So it was temporary?" I asked.

"It seemed pretty permanent when I ran into it," Brian said. "How deep would you have to plant a stake to make it immovable? Could someone easily pull something like that back out of the sand?"

"More importantly," I said. "Why? Why would it have been there yesterday and gone today?"

"Could smugglers have needed a way to temporarily tie up a boat, without leaving permanent evidence behind?" David said.

"Smuggling what?"

"Illegally caught fish? Drugs? People?"

I smiled. "I was thinking more along the lines that the stake had been left behind after someone dismantled a wedding tent or volleyball net."

"Would either of those things require something so sturdy?" Brian asked. "If the association put them up, wouldn't they know how many stakes they'd used? They must do that all the time. How could they forget one?"

I pulled my cell phone from my back pocket. "Let's check." I phoned Renée and left a message when she didn't answer. "Hey, Renée, quick question. David couldn't find the post that Brian ran into on the beach. Do you know of any reason why a sturdy metal stake would be pounded into the sand and then removed? Is it something your team does to secure recreational equipment or event stuff?"

I ended the call, and then immediately hit redial. "I'm asking for curiosity's sake only," I said. "Trying to solve the mystery of the missing post—like Nancy Drew." I laughed awkwardly. "I don't want you to think we're going to sue or anything."

Brian rolled his eyes as I stashed the phone back in my pocket. "Like that's going to reassure Renée," he said. "Isn't that what someone bent on litigation would say? It's not like the words *we don't plan to sue* are legally binding or anything."

I shrugged. "Clarifying my motives makes me feel better," I said. "Whether Renée believes me or not. I needed to *tell* her I wasn't bent on a lawsuit."

My phone pinged with a text alert:

We secure temp. beach equip. w/Day-Glo plastic stakes. Maintenance counts them. Environmental thing. Leave no trace, etc. Giant steel stake sounds dangerous. Not one of ours.

I texted back:

Did we confirm with you that it's NOT a historical artifact like the remnants of the Victorian pier/pavilion?

And Renée responded:

Not sure, but I've never seen it. Let me text the group that did feature on us for local history exhibit to be sure.

"Mom, you are such a slow typist," Brian moaned. "You have two thumbs, you know."

I continued pecking out my text message with my right pointer finger. "When it comes to texting, I'm *all* thumbs. But, you know, a track star who can't make it across the parking lot without readjusting his crutches might want to think twice about throwing shade about speed of any kind." My phone pinged with a response.

I read it and looked up at both kids. "Renée tells me that some local history expert doesn't know anything about a steel or iron stake on the beach."

My phone continued to ping with updates, including pictures of various brands of dog tie-out stakes one of Renée's contacts suggested we might have seen: **I've seen folks use these, along with long leads, to get around the leash laws.**

I showed the photos to the boys, but we all agreed they weren't sturdy enough to have been the stake that had tripped Brian.

"Would something that flimsy even hold a decent-size dog?" David asked. Belle barked. Apparently not, in her opinion. But I sympathized with those who wanted to offer their dogs more freedom than the state park's six-foot-leash law allowed.

David typed and scrolled furiously on his phone with both thumbs. My mobile binged again. "Send them that," David said, referring to the photo he'd messaged to my cell. "Ask if they've ever seen anything like it holding down anything on the beach."

I followed instructions. "Let's stop texting and get home," I said, brushing my hands on my jeans. "I'm desperate to wash my hands and face and take a walk somewhere I can breathe fresh air instead of dust."

"Can we go to the aquarium?" David asked. "Or rent kayaks in Elkhorn Slough? Grab a surfing lesson?"

"We'll see," I said, gesturing to urge them onward.

"That means no," Brian said.

"It means we'll see," I said. "We won't have time today since we need to see the orthopedist about Brian's leg. But make a list. We'll talk it over tonight."

"I can't surf," Brian said. "Stupid leg."

Brian seldom indulged in self-pity, but I felt he was entitled to a pinch of it, given the circumstances and our high expectations for the holiday, which had so far disappointed all of us.

"Sorry, bud. But we can't expect David to sit around with his leg up just to keep you company."

Brian grumbled unintelligibly under his breath.

David was uncharacteristically generous to his brother. "Maybe we can find stuff I want to do that is close to other stuff you and Mom can do while you wait for me. I'll be the guinea pig. If I try something that's no good, I'll save you the trouble. And if it turns out to be fun, we can do it together, later."

Brian pressed his lips together to stop them quivering. He stood up as straight as possible on his crutches. "Okay," he said. "Sure. Good idea."

The two boys flopped on the couch when we returned to the apartment. They fired up their computers, searching local recreational activities and tourist attractions.

I showered off the dust, taking extra care to scrub my scalp in case any stray spiders had tried to make a home there. I changed clothes. My beach wardrobe boasted nothing fancy. It was just an interchangeable array of washable layers. There was something freeing and refreshing about being able to dress quickly without looking, knowing that anything I pulled from the drawers would match.

"*Shh*," David whispered when I returned to the living room, combing out my wet hair.

Brian was zonked out. Healing required energy and his wound was a bad one that was forcing his body to handle pain while it rebuilt bone, soft tissue, and skin. For the near future, we'd have to plan on him falling asleep whenever he stopped moving. Poor guy.

I hated to wake him to head into town to see the doctor, but the kid was a good sport. The doctor was kind and efficient. X-rays revealed the bone was healing well with no sign of infection.

We'd been back home for only a few moments when I heard someone tromping on the wooden boardwalk outside the condo. A knock on the door startled the kids, but I'd been expecting it after hearing the footsteps. I opened the door, anticipating a maintenance worker or someone else who worked for Renée. I was wrong.

Chapter 17

Gel window stickers (for those old enough to be trusted not to eat them) can provide easily removable entertainment on a car, airplane, and hotel windows

From the Notebook of Maggie McDonald
Simplicity Itself Organizing Services

Friday, June 21, Late afternoon

"What are you doing here?" I asked the very serious, corporate-looking lawyer standing in my doorway. It was Nell Bevans.

"Hi Maggie," answered Nell. "Forrest sent me. We need to talk."

The first thing Nell needed help with was locating the condo that Forrest had rented for her to stay in while she finished up work for a client in Monterey and advised us in our dealings with local law enforcement and Jake's parents.

I helped Nell down our flight of stairs, across the boardwalk, and up a second steep flight to a one-bedroom unit close to the ocean. Only a hint of light lingered in the sky when I opened the curtains on the picture window. "It's dark now," I said, stating the obvious. "But in the morning you'll have trouble getting any work done. The view is guaranteed to distract you."

Nell dropped her briefcase, sighed, and kicked off her heels. "Stupid shoes," she said. "I had a meeting in Monterey with an investment group from Los Angeles interested in building a new hotel. It was all very corporate and trendy, but we were looking at a property on the water. With sand. In heels. Crazy. Absolutely nuts."

"It's good to see you," I ventured. "I was about to start dinner. Nothing fancy, but would you like to join us? Come barefoot if you like." We'd been in the trenches together for some time nearly a year ago, working to get Stephen out of jail. We'd been so focused on helping others that I hadn't learned much about Nell, yet here I was standing in her living room. I was glad to see her, but other feelings competed for my attention: fear, frustration, and a need to be a gracious hostess while at the same time fiercely protective of my family.

If Forrest thought we needed our own on-site lawyer, I worried that we were in more trouble than I'd thought. But I hesitated to ask. I wanted to assume that everything was okay. Too much had gone wrong already, and I wasn't sure how much more any of us could take.

Nell looked up. "I'd love to join you. I'll bring wine."

"I never say no to a free bottle of wine. We're having burgers. You aren't a vegetarian are you? Vegan? I'm sure I can..." I scrambled to think about what I had in the refrigerator that would feed a specialized diet.

"Relax, Maggie. I'm an omnivore. I've got fried artichoke hearts too. Can I bring those?"

"From the Giant Artichoke? Absolutely." Castroville, a few miles south of Watsonville, was the artichoke capital of the world and its twenty-foot tall concrete thistle was a local landmark. But the restaurant's deep-fried hearts were even more memorable.

"Come when you're ready," I said with my hand on the doorknob. But then I hesitated. "You still haven't told me why you're here."

"Probably nothing we couldn't handle over the phone. But I was down here and I have to stay within shouting distance of the group from Los Angeles, just in case their deal goes through. Forrest thought I might help out." After rummaging in her luggage, she pulled a pair of jeans, an oversized gray sweatshirt, and a bright purple T-shirt from her bag.

"I'm completely frazzled from the drive. It was bumper to bumper all the way from Moss Landing. Let me jump in the shower and into my comfy clothes. I'll bring the wine and the nibbles, and we'll catch up. I can't wait to see your boys. Great kids."

Nell peeled off her suit jacket. I made a quick exit before she stripped to the skin in front of me. In some ways, she reminded me of my friend Tess— completely allergic to the business outfits required for their professions. I was lucky. Sneakers and jeans were the perfect get-up for rummaging among other people's discards and dusty treasures. And they suited my personal style and temperament.

Later, while Brian monitored the burgers on the gas grill on our balcony, Nell updated us.

"It really is no big deal," she began.

"People tend to say that when something is a *very* big deal," I said.

"Forrest doesn't think there's any reason to be concerned. He expects the Petersons will cool off. They have more important things to deal with than a lawsuit. But Forrest doesn't leave anything to chance. The fact that you're all outsiders here makes him wary. He watches too many of those old movies in which a stranger comes to town and is blamed for everything that goes wrong."

"And how does that plot play out in real life?" I asked.

"Forrest asked me to approach the problem assuming that someone deliberately killed Jake, as unlikely as that may seem." Nell shook her head. "It sounds like a senseless, tragic accident to me, but Forrest's outlook is darker."

She hopped onto a tall stool and rested her wine glass on the balcony railing. "So, the first things I'll consider are motives. Who benefits from Jake's death? Was there an insurance policy?"

I started to tell her I had no idea, but she waved me off. "I looked into it. Jake Peterson had a small life-insurance policy through one of his jobs that will provide funeral expenses and a small payout to his girlfriend. In the grand scheme of things, it wouldn't be worth killing him for."

I gasped at the implication that Jen might have killed Jake over an insurance policy.

"I'm sorry. I get used to discussing these things bluntly at work. But that's how the insurance company is looking at it. The payouts are small, fraud is unlikely, and investigating Jake's death isn't worth the money they'd spend on an in-depth forensic analysis of his books. They might take a fleeting look at his finances, but that's it."

She took a sip of her wine before continuing. "Forrest wants you to refer any questions from the insurance, the cops, or the media to me. Don't talk to anyone about anything else to do with the accident. I'll handle any inquiries myself while I'm here. I'd like to have a crew shoot some still photos and video of Belle and the boys—"

"What on earth for?" I asked.

"To give to the news outlets."

"Don't TV stations take care of that themselves?"

"Most of the time, but if we provide them with footage, they won't mind so much if we decline interviews. And the video will help spin the story that the boys are wholesome, responsible citizens."

"Spin?" I asked. "It's not spin. They *are* wholesome and responsible. Is all this really necessary?"

"You never know. We need to be ready for anything. I might practice a little interrogation with the kids tonight. We'll make a game of it..."

"You make all these relationships sound confrontational," I said. "Remember, we've got friends in law enforcement. My kids are comfortable with everyone in the Orchard View Police Department."

"That may be a problem. Orchard View and Watsonville aren't the same. These cops don't know you. And there are few rules restricting law enforcement questions during an interrogation. They don't even need to tell the truth. They're on their home turf. You're not. And if you say something you shouldn't, you can't take it back or erase it."

"Sounds fun," David called from the kitchen before coming out to the deck and grabbing a fried artichoke. "Practicing with Nell, I mean, not being grilled by strange cops."

Nell smiled and her shoulders relaxed. "Forrest feels every civilian could use an advocate who evens the balance. Here, you're out of your element. Don't go it alone. You don't have to."

I appreciated Nell's advice and assistance and told her so. But something about the situation still bugged me. "Nell, I speak English. I know my rights. I trust the police, in general. I'm confident dealing with bureaucracy. Yet, you recommend I talk to no one without a lawyer."

"Right," said Nell, smiling, scooting forward in her chair and raising her eyebrows with the delight of a dog trainer who has finally taught a recalcitrant puppy to sit.

"What do people who don't know lawyers and cops do? What if they don't understand English, especially when they're under the stress of an investigation? What happens to them? Who do they have on their side?"

"Sometimes, they're savvy enough to request a lawyer, and one is provided for them. In the best case, they'll get an eager young public defender." She pursed her lips. "I worked for the public defender's office for two years."

"But you left to work for Forrest."

"The hours were brutal, and I never felt I could do enough. I met Forrest and liked his approach to the law. As he's fond of saying, the rich and famous are as entitled to representation as the poor and indigent. Our work with well-heeled clients makes it possible for us to do pro bono work." She sipped her wine. "It's a compromise. I wish the system were more balanced and fair, but it's what we've got."

She picked up a napkin and selected a steaming golden-brown fried artichoke heart from the cobalt-blue plate in the center of the table. "It's better than what's available to most people in most countries, particularly the poor."

I sighed.

Nell leaned against the railing. "It's a good thing these artichokes aren't available much beyond Castroville. I'd weigh five hundred pounds if I could pick them up every time I went to the store. They're delicious."

I smiled at her unconcealed effort to change the subject.

"This area is gorgeous," she said. "Tell me how you snagged this gig for the summer and what you've all been doing." She lifted her wine glass when Brian hobbled out to join us. "I know there's a story there."

"It'll have to wait," he said. "Burgers are up. All the fixings are on the kitchen counter. David's got the corn going, and there's salad. I'll meet you inside."

After dinner, Nell was having trouble keeping her eyes open, and the boys weren't much perkier. I said goodnight to all three and took Belle for a quick sniff and hygiene visit to the parking lot, scanning for skunks. Even my human nose, far less sensitive than any canine's, could detect they were around somewhere.

A hunting barn owl grabbed my attention and I watched it silently soar and then dive to pounce on an unwitting rodent. Renée had said that the association had installed owl boxes two years earlier as an environmentally sound solution to a population explosion among the gophers that tore up the lawns. Given the number of holes in the ground and mounds of sandy soil I'd seen, I wasn't sure how well it was working, but it was a treat to see the owl.

A young man in a black hoodie carried a load of what looked like rubbish down the ramp from one of the condos and dropped it with a resounding *thunk* in the back of a flatbed pickup with more rust than paint on its side panels. I wondered briefly if he was starting to clean up the dreadful condo we'd been assigned when we first arrived at the complex. Before I could investigate, Belle tugged gently on the leash, signaling that she was ready for bed. Chances were, the young man was just another homeowner getting his unit spruced up for the busy summer season. Maintenance people weren't supposed to work past four o'clock most days of the week.

I followed Belle up the boardwalk ramp and stairs and unhooked her leash. A few toenail clicks on the tiles followed by a contented sigh told me she'd conked out for the night on the floor between the bedrooms of her two favorite boys. They were in good paws.

But I was restless. I cleaned up the already mostly clean kitchen, poured myself a last glass of chardonnay, grabbed a blanket, and curled up in one of the cushioned patio chairs on the balcony. Listening to the waves and appreciating the relative darkness that made the Milky Way visible, I'd just started to relax when my phone rang, startling me into nearly spilling my wine.

Chapter 18

A sense of novelty and fun can change a disaster into an adventure. And a splurge can help everyone when you're at the end of your rope.

From the Notebook of Maggie McDonald
Simplicity Itself Organizing Services

Friday, June 21, Late evening

"Hey, Max. You've missed the boys. They're both out cold."

"What's that static? Do you want me to call you back?"

"Static? That's the ocean. I'm snuggled under a blanket on one of those cushy chairs on the balcony. You wouldn't believe how clear it is. No marine layer tonight. At least not yet. The view is sharp all the way to the horizon. In fact, the bay is so calm that it's a little hard to tell which stars are in the sky and which are reflected in the ocean."

Max, ever the romantic, responded with words that made me sorry he'd decided to stay in Orchard View to await the results from Howard's tests. It wasn't so much what Max said, but the way he phrased it that made me realize how much more room there was in a chair spacious enough for two. After I responded in kind and we were both miserably lonely, I filled him in on what the boys and I had learned and asked about the findings of his materials engineer.

"He hasn't had time to run tests, and he's careful with any statements he makes before he has accurate results, almost as if he were already practicing for a court appearance."

"Did he say anything that might be helpful?"

"I pressed him, but all he would say was that the piece of metal *could* have come from a propeller. I asked how an aircraft would operate if it were missing a fist-sized piece of metal from a prop blade. He said that they design propellers the way they do for a reason, and that even one with just a ding in the rotor would make an aircraft more difficult to control than a plane with a perfectly honed blade. Examining the prop is part of every routine safety check."

"Could someone have damaged it, but hidden its flaws from Jake?"

"I asked. Howard works at the community college on stage craft and says that their artists can paint a plywood and cloth set to look like metal that would fool him at a distance. Up close, he'd have to touch it to be sure it wasn't riveted aluminum. So, he wouldn't rule out the possibility. But, he said that a bogus or damaged prop would still have to pass the touch test."

"So with a little filler, careful sanding, and paint..."

"I couldn't say, and Howard wouldn't. He's going to look at the edges again under a microscope, specifically looking for paint and filler. He'll let us know tomorrow, probably with a report that is way more detailed than we need. That's part of the reason I wanted to stay up here, so I can nudge Howard if necessary and get the results as quickly as possible."

"It'd be difficult to paint the propeller without leaving a tell-tale odor, wouldn't it?" When I'd repainted the wrought iron railing on our front steps a few months earlier, the smell of the anti-rust paint was pervasive and unmistakable.

Max made a noise that told me he was considering the idea. "Maybe," he agreed. "But those hangars are full of the smells of solvent, fuel, and paint. I'm not sure that a brief application of paint would make a dent, particularly after it dried."

"So we really don't have any actionable information. Not until we get Howard's report or..." An idea slowly started to form and I laid it out for Max. "NTSB interviewed the guys in the hangar maintenance shop, right?"

"The mechanics David and I talked to seemed pretty impressed by the grilling they'd received from the feds. They still looked a little scared, I thought. David mentioned it too. He was glad he hadn't had to answer questions from them."

"If Joe and the other guys in the maintenance shed had seen someone messing with Jake's ultralight, I'm sure they would have mentioned it."

Max agreed. "They were eager to help. Jake was their friend and coworker. They weren't holding anything back as far as I could tell."

I trusted Max's assessment of the situation. He'd put in his time as a college professor and knew the age-group. He could smell a lie or even a twisted truth a mile off. If he thought the guys in the hangar had told him everything they knew, they almost certainly had.

"Did you ask them who has access to the hangar?" I asked. "And when? Do they lock it? Who has a key? Do they have separate locks for their tools and equipment? Have they had any break-ins? Are there security cameras? What about the parking lot?"

"*Whoa!* One question at a time. David and I touched on some of that. It seems theft has not been much of a problem. A number of people have keys and come and go at all hours without signing in or swiping into a security system. It's a fully equipped shop, so some folks even bring in projects they're working on that have nothing to do with their aircraft. There are some security cameras, but they're mostly for show—to give the impression of a high-tech system. The guys I talked to weren't sure the cameras still worked. One of the lenses pointed straight up at the ceiling."

"I guess that's par for the course," I said. "I'm always surprised when the CCTV footage on TV is crystal clear. Still, I might go back to the airport tomorrow and double check to see whether there are tapes or digital recordings of the camera feeds. I'll also find out if there was any point at which someone would have known Jake wouldn't be around. Do we know if he and Jen took a vacation recently?"

"What are you thinking?" Max asked.

"That if I wanted to damage a metal propeller, I'd need some kind of noisy cutting tool to do it. And I'd need to fill the gash with something, sand the whole thing smooth, and paint it. That would take time. I'd want to be sure no one else was around so I didn't have to answer questions, and I'd want to be sure the paint had time to dry before Jake came back."

"I'm not sure about ultralights, but I think regular aircraft are required to keep maintenance records and notes. Everyone says Jake was so meticulous. He might have kept records whether they were required or not. I wonder if he'd had the propeller off for maintenance recently. If Jake didn't service props himself, we may be looking at another location."

"I'm not sure I follow." I pulled the blanket more closely around me.

"Well, if I'd sent a part off to an expert for refurbishing and maintenance, and my life depended on that part, I'd use someone I trusted. I'd check it afterwards, of course, but if it looked a little different from the way it normally did, I'd assume that the appearance had something to do with some buffing or polishing process the expert had performed."

"So, as long as the propeller looked relatively normal and felt smooth, Jake might not have questioned what could actually have been a severely damaged rotor?"

"It's worth checking, don't you think?" Max asked.

I didn't answer. I was distracted by lights flashing on the surface of the bay and what seemed to be an answering flash from a neighboring condo complex. I tried to describe them to Max, who went directly to the worst case scenario.

"A flash? Like a gun flash?"

"I don't think so. Is it fishing season? Do they fish with lights?" I could hear Max clicking the keys on his computer as he tried to find out.

He read aloud from the Monterey Bay Aquarium website: *"Why are those lighted boats on Monterey Bay at night in summer? Commercial squid fishers use bright electric lights to lure these cagey cephalopods to the surface. Large purse seiners quickly encircle the concentrated schools and haul them aboard.'"*

He paused. "Apparently, the squid rise to the lights."

"It sounds like cheating," I said.

"Maybe so, but listen to this: *'Stadium-bright lights that shine green in the night have replaced the baskets of fire used in the [nineteenth Century.'* Were the lights you saw greenish?"

"I'm not sure. If so, that would explain the lights out near the horizon, but it doesn't account for the flashes I saw closer to the beach."

"Bioluminescence?"

"What's that?" I heard Max's fingers clicking on his keyboard in search of an answer backed up by research and experts. I forestalled another recitation. "I don't need a treatise, hon. Just give me the gist."

"Tiny oceanic microorganisms that light up at night—anywhere there's movement on the water.'"

"Awesome. A natural light show. The boys and I will watch for it. But it doesn't fit with what I saw. The flashes I spotted were man-made, I'm sure, and were coming from the beach or maybe even from higher up, in the condos."

"A resident searching for something under their sofa with a flashlight? A security light? Can you call the gatehouse and ask?"

"They'll think I'm nuts."

"Who cares, there might also be something very wrong happening. Which end of the complex are we talking about? And more importantly, how far away from your building? Are you and the boys safe?"

"It was on the far north end, where the property adjoins the state beach."

"Can you phone the ranger?"

"Is anyone on duty there at night?" I shivered, then gathered up my blanket and went back inside in search of safety and warmth.

"I saw one of their trucks patrolling around midnight when I was there."

I agreed to check with both the park ranger and site security, and text Max with whatever I discovered. I left a message with the park, asking them to phone me the following day if no one was on duty right now. I called the gatehouse. Vik Peterson answered.

"Right, Maggie," he said after I explained my concerns. "Some of the condos have security lights. The sensors sometimes get misaligned and animals set them off. I'll check it out. We've got a water leak in Building C that I have to address, but right after that, I'll head down to the north end."

I spotted another quick flash on the beach as I ended the call, but wondered if it was a result of my too-active imagination. The lights on the water seemed closer. I closed and locked the sliding glass door to the balcony, then pulled on the handle to double check that it was really locked.

I was tempted to close the drapes and jump into bed, burying my head under the covers, but I knew I'd be unable to sleep. Belle padded out of the hallway leading to the boys' rooms and tucked her ice-cold nose into my hand.

"What is it, girl?" I asked.

She tilted her head, whined softly, and wagged her tail. Then she padded toward the door and sniffed.

"Seriously? You need to go out?" I pulled my oversized sweatshirt protectively around my body. The last place I wanted to be right now was outside in the dark. Chances were, nothing was wrong. I tried to convince myself that there was a perfectly reasonable explanation for the flashing lights on the beach and they posed no threat to my family or the surrounding community. I tried. And failed.

Chapter 19

Consider off-peak times for beach visits and other excursions. Monterey Bay Aquarium can be packed like a sardine can during the height of the tourist season, but empty an hour before closing.

From the Notebook of Maggie McDonald
Simplicity Itself Organizing Services

Friday, June 21, Late night

I wrote a quick note to the boys, grabbed a flashlight and Belle's leash, took a deep breath and opened the front door. Belle did the rest. For her, this was just an ordinary hygiene walk. She headed straight down the steps and I followed.

It was a chilly night, with a slight breeze and unexpectedly clear though the moon disappeared behind a few stray clouds as I waited for Belle to attend to her duty. A small animal screamed and an owl screeched, announcing its success in snagging its prey. I turned on the flashlight and moved it in an arc to illuminate the parking lot. The beam of light revealed nothing but left me feeling vulnerable. Anyone who was up to no good now knew that I was in the vicinity, and that I wasn't just hopping in my car or taking out the trash.

My phone chirped a text, startling me. I curved my hands and body quickly round the too-bright screen, then sank to my knees to make myself a smaller target. Why I did that was beyond my ability to figure. Instinct, unreasonable fear, or a sixth sense?

The text was from Vik. **Leak still gushing. I'll get to you. I promise.** Belle sat next to me and leaned in, as though she was trying to read Vik's text. She whined and then stood, moving her feet in the near dance step she used when she was very excited or unsettled. She tugged northward. My heart sank.

But I sucked up my courage and followed her, slowly, jumping at every scuttling leaf or small animal sound, and a myriad of other benign night noises.

My hesitancy was, in part, warranted. The parking lots and walkways were well-lit for safety and security, but dark spots abounded. With my flashlight off and my phone in my pocket, I couldn't see the ground underfoot or sidestep the inevitable uneven boards or buckled pavement.

Maintenance worked hard to eliminate such hazards, but the humid coastal climate, changeable temperatures, sandy soil, and the perennial shifting of California's tectonic plates meant that trying to erase all obstacles to unwary feet was a losing proposition.

My ears strained to hear any noises that would warn me of nefarious activities before I stumbled on them. *What's my objective here?* I asked myself, stopping in my tracks as I realized I wasn't quite sure.

Of all my foibles, flaws, and quirks, Max most often cursed what he called my *nose for trouble.* I could almost hear him urging me to turn back and leave the investigating to Vik, the ranger, or anyone else who was trained and paid to conduct security checks. Regardless, I pressed on. When I reached the central courtyard in the northernmost building, I followed the boardwalk that led toward the beach. I eased open the reinforced glass door that protected the interior expanse of the condo building from sand and wind. Belle pulled forward, checking over her shoulder frequently as if asking, "Are we really doing this? A walk on the beach at this time of night? This is so cool. Why don't we do this every night?"

I ignored her enthusiasm, and nearly missed a step when a motion-sensitive security light clicked on at the top of the dune stairs. "Well, that's probably it," I said to Belle. "Mystery solved. What was I thinking? Not enough sleep and too much imagination about smugglers and pirates. Let's head home."

I was about to turn around when Belle growled, and I saw movement among the shadows at the water's edge. Without thinking, I dropped to my knees so I'd be concealed behind the tall beach grass. I tried to mentally turn down the volume on my breathing and Belle's, and turn up the volume on noises from the beach, particularly any sounds that didn't belong.

The security light clicked off, and I crept forward, craning my neck to see around the bank of dune grass while I remained in shadow. I put one arm around Belle to quiet her and make her feel more secure. Our posture had the added benefits of reassuring and warming me. It was hard to hear much over the sound of the waves, but I detected boat-like noises and voices. I squinted into the darkness, rewarded by flashes of cell phone lights and reflections on the water from the moon, which was working valiantly to emerge from behind a cloud.

Three men fussed with a small boat like a glorified kayak with a miniature motor, pulling it up on the beach out of reach of the incoming tide. One man secured a line around what appeared to be a metal post, which solved the mystery surrounding the stake that had tripped up Brian and then vanished.

But why would anyone land a boat here in the dark? There were better harbors all up and down the central coast. Could squid fishing be lucrative enough for individuals to take it up as a hobby or small business using kayaks instead of massive commercial boats with seine fishing gear? I doubted it. And there was something distinctly furtive about the movements of the men on the beach.

Why did I think they were men? The way they moved? Their size or shape? One of them called to the others, and I realized their voices, which were carried incredibly well across the sand by the wind, were deeper than those of most women. The words were unintelligible, but the meaning was clear. They were trying their best to do whatever they were doing quickly and secretly, before the ranger's next security sweep of the beach in his truck.

I was about to sneak back to the condo and phone the ranger again. But just then, the full moon escaped the cloud. Its light reflected off white plastic packages the men pulled from the hull of the kayak and transferred to a large duffle bag on the sand.

I'm no expert on drugs or drug smuggling. Like most people, I know only what I've seen on television, and I'm smart enough to know that studios take many liberties with the truth in their quest for visually engaging programming. But the bread loaf-sized packages had the appearance and apparent weight of the parcels that television actors portraying drug agents pulled from tire wells and other secret hidey holes whenever they uncovered a drug-smuggling ring. I knew I'd seen them before. Recently. But where?

The moon illuminated the scene long enough for two of the men to disappear with duffle bags behind the dunes in the state park. The kayaker cast off and vanished in the distance.

Once they were out of earshot, I whispered to Belle. "What did we just see? We need to call the ranger. And the sheriff. And who else? The DEA? Nell?"

I shivered, chilled down to my bones, more by the potential danger of the situation than the temperature of the air. Belle and I flew over the bumps in the parking lot and up the stairs to our condo. Once inside, I leaned against the door, barring it against potential threats to my family. I struggled to organize my racing thoughts.

David emerged from the bathroom, squinting and rubbing his eyes. "What's up, Mom," he asked. "Everything okay?"

I paused before answering, but before David could formulate another question, my phone pinged with a text message. I glanced at the screen and sank into a nearby chair, willing the message to disappear or resolve into something more helpful and friendly. It didn't. I passed the phone to David. He peered at it and read:

"Go home or else. Your kids are going to jail."

He looked up. "Mom?"

I stared at my eldest son, mouth gaping, unsure what to say.

"Mom?"

Brian must have heard me come in, felt David stirring, or sensed a change in the atmosphere. He hopped out of his bedroom, using the walls for support instead of his crutches.

"What am I missing?" He mumbled, making his way to the counter stool that was becoming his favored perch. David passed him my phone. Brian's eyes grew wide as he read.

"How did they get your cell number?" Brian asked.

I shivered, thinking back to the number of cards I'd handed out and to the card I'd slipped under the tabletop at Beach Street. Heck, I kept a stash in my car and in the pockets of all my jackets. I could have dropped some in the grocery-store parking lot, at Starbucks, the airport, or any one of a number of other places. And any random stranger with sharp eyesight might have been able to read the number through the car window.

Robot-like, I pulled mugs from the cupboard and heated water for tea. I popped bread in the toaster. I was stalling for time.

"Mom?"

I retook my seat at the table and was soon joined by David. Belle sat glued to Brian's side, thumping her tail softly as if hoping she was reading the situation wrong and we'd soon assure her everything was okay.

"Should we go home?" I asked myself aloud, not expecting answers from the boys.

"No way," said Brian.

"You said we could invite our friends," David said. "We can't leave now."

"This text, if it's not some stupid prank, says there's something going on here that isn't right," I said. "Someone is trying to warn us off."

David broke the tension with well-timed sarcasm. "Do you think they're giving us just a little too much credit?"

Brian smiled, but he still looked worried. "We have to stay, Mom. It's what we do. We can't let the bad guys win."

If we'd been home, I'd have agreed with him in a heartbeat. Max and I had always tried to do the right thing and to instill the same ethic in our sons. But that was easier said than done, and much easier to accomplish in the company of the trusted friends, neighbors, resources, and law enforcement experts we knew at home.

Here, I was fairly sure that Vik Peterson, Renée, and the sheriff were honest and conscientious, but I was basing that on first impressions, gut instincts, and the hope that we hadn't already aligned ourselves with a den of thieves and cutthroats who would threaten children. How much did we really know about them?

"Mom?"

The water for tea boiled and the toast popped up. I buttered the slabs, plopped tea bags in the pot, and poured water over them, still sifting our options. I spoke slowly, formulating a plan on the fly.

"We need to call your father," I said. "That's the first thing. But that can wait until morning.

"I'm texting him now," said David. "If he's awake, he'll call us."

"Good idea. I think we also need to call the local authorities, along with Stephen. I'd like to ask what kinds of contacts he has in Santa Cruz County to help us out." I glanced at the boys in an attempt to measure their level of anxiety. Both looked calmer than I'd expected. Had events in the past few years made them immune to threats?

All of our problems were bigger than I could solve tonight. In the end, we finished our tea and toast, left messages for Stephen and Max that would remain unanswered until the morning, and made a brief list of approaches to our problem that would be better left until after we'd had more sleep and a hearty breakfast.

I feared we'd all lie awake fretting, but I was wrong. I slept so soundly I didn't stir when the boys and Belle came to join me on the king-sized bed—something they hadn't done since they were small. I felt I'd only just fallen asleep when my phone vibrated with a text from Renée.

"Kids sick. All vomiting. Spending today holding babies and doing wash. Take the day off."

I wondered if the children's illness had made Renée lose sight of the fact that today was Saturday, or if she expected me to work seven days a week. I decided it didn't matter at the moment, and we could clarify our work expectations later.

Do you need anything? I typed. **Bananas? Rice, Applesauce? Toast?**

We're all set. Thanks. See you tomorrow. Or maybe the next day.

What can I work on here? I texted. My stomach felt a little queasy when I read her response.

That condo you were assigned when you first got here needs clearing out. You can tackle that...

Suddenly, I recalled where I'd seen bread loaf-sized bags encased in plastic. And everything I thought I knew about what was happening within and around the condominium complex changed.

Chapter 20

Allowing older children to participate in planning activities may result in less grumbling. Results may vary.

From the Notebook of Maggie McDonald
Simplicity Itself Organizing Services

Saturday, June 22, Morning

I hesitated to respond to Renée's text suggesting that I clear out the revolting first-floor condo. My fingers hovered over a series of alarmed and disgusted emojis. But then I remembered the white, plastic-wrapped, packages I'd seen in that apartment—the ones I'd assumed were part of an abandoned craft project. I decided to at least poke my head in and verify that my recollection was accurate. If the rest of the dwelling was as dreadful as I remembered, I'd recommend a professional cleaning done by a crime-scene clean-up operation certified to properly handle and eliminate biohazards.

Did Renée know about the drugs? Was she or someone else at Heron Beach part of the smuggling operation? What had happened to the condo's owner? Had he or she run afoul of a drug deal gone wrong?

Renée didn't wait for a reply. **...or not.**

I settled on typing, **I'll let you know after I've had a chance to wake up and think about it. We had a rough night here ourselves.**

Not sick I hope?

Everyone healthy. I'll check in later.

I put down the phone with every intention of going back to sleep. But I couldn't. As gently as possible, to avoid disturbing Belle and the boys, I crawled out from under the covers and waited as Belle lifted her head, sighed, and oozed off the bed to follow me in slow motion, making it clear she was beginning to disapprove of my sleeping habits or lack thereof.

I made a quick cup of coffee with the unit's early model pod machine, which groaned through the whole process, leaving me with a mere six ounces of weak, lukewarm coffee. I gulped it, pulled on my warmest coat, shoved my phone into the pocket and my feet into my flip-flops, and grabbed Belle's leash.

This early in the morning, I didn't hook the leash to her collar. There would be no one stirring for her to bother. She knew to stay close and her obedience to my emergency recall command was reliable. Belle caught up on her pee-mail. I phoned Max. While I waited for the call to connect I tried to appreciate the rainbow sherbet-colored sky that accompanied the sunrise. The whole area was an excruciatingly beautiful yet fragile environment with an vast array of wildlife. Many of the species that thrived here existed nowhere else. In many ways, it seemed a holy place to me, and it broke my heart to think that there were bad guys who insisted on disrupting its serenity.

I tore my gaze away from the sky and focused on my phone. My call hadn't gone through. I punched speed dial again and reached Max's voicemail.

"Max, what are the chances you can come back to the beach today and work remotely from the condo here next week? I think we need you with us. Call me when you wake up, and I'll fill you in. We may need Stephen's team, too."

I'd meant to call Stephen earlier in the week, but had I? In the confusion following the death of Jake Peterson, I must have forgotten. I checked my call history. Nothing. Which made sense. If I'd left a message for Stephen, he would have returned my call. He was that kind of guy. I glanced at the time. It was still early, but not for Stephen, whose chronic insomnia meant he was typically awake outrageously early. I hit speed dial and waited while it rang and went directly to his voicemail; "My phone's off while I meditate. Leave a message. I'll call back."

I smiled at the image of Stephen, who resembled the iconic Mr. Clean with a beard, accompanied by his ever-present mastiff Munchkin, meditating. It wasn't that I begrudged them the serenity. Both of them had long struggled with PTSD and had found solace in helping others. But I thought of them both as perpetual-motion machines. Max called Stephen the "ninja marine" or the "caped crusader" thanks to his uncanny ability to be on the scene whenever he was needed. In fact, I wouldn't have been surprised to discover that, seconds after I'd decided I needed his help, he was already on his way.

"Hey Stephen," I told his voicemail. "I'm hoping I can convince you and maybe your pal Rocket to spend a few days at the beach. I'll spring for a condo with a great view. Munchkin will be welcome as a service dog, but you may need to bring his paperwork."

Frustrated by my inability to reach either Max or Stephen, I stuffed my phone back in my pocket, pulled up my hood against the early morning chill, and called to Belle. "Time to head in."

Belle bounded toward me from behind a hillock of beach grass on the edge of the parking lot. Her ears extended from her head like airplane wings. Her golden retriever grin lifted my spirits—until she screeched to a stop next to a rustic shingle-covered garbage and recycling shed, barking a wary but still cheerful hello.

"Belle, now."

She yelped and pelted toward me with her ears drooping and her tail between her legs while a black and white cat-sized creature ambled into view from behind the rubbish shed. As soon as my brain formed the word *cat*, I knew I'd been wrong. The unmistakable stench of angry skunk made my eyes water and my nose run. Belle had gotten the full force of the spray right between her eyes. She whined, rubbed her face on the grass, and then against my leg.

At home, we had all the supplies necessary to deal with a skunk emergency. Here? I was at a loss. I couldn't put her in my car and drive to town for supplies—I'd never get the smell out of the upholstery.

"Oh, Belle," I said, turning my face away. Her eyes were nearly swollen shut. She whined in pain and embarrassment. I clicked her leash to her collar, and she stayed glued to my heels for guidance. I briefly considered hiking to the state park's outdoor showers, but water alone couldn't cope with a skunk's oily spray, and the park was too far to shuffle in my flip-flops. I hustled her back to the condo and quickly through the front room to the shower enclosure in the boy's bathroom. I turned the exhaust fan on high and called the gatehouse.

"Vik?"

"Nope, Lenny. The night guard. Your dog just get skunked?"

"You saw?"

"Hang tight. I'll bring you our anti-skunk kit."

"Anti-skunk kit?"

"Thanks to a homeowner who wanted us to be ready for any emergency. He had two huge puppies who never learned. Told me they had a black and white kitten at home that the dogs adored. Skunks around here kept trying to teach those pups, but the goofy mutts couldn't tell the difference 'tween cats and skunks—until it was too late."

Lenny delivered promptly. I followed the instructions on the three-by-five card in the package, mixing peroxide, baking soda, and dish soap as directed. By the time the boys woke up, I had turned on all the unit's fans, opened the sliding glass doors and windows to the brisk sea breeze, and sprayed an odor neutralizing product inside and directly outside the condo. Using the shower and a bucket, I'd washed Belle thoroughly—twice with the homemade peroxide mixture and once with a commercial anti-skunk shampoo that was also in the kit. I'd wiped down the shower walls with a solution of vinegar and water and then soaped up my own hair and skin.

My clothes spun in the washer and Belle slept at my feet on the kitchen tile. I sucked in the smell of fresh coffee and cinnamon from a coffee cake I'd popped in the oven in an attempt to replace the noxious skunk odor with a more pleasant aroma. I thought I'd completely obliterated the skunk's perfume until the boys emerged from my bedroom, pulling the edges of their T-shirts over their noses.

"Belle!" they cried, waking the exhausted dog who roused and bounded toward them as they backed away.

"She's clean," I said. "As clean as three baths could get her."

"But she still stinks," Brian said, gagging. He gave me a morning hug and then pushed me away. "Or maybe it's you."

"We both smell much better than we did a half hour ago. Guess what? You can bathe Belle as often as you like. And I'm sure she'd love to accompany you into the ocean."

David was brave enough to sniff her fur. "Not bad. Mr. Skunk didn't score a direct hit?"

"Mr. Skunk is a sharpshooter. He got her right between the eyes. But this is a full-service resort. The gatehouse provided a skunk kit that worked like a charm. I'll need to restock it and get one for home. Maybe give it as gifts to our dog friends."

Brian hopped to the table without his crutches. "Maybe this family shouldn't take vacations anymore. We can't catch a break. Can we go?"

"Home? Cut and run? Our mom? Never," said David. "What's the plan?" He tapped his brother's side with the back of his hand. "You've got to know she's got a plan."

I took a sip of my now cold coffee and filled the boys in on my plans to summon our team of protectors and crime fighters. Stephen called, saying he'd be on his way as soon as the morning traffic died down. He'd use the next hour to check in with law enforcement contacts in Santa Cruz County, where he said the sheriff had trained under the same mentor as Jason Mueller, our friend and Stephen's husband. "I'll let Jason know what's going on with you all and see if he has any other ideas," Stephen promised. "I'm glad you called. Now hang up the phone so I can get to work."

Stephen's tone was friendly and cheerful, but his military background revealed itself despite his efforts to keep things light. He was issuing a direct order for me to skip any gracious chit-chat so he could get on with the job at hand.

I was able to let Max know about Stephen's impending visit when he called, frantic. "The line was busy and I've spent the last few minutes imagining dire scenarios."

"Sometimes imagination is a terrible thing," I said. It was one of our most frequently employed family proverbs.

"When my children recently witnessed a fatal air crash, my youngest has injured his leg, and my fiercely independent wife says she needs back up, I think it's reasonable to go straight to the assumption that global nuclear war is on the horizon," Max said.

"Eminently reasonable."

"Enough chit-chat. Put me out of my misery and tell me what's *really* going on."

I signaled to the kids that they should listen in as I recounted my pre-dawn spying expedition with Belle. I wrapped up with "...and then Belle got skunked."

"We really can't catch a break, can we?"

"Brian says we should give up on the idea of family vacations."

"We'll have to change that mindset," Max said. "Maybe the problem is this bogus idea of a *working vacation*. Everyone knows those are way more work than they are vacation."

"This one's torture," I said. "But Renée's in a tight spot, and we're all falling in love with the location despite everything else. Yesterday I spotted six species of migratory ducks on my way to the car."

"Yet you missed the skunk."

"I'm now acutely aware of the skunk," I said. "And Belle won't go anywhere near a garbage bin for a good long time. But, more importantly, I've got my eyes peeled for danger and I've called out the cavalry. Nell's here to help with the legal end of things, Stephen, Munchkin, and a member of their military security team are on their way, and Jason's promised to run interference with the local cops." My voice softened as I touched on the most comforting part of my plan. "And you're coming, right?"

"Can you all sit tight until I get there?" Max said. "You're safe in the condo, right?"

"As far as I know, but I want to get groceries so we can feed everyone, and I need to restock this skunk kit before we need it again or before some other hapless vacationer takes a hit." I glanced at my watch. "I have time to head into town and back and still get lunch ready for when you arrive."

"Let me do that. Sit tight. Please?"

"I'll do my best," I promised. "I'll text you the list for the skunk kit. Keeping your two active boys and Belle under wraps will be the trickiest part."

"Anywhere you go, you all should go together," he said.

I promised I would heed his advice and we ended the call.

David wanted to body surf, which I okayed despite Max's warnings because it would give Belle another cleansing bath. David donned his wetsuit. Brian emerged from his room wearing a long-sleeved rash guard and had rigged up a complicated system of layered trash bags and duct tape to protect his injury. I examined it skeptically. "Aren't you supposed to keep weight off your foot for at least another few weeks?"

"I can hop to the water. I'm buoyant. I won't need to put weight on the foot in the water. Water's the perfect place for me."

"You're not seriously letting him do this?" David asked.

I shook my head. "Sorry bud. Not yet." Brian deflated as only a teenager can, as though he was returning to a liquid state. I relented. Sort of. "Tell you what. You've got all that stuff on. Would you consider trying it out in the shower first? Just to make sure it's watertight? Then you'll know if you need to tweak your design and you'll be all sent to go in when the doctor says you can. We'll start with a calm day when you're not likely to get knocked off balance by a rogue wave."

Brian begrudgingly accepted the wisdom of my words, and emerged from the shower a quarter-hour later with his hair dripping. "Foot's bone dry," he said. "It's a win."

I congratulated him and suggested he try out his crutches on the sand. Belle and David went with him. "Avoid any trash cans," I urged. "Those little stinkers can spray fifteen feet."

"On the beach?" David said. "What kind of self-respecting skunk spends time at the beach?"

"According to the all-knowing skunk kit, the local ones do," I said. "Their favorite foods are bird eggs and picnic remains. Unfortunately for us and the birds, the beach provides a fertile hunting ground for both. Just keep a sharp eye out. Keep track of time, too. I need you back up here in an hour. Dad and Stephen are coming. I'll hang a beach towel over the balcony railing when it's time to come in. Keep our unit in view while you're out there."

I let them go with only a few qualms. My plans didn't adhere to the letter of the law as dictated by Max, but the condo I wanted to investigate was the closest one to the beach and not far from where David would be body surfing. I could keep an eye on them easily.

I phoned Nell, asking her to join me for breakfast. I then amended my invitation to coffee and cake knowing that she appreciated specificity, was an early riser herself, and had surely finished breakfast hours earlier. She arrived as I was finishing my call to the rental agency to reserve a two-bedroom condo for Stephen, Munchkin, and whatever reinforcements they brought with them.

"I'm afraid we require very specific paperwork to admit a service dog," said the officious clerk with a sniff. "Apparently we currently have a contract employee on site with a dog. I don't know who allowed that, but we're protesting it. We don't want to set a precedent. It will cause all sorts of trouble."

I refrained from telling her I was the guilty party and asked her to text me details specifying the paperwork she'd need before she'd hand over the keys to Stephen and Munchkin. I had to send a text reminding her, but then I forwarded it to Stephen.

"If you have any trouble with that, let me know," said Nell, who'd arrived while I was on the phone. She cut herself a generous slice of the fragrant orange cinnamon coffee cake. "There's no question in the law. Munchkin is a service dog, permitted wherever Stephen is allowed."

"Can you still smell skunk in here?" I asked.

Nell sniffed. "That was you? The stench woke me up."

"It was more Belle than me, but yeah, we're responsible," I said. "Can you still smell it?" I reached for the spray can of odor neutralizer.

"I can," said Nell. "But it's faint. I wouldn't have known that this was the guilty condo. She sniffed again. "Nothing like the smell of the beach, even when it's tinged with skunk." She smiled reassuringly. "I'm sure your rental deposit will cover an extra cleaning if the agency complains."

"The condo comes with the job, so I'm not too concerned," I said. "I was more worried about Stephen and Munchkin turning tail and running, and maybe Max asking for a temporary separation." I was kidding on both counts, which I didn't need to explain to Nell, who'd met all the parties I'd mentioned on previous adventures. I wondered if I should tell Nell about my unappealing excursion to the noisome condo, but she must have read my thoughts.

"I know that look," she said. "What plans are you cooking up?"

I explained and Nell was game.

I prepared to subject my senses to what my nose would assume was a violent assault. The second one this morning.

Chapter 21

When traveling with small children, your carry-on luggage should include an emergency change of clothing for every member of the family.

From the Notebook of Maggie McDonald
Simplicity Itself Organizing Services

Saturday, June 22, Morning

I eased the door to the small condo open, expecting a swarm of flies. My eyes watered and I swallowed hard to tamp down my gag reflex. The overwhelming smell of death, damp, and decay had grown stronger since my last brief visit.

I glanced at Nell, who had buried her nose in her elbow and was squinting as if narrowing her field of vision would diminish the odor. "You're not going to try to clean this yourself," she said.

I shook my head. I'd worn a pair of rubber boots I'd found in the depths of the master bedroom closet in our condo. I'd have to scrub them or replace them after this. I toed a pile of something green and fuzzy out of the path between the front door and what appeared to be the former resident's work area.

"Don't touch anything," Nell said. I assumed she was concerned about preserving fingerprints and evidence, but she clarified her statement quickly. "Breathing this air has to be unhealthy. This apartment needs a biohazard team and will have to be gutted. There's no way they're going to get this smell out of the sheetrock. Ever. People complain about lingering cigarette smoke when they buy or rent a home from a heavy smoker, and that's nothing compared to this." She gagged and coughed.

"I only need a moment here," I said. "Wait outside if you want."

But Nell gamely and loyally stood by me. She pointed toward a stack of plastic wrapped packages packed neatly into cardboard boxes next to the fireplace. It was the only tidy corner of the room. "Is that what you were looking for? Do you think it's drugs?"

"I'm not sure. But that's why we're here. I want to get those packages tested so we can be certain." A pile of canvas hung precariously half-on and half-off the end of a threadbare sofa. Now faded and covered in mildew, the cloth had once been the high-visibility hue referred to as safety- or blaze-orange in state and federal safety statutes, but which my kids had dubbed *please-don't-lose-me* red.

I grabbed a plastic bag and a swatch of the cloth, then dashed back outside, followed quickly by Nell. I let the door swing shut and heard it lock behind me. In unspoken agreement, Nell and I headed straight to a bench built into the landing on the staircase over the dunes. We sucked in great quantities of fresh sea air before we were prepared to speak. I coughed like a life-long smoker to expel the noxious air from my lungs.

"What *was* that?" asked Nell. "Were they butchering animals? What would cause a stink like that? I searched for a dead body. Why haven't the neighbors complained?"

Nell's questions were the same as mine had been. I could only speculate. In the meantime, I dialed Renée and had started to leave a message when my phone rang. I accepted the call from a breathless Renée, with the sounds of happy kids in the background. "Sorry, Maggie, we were outside. These babies bounced back fast. You'd never know they'd been up vomiting all night. What's up?"

I took a deep breath. "I hope you budgeted for a hazardous material cleaning service for this apartment," I said. "It's way beyond anything that I'm willing to handle. Your staff shouldn't try either. It's a definite biohazard, and you'll need a qualified expert to tackle it as soon as possible. I can't believe the neighbors haven't complained. Nell and I lasted only a few moments without rebreathers."

"It's really that bad?"

"Nell assumed it was a crime scene. So did I when I first saw it."

"No way," Renée said. "Mrs. Nesbitt? She'd never—" I heard strange sounds from the other end of the phone. "No, Aiden. It's not a teething toy. Here."

Renée began again. "Mrs. Nesbitt fell and broke her hip. After a stint in the hospital, her daughter Barbara helped her move into rehab. The plan is for her to go to an assisted living facility in Soquel. Cute place. Great staff. Barbara told me she was waiting for her brother to help her move Mrs. Nesbitt's furniture, and then they were going to put the unit on the market."

"At this point, they'll need to gut it. It's a mess."

"Seriously?" Renée paused. "I guess time got away from us. But come to think of it, Mrs. Nesbitt's fall was back before Christmas. Yikes! It's been nearly six months. I've been so busy with the new job. I should have sent a cleaning crew in there long ago to empty out the fridge and garbage."

"I think the power is off, so any food is long since rotted. Mrs. Nesbitt must have been preparing a meal when she fell because there were moldy green items on the floor and the counter."

"Gross!" Renée said. Now that she was finally beginning to grasp what I'd been trying to report about the condition of the apartment, I shifted gears. "Could the former resident have been involved in drug smuggling?"

"*Mrs. Nesbitt?* Never."

"There are cartons of plastic-wrapped white packages stacked in the living room."

I'd expected shock or disbelief, but Renée snorted once, twice, and followed up with gales of laughter. Her delight was confounding but also contagious, and I smiled without wanting to. "What's so funny?"

"Mrs. Nesbitt had a cottage industry in her unit, but it wasn't drugs." Renée snorted again. "Sorry, I can't help it. Mrs. Nesbitt and drugs. That's priceless. She was recycling. An eco-warrior."

"Those bags don't look like any eco project I've ever seen."

"Kapok."

"Kapok?"

"You know, the stuffing from those old bright orange life jackets we all wore when we were little. They don't use it much anymore, but it's a natural, sustainable product, and there's a guy in Southern California who is mixing it with rayon remnants from the fashion industry to make those floating berms for oil spills. Recycling material to clean up the ocean. Genius."

I thought of the pile of orange canvas and fingered the swatch in my pocket. "There's a market for that?" I asked.

"Not much, but Mrs. Nesbitt felt like she was doing some good."

"Where'd she get the old lifejackets?"

"I'm not sure. Someone sent her a box or two a month, and everyone who lives here year-round and walks the beach knew about her project.

If we found one washed up on the sand, we'd wash it off and drop it in front of her door."

I smiled at the quaint and hopeful neighborliness of the story Renée was spinning, but I wondered how much of it was true. Was kapok really used for oil spills? Was there truly a market for mildewed material that had been soaking up seawater for months or years? Or was Renée covering up a drug trade that thrived in this quiet community out of the reach of the sheriff's routine patrols? I needed more details.

"So she removed the orange covers and all the straps and buckles and saved the kapok pouches," I said. "How did she get the plastic packets to her buyer? I didn't see any mailing materials other than the cardboard cartons. It sounds as though she was essentially housebound before her fall."

"I'm not sure of the details, but some young kid from town, maybe her grandson, did her grocery shopping every week or so. He brought cartons of lifejackets, too, and took away the kapok pouches. I think he drove a silver pick-up. Or maybe it was covered with primer paint. I never paid much attention. Vik might know, since he had to let the kid in through the gate."

I wondered if Grandson Nesbitt was the youth I'd seen in the parking lot, but I waited to ask until we'd tested the contents of the packages. If Renée was naïve enough to believe her far-fetched story, I didn't want to shatter her innocence, nor her adoration of the great icon of green living, Mrs. Nesbitt.

"Wow, that sounds like a nifty set-up," I said, cringing when I heard the false note in my voice. I doubted I was fooling anyone. Nell rolled her eyes. "But as homey as that sounds, her apartment is no longer cozy and safe. It's a biohazard that needs immediate cleaning before it attracts rodents and other pests I don't want to even think about." Nell crinkled her nose, but I heard nothing from the other end of the phone.

"Renée? Are you there? This is serious. It's becoming a public health issue. A liability problem for the association. If you deal with it now, I can avoid calling the health department."

"You'd rat me out? You're supposed to be working for me." Renée sounded angry, hurt, and scared. But it couldn't be helped. My professional ethics and my insurance policy dictated that I promptly report dangers to public health and safety.

"Let's take care of the problem so I won't need to bother the authorities," I said, glancing at my watch. It was nearly time for Stephen and Max to arrive, and I'd promised I'd be dogging the footsteps of my offspring. "Renée? I've got to go. Do you want to call a hazmat team or do you want me to? I don't have any contacts in the area, but I can look into it. Police departments usually have lists of services that are licensed for this type of activity. I can call Sheriff Nate."

"No, no. I'm about to feed the kids their lunch. After that, they'll nap. I'll have time to call. I'd like to see if I can negotiate an exclusive contract that would snag us a lower cost introductory service."

"Good idea," I said, still wondering whether Renée was as squeaky clean and honest as Tess had told me she was.

I ended the call and waved the kids in from the beach, where they seemed to have given up body surfing in favor of digging giant pits in the sand. Belle helped.

Nell and I dashed upstairs and set the kitchen to rights while we waited for Max and Stephen. On a whim, I texted Renée with an invitation to dinner, kids and all. I wanted to see what Stephen made of Mrs. Nesbitt's story. Thanks to his law enforcement experience with the military, and his close association with the Orchard View Police Department and its chief, Stephen Laird had a finely tuned ability to separate fact from fiction.

The kids came up from the beach, interrupting my melodramatic train of thought. "How'd the leg encasement work?" I asked Brian, meeting him with a chair he could sit on outside to remove the sandy wrappings. David, shivering, made a bee-line for the shower.

The sound of ripping duct tape nearly obliterated Brian's words as he called out. "Dry as a bone," he said. "No sand. No water. And I bet I can get out of this faster than David can get out of his wetsuit."

I congratulated him and added garbage bags and duct tape to my grocery list. Brian hopped inside, stashed a ball of plastic and tape in the garbage, and collapsed on the sofa. I pulled the bag of white material from my pocket and plopped it on the counter, but then immediately lifted it off, fearing whatever contaminants might have adhered to its service.

Nell ripped a length of paper towels from the roll on the counter and used them to pick up the plastic-wrapped package. "I'll take it back to my condo," she said. "We need to get it tested."

"Does Forrest have a lab he uses? One whose results will stand up in court? I don't know who we can trust down here. If a little old lady is part of a long-standing drug ring, who else is involved? Renée seems to have at least been aware of the comings and goings of Mrs. Nesbitt's operation, and the sheriff and ranger could be in on it too."

"I'll get a messenger from the lab Forrest uses down here tonight," Nell said, opening the front door and preparing to leave. "There's no secure chain of evidence here, but if we find something, no doubt the other packets in the condo could be tested."

Before she closed the door, she poked her head back inside. "I think after handling this I should take a shower before I come back down here for lunch if that's okay? Do I have time?"

I nodded. But just as the door closed behind Nell, she opened it again. "If you suspect Renée, why did you invite her for dinner?"

"Keep your friends close, but your enemies closer," I said, realizing I wasn't sure Renée belonged to either group. She was my client. "Whoa. That sounded way more dramatic than I intended. The truth is, I don't really suspect Renée. My friend Tess put me in touch with her, and I trust Tess's judgment but..."

"But?"

"I still want those packages tested for drugs. I want to get to the bottom of this, for my own peace of mind and the safety of my family."

Chapter 22

Assigned seats in the car may forestall arguments over who sits where. Hanging a storage organizer with each child's toys, activities, and snacks nearby may help establish ownership over each kids' territory.

From the Notebook of Maggie McDonald
Simplicity Itself Organizing Services

Saturday, June 22, Lunchtime

Max and Stephen arrived with Stephen's elusive friend Rocket, whom I spotted in my peripheral vision as he moved silently, like a shadow, past our apartment to the one next door that I'd rented for our security team. Stephen didn't bother to explain. I suspected Rocket would do a quick reconnaissance tour of the area and then grab some rest to prepare for a sleepless night spent assuring our safety.

"Any trouble getting Munchkin through the gate or the rental agency?" I asked, rubbing the soft ears of the giant mastiff.

Stephen smiled. "Rocket glared at the desk clerk, who hastened to tell us that you'd explained Munchkin was a service dog and retired marine. She thanked him for his service, handed him a biscuit, and then discreetly removed dog slobber from her hands with a tissue." Munchkin was a quiet, dignified gentleman, but he left a trail of slobber wherever he'd been. Snails would be envious. It was his superpower.

"Any more threatening texts?" asked Stephen.

I handed over my phone, saying, "Not yet, anyway. Maybe he had a wrong number?"

Stephen clicked and scrolled. "I'm looking to see if there's any clue to his identity, but I'm going to have to get someone more techie to take a look."

"Want to help us dig more sand pits on the beach after lunch?" Brian asked, knocking back a pain pill that was well earned, seeing as how he'd just completed his most active morning since his injury. "We were going to dig pits for fires for marshmallows, but we got a little carried away. We're thinking they'll be great for spying on pirates or smugglers."

"Seriously or pretend?" asked Stephen.

Brian and David looked at each other, then back at Stephen and shrugged.

Stephen glanced at Max and I before replying. "Rocket's getting the lay of the land right now. We'll confer. If we think you'll be safe, then it's up to your mom and dad whether they want to let you watch for bad guys tonight from the safety of your bunkers."

The boys could have sustained whiplash from the speed with which they swiveled their heads. "*Puh-leese*," Brian said.

"We'll see," I said, even knowing they were among the most annoying words parents could use in response to their offspring's requests. "But there's no reason you can't make those pits bigger and deeper while we decide." They disappeared to refashion the duct-tape and garbage bag protection for Brian's leg before heading out again to the beach. With any luck, and with all the fresh air and exercise they were getting, they'd be safely asleep before any smugglers arrived on the beach.

Max picked up his backpack from the floor near the door and brought it to the table. He pulled out a paper bag and placed it in front of him with a metallic *clunk*.

"The chunk of metal David found?" I asked. "Did Howard finish his report?"

Max nodded. "He thinks it's part of a propeller. Says the size is right for a small ultralight with limited range. The sheriff will pick it up this afternoon."

"Can we trust the sheriff?" I asked.

Max raised his eyebrows and Stephen leaned forward. "Can't we?" Max asked.

Nell and I filled them in on everything we'd seen and learned since I'd last spoken with Max. I told them of our growing sense of wariness. Sitting around our table in the company of friends, our anxieties seemed silly. But Max and Stephen appeared to accept them at face value.

"Howard took a ton of pictures and measurements using a scanning electron microscope," Max said. "We've got a copy of the report for the sheriff, but we also sent a copy to Jason. This piece"—he pointed to the evidence bag—"really needs to go to the NTSB, but Jason suggested that, for political and chain-of-command reasons, we let the sheriff pass it along to them." He glanced at Stephen for confirmation.

"Too bad we can't make a copy of a chunk of metal, just to be safe," Stephen said, rubbing his beard. "But Jason believes that the report, along with testimony from David about where he found the part and from Howard about his findings, will hold up in court."

"So you already considered what might happen if the propeller piece vanished in the sheriff's custody," I said. "Does he have a reputation for shady dealings?"

"Not at all," Stephen said. "But you know Jason. He likes to consider every eventuality."

I nodded. "Did Howard have any idea what happened? Does his report confirm our suspicion that someone tried to sabotage Jake's ultralight?"

"Yes and no," Max said. "He said the piece of metal was tampered with in a way that might have allowed a little plane to operate properly for a short period. But with continuous pressure on the propeller blades, the tip could have bent or broken off. Any propeller that's not balanced will cause problems for the pilot and the plane."

"Enough to cause a crash?" I asked. "Enough to charge someone with murder?"

"That's where Howard's report gets a little fuzzy," Max said.

"Could he explain how David found the chunk of metal so close to the crash site?" I wasn't completely clear on the physics of the situation, but I couldn't figure out how a piece of the propeller could have broken off and caused a problem in flight, but still have been found so close to Jake and his downed craft.

"Howard wrote that the sample appeared to have been tampered with by someone who expected it would fail mid-flight. He didn't think the damaged propeller could have held up for more than a few minutes. But, he said he couldn't say how long it took for the blade tip to completely separate from the rest of the propeller. Based on his findings, Howard said it was possible that the tip had been badly bent and the jarring of an emergency landing or a crash could have caused it to separate completely."

I sighed. "That's a relief." Then I replayed my words and felt a need to clarify my thinking. "I mean, it was obviously dreadful for Jake, Jen, and the Petersons. But I'm glad to know there's a way to explain how David could have found the part among the wreckage instead of somewhere along the ultralight's flightpath."

The clomp of footsteps on the stairs followed by a knock at the door saved me from further explanation.

Max answered the door. It was Sheriff Nate Sanchez, who'd apparently arrived to take possession of the evidence. Max introduced himself and invited Nate to join us at the table. I grabbed a clean mug and poured him a cup of coffee. Nell passed him cream and sugar, but he took it black.

"Thanks," he said, taking a sip. "It's been a long day."

Stephen offered Nate a cookie from the few remaining on a plate that had been piled with treats less than a half-hour earlier. Stress and over-indulgence in carbohydrates always go together, in my experience. If the cookie plate was any indication, we were all way more anxious than was good for us.

Max handed Nate the paper bag and started to explain its contents. Nate waved his hand in the air. "I've read the report. I'll make sure this and the paperwork get to the NTSB, but I doubt it will change their findings. I've heard they're expected to rule the crash an accident."

I wasn't sure who the sheriff could have heard from. From Max and David's report on their conversation with the mechanics at the Watsonville airport, NTSB reports were closely held secrets until the findings were released, months or even years after a crash occurred. Most events were deemed accidental, but it was the *cause* of the accidents that the federal agency hoped to uncover. Their ultimate goal was to propose evidence-based safety measures to prevent future lethal failures of our transportation systems. Was the sheriff trying to allay our fears or throw cold water on our interest in the case? Either possibility could prove to be true. And both would be within his job description. I was so used to our friends in the Orchard View Police Department sharing details of their cases with us, that I wondered if I'd imagined Sheriff Nate was hiding something when, in reality, he was just doing his job. I sighed and topped off my coffee mug, then lifted the pot to the others. Nell pushed her cup toward me. I filled it.

Sheriff Nate tilted his mug back, took a swig of his coffee, and set it firmly on the table as if punctuating the conversation, full stop. He stood, thanked me graciously, and then handed Max what looked suspiciously like the paperwork delivered by process servers on television. Max raised his eyebrows, and the sheriff confirmed my suspicions. "A subpoena," he said. "We'll expect David, Brian, and Maggie at the district attorney's office on Ocean Street in Santa Cruz for depositions Monday morning," he said in a voice that was far more formal than he'd sounded since he'd arrived and introduced himself to Max.

Max stiffened, but before he could protest with the fury of a protective father and husband, I jumped in. "Seriously? A subpoena? All you had to do was ask. We're happy to help."

Sheriff Nate bristled. "We're just being thorough."

"We'll be there," I said. "With our lawyer." I nodded to Nell, who stood. In a T-shirt, jeans, flip-flops, and a messy ponytail, she looked neither as scary or accomplished as I knew her to be. But I wasn't worried. My previous work with Nell and Forrest had taught me well. In legal skirmishes, it never hurts to be underestimated by your opponent.

Sheriff Nate's nostrils flared, but he spoke slowly and calmly. "That's not necessary," he said, echoing the words I'd used moments before.

I responded in kind. "We'd like to be thorough."

The sheriff showed himself out and closed the door softly, indicating he had a greater command over his emotions than I'd thought. If he had allowed any of his feelings to leak out, I felt sure he would have slammed the door and stomped down the stairs.

In Nate's absence, I could hear the *tick* of the battery-operated wall clock and the *hiss* of water dripping on the defrost heaters in the refrigerator. Belle sighed. I was afraid to speak, terrified of what the subpoena meant and of what might happen on Monday. I wasn't alone in my fears.

Stephen voiced my unspoken anxieties. "That means we have until Monday morning to figure out what's going on here, who's behind it, and how it's all related."

Max took an audible breath. "That doesn't leave us much time."

"We can only do what we can do," said Nell, gathering up her things and stashing a cookie in her pocket. "I'll call Forrest and work out a plan for Monday and a backup plan, just in case." Shoulders back, chest out, chin high, she looked each of us in the eye and strode out of the apartment, not-quite-slamming the door. She was confident of her ability, as always, but angry, too. We were in good hands, but that didn't stop me from reaching for the last cookie on the plate.

"Shouldn't she be interviewing you and the boys?" Max said after the door closed behind Nell. "Taking down the details on a legal-sized yellow pad?"

Stephen let out a breath and placed his hands flat on the table. "Nell and Forrest will do what they do best. The rest is up to us. How 'bout you show me this crash site, the place on the beach where you saw the smugglers come in, and the farms you told me about."

The walk would do us all good, burning off nervous energy, and familiarizing Stephen with the lay of the land. But I wondered if it would be enough, what the rest of the weekend would entail, and what would happen on Monday if we weren't able to uncover some earth-shaking new evidence within the next forty-eight hours.

Chapter 23

Pack a garbage or laundry bag to collect the whole family's dirty laundry in one spot. This tactic is helpful if you need to wash clothes during your trip, and makes it a snap for any family member to quickly start the laundry chore once you're home again.

From the Notebook of Maggie McDonald
Simplicity Itself Organizing Services

Saturday, June 22, Afternoon

We'd returned from our hike, washed the sand from our feet, and had started dinner preparations, when my phone rang. I didn't recognize the number.

"Hello?" I spoke tentatively, fearing the call might have originated with the Petersons, a news outlet, or the person who'd sent the threatening text.

"Maggie? It's Jen. Jen Amesti, Jake Peterson's girlfriend. We met at Starbucks?"

"Of course. Jen. How are you?"

"Did you say you had connections in law enforcement?" Jen asked, squishing the words together and voicing them in a single breath. Before I could respond, she raced on. "Jake's house. Someone broke in. All his camera memory cards are gone. All his research. All the pictures recording our life together." Her voice broke, but she cleared her throat and barreled on. "I checked with his roommates, his parents, his department at the university, the landlord, and the sheriff's office, and none of them have the memory cards. They're gone. I have to get them back. I have to." Her voice broke again. "Can you help me? I don't know who to talk to, who to trust, or what to do."

"He didn't back them up?" I asked, and then kicked myself. That was the first question people *always* asked when someone was distraught over losing something stored digitally. Obviously Jake hadn't backed up the memory cards, or Jen wouldn't have been so upset. We *all* know we should back up our computers. No matter what kind of project I was working on with a client, I would also suggest they buy easy-to-use automated cloud backup systems for their digital devices. But most of us learn those lessons the hardest way possible, when we haven't backed up our prized work, research, or mementos. Losing data sucks. It's never helpful and often downright cruel to ask a sufferer why they neglected to back up their files. Doing so was the modern equivalent of kicking a guy when he was down.

Jen's helplessness overcame her and she burst into tears. I fought against absorbing her despair and struggled to think of something, anything that could help her locate the photographs that represented her memories of her beloved Jake, but which my gut told me could also hold the key to his murder.

"Jen?" I spoke slowly and gently as I would with a skittish dog or horse. I needed to be sure she was listening.

"Sorry." She sniffed. "Go ahead."

"My law enforcement friends are here with me now. We're just starting dinner, but we can save a plate for you, or you can join us for dessert if you want to come over. We can talk it through and figure out our next step."

"*Our* next step? You mean you'll help me?"

"Of course. Helping you helps my kids, and though I never met Jake, I've become surprisingly attached to him. We'll put our heads together and solve this thing." I spoke with a confidence and cheerfulness that rang false as I replayed my words in my head. But it was enough to buck up Jen.

"I'll be right over," she said. "Heron Beach? What's the number?"

I gave her directions, since GPS was useless inside the security gates, and told her we'd see her soon.

As I ended the call, Max, Stephen, David, Nell, and Brian all pelted me with questions. A knock at the door made me feel assaulted from all angles. I pushed back my hair, took a deep breath, smoothed out my T-shirt and opened the door, slowly.

"Renée." I hugged her with relief, having nearly forgotten I'd invited her. We weren't quite at the hugging stage of knowing one another, even in instant-intimacy California. Renée recoiled slightly, then hugged me back and handed me a bottle of wine and some flowers.

"You shouldn't have," I said. "Really. How on earth does a working woman, who unexpectedly finds herself the mother of three tiny children, find time to breathe, let alone focus on social niceties? Where are the kids?" I searched behind her as though she'd been hiding them behind her back.

"Another neighbor, bless her, has taken them for the evening. If you hadn't invited me to dinner, I probably would have made do with popcorn and fallen asleep on the couch. How can three such tiny people be so exhausting?"

"It's the mystery that haunts parents everywhere," Max said, taking Renée's jacket and handing her a glass of wine. "But we've got a few other problems on our hands, including a new one Maggie was just about to tell us about. Have a seat."

David brought in a plate of chicken from the grill. Stephen handed her the salad bowl, introducing himself and Nell. Max, who suddenly realized Renée had no idea who he was, retroactively said, "I'm Max. Maggie's husband and father to these two." He waved his hand toward Brian and David.

Everyone turned toward me, apparently expecting me to quickly recount the details of my phone call from Jen. But I hesitated, squinting at Renée. *Could we trust her?*

Renée looked up from preparing her plate. No one spoke. My thoughts raced. Tension in the room built. She glanced around the room. "You're giving me the heebie-jeebies," she said. "What is it? What's happened?"

I decided it wouldn't hurt to fill her in on Jen's phone call. If she was behind the theft of Jake's memory cards, she already knew everything I was about to say. More likely, she wasn't involved in this tangled mess of criminal activity, and we could trust her.

I took my seat at the table and poured myself another glass of water and another glass of wine, trying to remember to alternate sips. I recounted the details of Jen's phone call.

"So, what do we think?" I asked when I'd finished my tale. "Who stole Jake's stuff? How do we get those memory cards back?"

Stephen stood and picked up his phone. "Jason has a contact in the local police department. I'll ask him to double check what the sheriff's office told Jen. The deputies may have picked up the memory cards but weren't ready to share that information with Jen." He stepped away from the table and into the hall leading to the boys' bedrooms. The sound of his low rumbling voice told us he'd reached Jason.

As he finished the call and returned to the table, there was yet another knock on the door. Stephen answered it and introduced himself to Jen. The condo, which had once seemed spacious, was growing crowded. The boys moved, unbidden, to lean on the sill of the dining area window. Then David opened the door to the balcony and brought in two patio chairs. He positioned them so that Brian could sit and keep his still-healing foot raised.

When everyone was mostly settled, Stephen cleared his throat. "If I may, I'd like to summarize where we are to bring everyone up to speed. We don't have much time left to solve this thing, and we'll need to work fast."

After Stephen reviewed the list of suspects and some of the outlandish scenarios we'd proposed to explain all the goings on and tie them together, I glanced at Jen and Renée, expecting them to be first to ask questions. But Jen had covered her mouth and was blinking rapidly as if trying to bring the room and Stephen's words into focus. Renée shook her head and laughed nervously. "I can't believe all this has been going on and I knew so little about it." She scoffed. "I mean, I knew about Jake and the Petersons' accusations, of course, but smuggling on our beach? Mrs. Nesbitt being a drug runner? Bad guys on the farms and in the state park? Talk about conspiracy theories. I'm surprised you haven't lined the windows with aluminum foil. For heaven's sake. I've lived in Watsonville all my life. These are my friends. My family. Most people in town are both. Are you all stark raving mad?"

I think Renée must have expected us to laugh off our suspicions, or at least be amused by her suggestion that we were all crazy. But we met her accusations with silence.

Stephen once again filled the gaping chasm in the conversation. "It does sound crazy, particularly when it's all laid out at once. But something is certainly happening here that someone wants to keep secret. Someone tampered with Jake's ultralight and someone wants to stop Maggie and the kids from investigating. Show her that text you got, Maggie."

I unlocked my phone and started scrolling, getting a quick reminder about how crazy the past few days had been. I found the still-terrifying message, shivered, and handed the device to Renée, who read it, then looked up. Her face reflected her dismay and disbelief.

"You've got to be kidding. You believe this?" Renée held up the phone. When no one answered, she said, "Seriously? If you do, why are you still here? Why not go back home and forget you ever heard of Heron Beach and this project?"

For a moment, no one spoke. Then David said, "Because that's not what our family does. My mom said she'd help you get your office organized, and she will. If there's something bad happening here that could endanger us, it would threaten your business too. You need to be as concerned about your safety as we are about ours."

"Imagine the liability," said Nell.

"We are *not* going to sue, no matter what happens," I said. As Brian had observed earlier, the words were those most often used by someone who would eventually bring a lawsuit and did nothing to reassure Renée. She still looked as though she thought she'd landed in a nest of paranoid lunatics.

Everyone began speaking at once, and the noise level grew excruciating until Stephen whistled in a way he must have perfected in his military days. It worked.

"Here's what we need to do," he said, counting off the individual parts of our project on his fingers. "We need to locate those memory cards for Jen, find out who took them, and why."

He took a sip of water and continued outlining our tasks. "We need to test the package Maggie lifted from Mrs. Nesbitt's apartment so we can either rule out the old lady's part in this or add her portion of the scheme into the mix. We need to get a computer expert to trace that threatening text. We need to find out who drives a silver pickup truck and was looking after Mrs. Nesbitt, and whether it's the same person that Maggie saw in the parking lot. Renée started to speak, but one look from Stephen silenced her.

"I want to hear what you have to say, Renée," Stephen said. "You know the people around here better than anyone. But let me lay all this out first." He looked over his shoulder at Brian and David. "The boys want to watch for smugglers from the pits they've dug on the beach. I need to check with the ranger and let him know what they're planning since the beach officially closes at ten o'clock. We don't want him driving his truck into one of your bunkers in the dark, either."

Stephen spoke his last sentence in a lighter tone than he'd used all evening, and a tension-busting peal of laughter started with Brian and David and moved around the room. Stephen grinned, but then brought us back on task. "Renée, is there a place on the property where we could observe those fields behind the ridge? Where no one would see us?"

"Do you think there's something illegal going on up there? If there were, surely Vik or Lenny, the night guard, would have seen the lights and reported them."

"We need to check it out anyway," Stephen said, in a voice that brooked no argument. I was used to seeing him take charge of a roomful of citizens and volunteers back in Orchard View where his law enforcement experience was well recognized and his standing in the community had bought him some clout. I was surprised to see that his kindness, firmness, confidence, and leadership skills worked almost as well here, where he had no connections or credentials and was unknown to Jen and Renée. The two women seemed to trust him implicitly, as I had when we'd met him on our first day in Orchard View.

"Renée, I know that you trust all the local people who we've listed as suspects," Stephen said. "My partner Jason Mueller, who is chief of police in Orchard View and has connections all over the state, is running background checks. The ranger here in the state park, Charlie Adams, is a well-known straight shooter, as honest as they come. Jason says we can rely on him. But are there people here you don't trust or have been wary of before? Who are the usual suspects?"

Jen and Renée looked at each other. Jen whispered, "*Oh-Oh?*" Renée clarified. "Oscar Ochoa. Oh-Oh. He's a local street gang leader. I'm sure the Watsonville cops have their eye on him."

Jen cleared her throat and added, "Jake was good friends with Oh-Oh's little brother, Dom. Domingo. Oscar once accused Jake of being a pedophile and grooming Dom and some of the other boys."

I gasped, but Jen waved her hand. "Dom must have convinced Oh-Oh otherwise, because as far as I know, Jake was never threatened after that one time. Dom had a serious case of hero worship, but it wasn't anything more than that. Jake wanted the kid to take science classes and study hard and go to college. I think Oscar wanted that, too. He and Jake were on the same side. They both wanted something more than the gang for Domingo."

Renée interrupted. "I went to school with Oh-Oh. He had gang connections, but I never thought of him as a bad guy. Last I heard, he was talking with some outfit in Los Angeles or New York that provided seed money to gangs wanting to start legitimate businesses."

"You're kidding," I said.

Stephen smiled. "No, it's true. A gang in New York launched a company that does street fashion. The design part and the connections are all new, but it turns out some of their taggers had a great artistic vision. Manufacturing and distributing illegal drugs aren't all that different from what legitimate businesses do: handing out samples to influential people, and letting word of mouth work its magic."

"I want to hear more, but I don't want to get off track," I said. "Could we be looking at the start of a gang war here? Some higher ups could be miffed that this Oscar character is thinking about shifting gears. I heard somewhere that the only way out for gang members is to fall off the radar and disappear with a witness-protection program level of secrecy."

Stephen leaned forward. "Maggie's right. We're getting pretty far afield here. Let's go where the evidence takes us and just observe what's going on tonight. If the bad guys show up, their movements will direct our next steps."

Stephen handed out assignments. Brian and David's job was to increase the size of their sand pits. Stephen would check in with Jason and the ranger. Max and I volunteered to keep everyone supplied with snacks and coffee since it was shaping up to be a long night.

Renée and Jen worked on providing detailed descriptions of some of our suspects and scoured the internet for photographs of all of them.

Nell retired to her own condo, saying there were a few things she needed to check on. When I took her a plate of dessert later, she was on the phone. She answered the door, mouthed the words *thank you,* took the plate, and closed the door without telling me anything. Though she hadn't said a word, her air of confidence, determination, and focus continued to buoy me. As I walked back to our condo, however, I felt my anxiety level rise again as my brain began flitting among all the different ways that our plans could go wrong. But then I thought of Rocket. And Stephen, and how successful we'd all been before when we'd worked together to set injustices to right. "We'll do it again," I whispered to myself. "We have to."

I hoped I'd have no reason to doubt my words.

Chapter 24

Plopping a paper or reusable silicone cupcake-tin liner in your car's cup holders converts them to useful (and easily cleanable) snack containers.

From the Notebook of Maggie McDonald
Simplicity Itself Organizing Services

Saturday, June 22, Late afternoon

Within moments, the condo emptied. I was alone. Nell had given Stephen the wrapped package I'd picked up from Mrs. Nesbitt's filthy condo. He'd called a testing service that Jason had recommended—one that was accredited to provide court-admissible tests. They'd agreed to analyze it immediately, and Stephen had taken the sample to the gatehouse to meet a messenger who'd been dispatched to pick it up.

Max and the boys were on the beach, perfecting the design of the bunkers from which they'd spy on the smugglers. We'd called the state park and talked to Ranger Charlie Adams, who said he'd stop by on his next drive down the beach. Jason told us he knew Charlie and trusted him, but the park ranger/law enforcement officer was skeptical about the advisability of under-aged civilians getting anywhere near a drug-smuggling operation. In general, the park system was cracking down on existing laws that closed the beaches at night. With staffing cuts, the efforts were easier in theory than in practice. In any case, Charlie appreciated that Jason had vouched for the kids, but he insisted on checking out Brian and David himself.

I was about to join Max and the boys on the beach when I started at the sound of knuckles rapping on our front window. I peered out. A tall, scarecrow-thin man in a Smokey-the-Bear hat leaned against the stairway railing.

"Ma'am," he said, removing his hat. "I'm Charlie Adams. We spoke on the phone."

"Yes," I said, "We met on the cliff after Jake's crash, and again at Beach Street Café." I invited him in and offered coffee, which he declined. "I spoke with your husband and your boys on the beach just now. Nice family."

I smiled in thanks as he continued. "We sometimes have problems with people digging tunnels and pits in the sand that collapse upon them with tragic results, but your men seem to have safety well in hand. Your boys seem calm and sensible, and showed me their cell phones and a police-issue radio they were planning to use to stay in touch with adults." He scratched his head. "Where'd they get that equipment?"

I explained our family's relationship to the Orchard View Police Department and handed one of Jason's business cards to Ranger Adams. "Feel free to check," I said.

Charlie grinned. "I already have. I just wanted to see what your answer would be. Jason vouches for you and says you have law enforcement-trained personnel here with you."

I nodded, and recited as much as I knew and could remember about Stephen and Rocket's résumés.

"I look forward to meeting them both," said Charlie, though I explained Rocket's elusive nature. "And I've talked to your boys. If anything happens on the beach tonight, their job is to stay hidden in their sand pit. If they decide they can't do that, the only direction they're allowed to run is toward the stairs and straight back to your condo, from which they're to call the gatehouse, me, you and your husband, and Stephen. They nodded solemnly when I gave them their orders, but I wanted to double check. Can they do this safely? Will you sign a waiver in case someone gets hurt? If you or your husband need help to say no to this plan, I'm happy to be the official bad guy and tell your boys I'll award them a steep fine if I spot them anywhere near the beach after hours."

"Thanks," I said, meaning it. I approved of law enforcement officers who took their vows to serve and protect seriously, and were flexible in the ways they applied the law, their instinct, and their discretion in dealing with their communities. "The boys are sensible, and they will take direction or orders from Max and me, from Stephen and Rocket, and from you. Our friends in Orchard View have taught them to trust and work with the police."

"Good," said Charlie, nodding and returning his hat to his head. "I'll check in with you all tonight. My hope is that the boys will have a lot of fun, but will be disappointed when no bad guys show up."

"I'm with you," I said, thanking Charlie again and showing him to the door. Before he left though, I thought of a few questions. "Is smuggling a big problem? What is the chance they'll run into real drug dealers tonight? Gang members? Do you think they'll be armed?"

He responded patiently and calmly. "Honestly? We're much more likely to get calls about heart attacks, drunks, and out-of-control beach fires than anything else. Maybe a stray dog or an injured sea mammal, but it seldom gets more exciting than that even on the big summer holidays like July Fourth. Certainly not at this time of year. Most nights I look at the stars and fight to stay awake and alert."

I let out a breath. "Sorry. I'm a bit of a worrywart, especially when it comes to my kids."

"Rightly so, ma'am. Rightly so." He touched his hat brim and turned away. I watched him descend the stairs stiffly in his work boots and then called to him. "Ranger Adams?"

He turned with his hand on the rail.

"They've spent nearly the whole day body surfing and digging in the sand. My guess is that they'll sleep through any nighttime adventures on the beach."

Charlie smiled, nodded, and returned to patrolling the beach.

* * * *

The boys set out at nine o'clock equipped with a thermos of hot chocolate, snacks, flashlights, blankets, and warm, waterproof jackets. The marine-layer had come in at four o'clock in the afternoon, and we'd suggested they might like to postpone their adventure for another night. We might as well have tried to stop the tide.

Max and Belle and I checked on them before we went to bed. Belle seemed eager to join the boys, but they feared she might bark at the smugglers and either give away the boys' location or scare the crooks away. Both kids seemed warm, content, and excited. We had them check their phones and radios and then said good night.

"Stay far to the right as you head up the steps," I told Max. "Otherwise you'll trigger the motion sensor and blind us with the security light."

I'd planned to stay awake, keeping watch over the boys and the coastline from the living room window. The second time I nodded off, I decided to leave the night watch to the boys, Charlie, Rocket, Stephen, and Munchkin. What were the chances that anything would happen anyway? The smugglers, if that's what they were, had already dropped off a load of contraband this week. How often would it make sense to do that? Daily? I didn't think it would be worth the risk. I joined Max under the covers. Fast asleep, he, like me, was fully dressed with his boots by the side of the bed, prepared to leap to action if called upon to do so.

* * * *

At three in the morning, I was jolted awake, though I wasn't sure how or why. I stopped in the bathroom first and then crept to the window to peer out. I gasped. A flashlight bobbed on the beach, not far from the boys' sandpit.

"Max, wake up. They're here." We scrambled into our shoes and jackets, leashed Belle, and flew down the steps from the condo to the boardwalk and then down the second flight of stairs to the beach, keeping left to evade the motion sensor and protect our night vision. Half running, half stumbling, across the sand, we nearly fell into the pit. Max shined his light into the faces of men who'd joined our boys, nearly blinding Stephen, Rocket, and Charlie. I sat back, breathing hard.

"False alarm. We thought you were bad guys," I said.

"Not tonight," said Rocket. I couldn't remember if I'd ever heard him speak before.

"The ranger was telling us about when his dad was in the Coast Guard," Brian said. "And German spies tried to land."

"Cool," I said, hunkering down, scrunching close to David, and covering my legs with the blanket. Max glanced up at the glittering sky then out to sea. Shrugging, he joined us, scooting in between Brian and Belle. Munchkin licked his face in welcome.

Charlie took a deep breath and launched into his story. "I'd just told the boys that my dad was barely old enough to enlist in the Coast Guard during World War II. I think he joined up because they patrolled the beach with German Shepherds, and he'd always wanted a dog. He claimed his job was walking on the beach at night and chatting to pretty girls who admired his dog. But the Coast Guard had received a report that there were German submarines off the coast, along with a credible rumor about a plot to land spies on the night of the new moon. Sure enough, 'round about midnight, the dogs started barking, and a rubber raft came ashore carrying five men. They caught three of them, but two escaped over the dunes. Happened not far from here, in fact."

"What happened then?" Max asked. "Did they catch the other two? I've never heard of spies landing on our shores in the 1940s."

Charlie nodded. "They hushed it up at the time, but the Germans tried it more than once."

He poured steaming coffee from a thermos into a red plastic mug, and then held up the thermos, offering some to the rest of us. We shook our heads. "No thanks. Go on," Max said. "This history is news to me. What happened?"

"You have to remember that, back then, there weren't so many people living around here, and everyone knew one another. The Germans made their way to the train station planning to hop a bus into San Francisco and the U.S. Army's Western Defense Command at the Presidio. They looked, spoke, and dressed like Americans, and their papers seemed legit."

"So, how'd they catch 'em?" asked David. "Was there a secret code or password they didn't know?"

"Nothing quite so romantic. The same townspeople took that bus every week up into the city. They knew right away that the men weren't locals. A young Army nurse on leave was headed back to work at Letterman Hospital and phoned her boss before the bus took off. A contingent of military police met the spies when they got off the bus in San Francisco."

"Did your dad get a medal or anything?" Brian asked.

"Better than that," Charlie said. "He met my mother. She had a job babysitting for the summer and was taking the kids to the beach. They wanted to meet the heroes who caught the spies. My mom liked German Shepherds. One thing led to another and here I am."

We chatted a little longer before Charlie left to continue his rounds. He gave us each his direct line and waited while we programmed the number into our phones. We watched as his truck's red taillights disappeared into the darkness. The tide had come in. Waves crashed on the shore, sometimes hard enough to shake the sand. I shivered and snuggled closer to David, who yawned. "Looks like our big adventure is a bust," he said.

"*Hmm,*" I said in a whisper as I squinted into the darkness beyond the bunker. "Look there."

Coats and blankets rustled as everyone shifted to peer over the edge of our hiding place at what looked like a small kayak paddled by one man. I thought that a second man waited on the shore, though it was hard to tell in the nearly complete darkness. But then he called out. Rocket pulled on a pair of what I assumed were night vision goggles that made him resemble a cyborg. He scrambled silently from the bunker and disappeared. Stephen tapped at the dimmed display of his smartphone, and I assumed he was alerting Charlie to the smugglers' arrival.

Max held Belle close to his side in an effort to keep her comfortable. The safer she felt, the less likely she was to bark. But she sniffed, and Munchkin lifted his ears.

Stephen peered over the rim of our bunker, keeping an eye on Rocket. Every muscle in his body seemed tense, like a cat poised to launch itself at a mouse.

The police radio crackled. David grabbed it and turned down the sound. He looked up. By the dim light of Max's shielded flashlight, I could see David's face was filled with alarm. "Someone's had a heart attack at the campground," he said. "And the shower building is on fire. Charlie's responding. We're on our own." He jerked his head in the direction of the men with the kayak.

I tried to dial 9-1-1, but there was no response from my phone. I squinted at the screen, wishing I'd thought to wear my glasses. "No battery," I whispered. "I'll go back to the condo and phone the police and the gatehouse." I put my hand firmly on David's shoulder and stared at Brian. "You two listen to your father and Stephen. Stay put."

I ran to the steps, keeping my head low and, I hoped, out of sight in the darkness. But as I crested the top of the steps the security light clicked on and illuminated me like a stage light, announcing my presence to the bad guys and anyone else in the vicinity. I froze, hissed, and then dropped to my knees below the level of the dunes. How could I have forgotten the motion sensor? No way could the bad guys miss that. I crouched deeper as Belle barked and I heard the unmistakable sound of a gunshot.

Chapter 25

Need an easy way to contain dirt and debris on a car trip? Cover your rear passenger seats with a fitted sheet or mattress protector. As often as necessary, the sheet can be removed and shaken out or laundered.

From the Notebook of Maggie McDonald
Simplicity Itself Organizing Services

Sunday, June 23, Early morning

"9-1-1 Watsonville," said the dispatcher who answered my call. "What is the emergency?"

I introduced myself, explained I was at Heron Beach, and that we suspected smugglers were transporting heroin. "If you hurry, you can catch them. I heard a gunshot." My thoughts weren't as organized as I'd have liked, but I hoped the experienced officer could make sense of them and send help immediately. My hopes were dashed.

"I've recorded your call and alerted our officers. They'll respond as soon as possible."

"Right away?"

"We're responding to a heart attack and fire at the state beach campground and a three-alarm fire with casualties at the apple juice plant," the dispatcher said. "I have no one to send at the moment, but we'll get an officer to you as soon as we can. Within the next thirty minutes, I'm sure." She'd sounded mature, poised, and in control when she first answered the phone but now seemed younger and more flustered in the face of so many demands on the local emergency teams. I could hear more phones ringing unanswered in the background. "Thank you," I said, and ended the call.

I didn't feel thankful. I was angry and scared. I closed my eyes and leaned against the frame of the open front door. I needed a moment to catch my breath. Everyone I loved most was on the beach and in danger. That's where I needed to be, whether I could be of help or not. I grabbed a spray bottle of window cleaner and a flashlight from under the kitchen sink and dashed back to the beach.

It was chaos. From the top of the dunes, I could hear Munchkin and Belle, doing their best impressions of attack-trained dogs, snarling and barking. I squinted into the darkness. Waiting for my eyes to adjust and tell me where I could help most, I missed what was right in front of me.

I descended the steps and gasped as I was grabbed from behind by a bulky, fishy-smelling man. I raised the bottle of window cleaner and pulled the trigger, spraying directly behind my head. I heard a groan and the strength of the arms holding me lessened. My own eyes stung. I hoped that at least some of the vinegar-based fluid had reached my attacker.

I hit him over the head with the flashlight and escaped, charging toward Brian and David in the sand pit. Lights bobbed in the darkness, growing larger as they approached us. Rocket and Stephen had subdued two of the men. After marching the bad guys toward us, they ordered them to sit on the cold damp sand.

Rocket cuffed my attacker, dragged him roughly to his feet, and pushed him to the ground next to the other two men. He met the description of the gang leader, Oscar Ochoa—Oh Oh. He looked familiar to me and I realized I'd seen him before, when we'd had breakfast at the Beach Street Café. Charlie had been there too. If only we'd known then what we knew now, we could have arrested him then.

The other bad guys seated at Stephen's feet were not much older than Brian and David. I didn't recognize them, but where Oscar appeared sullen and defiant, the younger boys craned their necks to look Stephen in the eye, chattering rapidly in Spanish.

Max hugged me hard, then stepped behind me to make room for embraces from both of our boys. Belle sat on my foot and leaned hard into my leg. Her head pressed tightly against my knee, gazing up at my face until I reached down to massage her ears. "Are you all okay?" I asked. "I heard a gunshot. Is anyone hurt?" I stepped back from the boys and Max, scrutinizing their bodies for blood and injuries. Tears ran down my face from the vinegar spray.

"We're fine," Max said. "Let's get inside where we've got light and warmth. I'll fill you in. You need to wash out those eyes." He took the bottle of window washing fluid from me and scanned the label. "Looks like this stuff won't do any permanent damage to your vision, but we'll call poison control to make sure that a good rinsing is all your eyes need.

"But what about them?" I asked, tilting my head toward the three men crumpled on the beach. They stirred and Munchkin growled, the hair on his back standing up in a ridge like a Mohawk.

"Leave them to Rocket, Stephen, and Munchkin. They've got this."

Stephen dragged the men to their feet, and they lurched over the sand in the dark. With their hands cuffed behind their backs, their balance was off, and they stumbled frequently. One cried out as he banged his shin on the steps. I almost felt sorry for him.

We waited until they crested the top of the stairs before we started back to the condo. "Rocket fired the shot," Max said. "Blanks. He was trying to get the smugglers to focus on something other than you, silhouetted by the security light."

I winced. "That was stupid of me. I was so focused on getting help that I forgot about the sensors."

"No harm. No foul," Max said, reaching out his hand to help me up, and we trudged over the dunes to our condo.

"Where's Stephen taking them?" I asked.

"Gatehouse. Waiting for the sheriff's men."

"Yeah, about that. It might be awhile." I waited until we returned to the condo and had removed our shoes and damp jackets before explaining about the multiple emergencies that were delaying the first responders. I made tea and toast, which we ate, barely noticing what we were doing. We sat without talking. Though questions flitted through my head, I was too tired to utter a coherent thought. I would have fallen into bed if I'd had the energy to stand and walk the few feet separating me from my pillow.

We must have left the front door unlocked, because Stephen knocked softly and then entered, collapsing into the only empty chair in the living room. Munchkin padded silently after him, sniffed a hello to Belle, and flopped at his feet with a sigh.

"Rocket's got them," Stephen said, echoing Munchkin's sigh with one of his own. "We locked Oh-Oh in a back room, and his sidekicks are so scared that they're telling us everything. They're just kids. They'll need to repeat it all to the sheriff, of course, but Rocket's listening carefully. If their story changes, he'll know.

"Have you learned anything so far?" I asked, yawning before I could cover my mouth or apologize. I started an epidemic. When we'd recovered, Stephen summarized the kids' confession.

"The kids are working for Diego Baker," Stephen said.

"The traditional farmer with the fields south of the organic farm and the barn," I clarified.

"They're smuggling, but they say they don't know what they're bringing in," Stephen said. "They meet a fishing boat twice a week. The boat drops a pallet. It floats. One of them tows it behind the kayak until they bring it up on the beach, break up the load, and they both carry the packages uphill to the barn."

"What's the connection to Jake's death?" I asked. "And Mrs. Nesbitt's mysterious packages?"

Stephen shook his head. "We're not sure yet. We didn't want to slow their roll or give them a chance to think about the consequences of telling us everything. So, we didn't ask questions." He cleared his throat and took a sip of his tea. "But, right now anyway, it looks like there's no connection between Jake and the smuggling. And I'm still waiting for the labs on Mrs. Nesbitt's piece of the puzzle."

Stephen stood and brushed sand from his jeans. He looked down, froze, and blushed. "Sorry about the mess," he said.

"Don't worry about it. I think I brought in half the dune on my shoes. It'll vacuum up tomorrow."

* * * *

In the morning, I was awakened by a phone call from the district attorney's office saying that something had come up and our deposition was now scheduled for Tuesday afternoon. I hoped the delay was a result of the workload generated after authorities rounded up the smuggling ring. I was glad for the reprieve, since there was so much we still didn't know about what had happened to Jake, except of course that Brian and David had nothing to do with his death.

I talked it over with Max. "The most reasonable explanation I can think of is that Jake saw something he shouldn't have, and someone tried to scare him off, or worse, killed him."

"Tampering with an aircraft is a felony," said Max. "And any death that occurs during the commission of a felony is charged as murder. Even if the culprit only meant to scare Jake by hobbling the ultralight, that person is now a murderer." Max spoke with conviction, though I knew his only legal background came from television. As a result, his store of expertise was a mixture of American military and civilian laws, along with a pinch of British, Australian, and New Zealand legal precedents. A broad smattering of knowledge from dubious sources, to be sure.

I continued brainstorming. "Even if we've nailed the smuggling ring, it doesn't explain the missing memory cards from Jake's camera."

"Jake could have taken pictures of something incriminating without knowing what he'd done," Max said. "Or someone could have suspected that he had. Wouldn't be the first time some innocent person was killed for no reason."

I frowned. "I hate that idea."

"Real life is never as tidy as it is on television."

"Sorry. I just wish it were as easy as Gibbs and his team make it look on *NCIS*. There are never any annoying loose ends." I cradled my coffee mug and inhaled the steam. "So, you think we should discard the traditional motives?"

"What do you mean?"

"Follow the money. *Cherchez la femme*."

"Hmm. Greed and lust. How would that play out?"

"Jen's beautiful and accomplished. Could someone have wanted her for themselves?"

"Himself, you mean?"

"Or herself."

"Good point," Max said. "We don't know much about Jen or her friends. Does she have family? Could one of them have been retaliating against Jake for hurting her with the breakup? For sending her far away to graduate school?"

I thought for a moment and then outlined what might have been the strategy of our imaginary villain. "Jen said she'd offered to apply to a local university and wait a year. Jake wasn't ready to commit. So, Jen looked to the East Coast and Southern California, making it Jake's fault that she's considering a move. If our killer had romantic designs on Jen, getting Jake out of the way would have served the dual purpose of keeping her in town and removing Jake as a competitor for Jen's attention.

"And what about money?"

Max's question stumped me. "Aside from ill-gotten smuggling gains that would be at risk if Jake spilled key evidence to the authorities, I don't know of any financial angle on this case, do you? It's not like Jake was getting buckets of money from lucrative grants that would go to someone else if he wasn't around. He hadn't nabbed a plum job that someone else wanted. People don't murder others over jobs at the Jumping Bean or Starbucks, do they? Or graduate assistantships?"

Max shook his head and we went back to reading the paper and sipping our coffee. As soon as the kids were up, though, we wanted to check out the beach and the barn, and see what we could piece together about events that had unfolded after we'd gone to bed.

Brian wasn't up to the long hobble on his crutches and elected to stay home. David, Belle, Max and I set off.

Tide and the wind had obliterated any footprints that had been left in the sand near the shoreline the night before. Only tire tracks from Charlie's truck and remnants of the deep pits the boys had dug remained as reminders of the previous evening's activities.

"Looks like we almost caught something else," David said, pointing to twin wheel tracks. They narrowly skirted the edge of the pit.

"I'm glad you didn't," I said. "We'd waste the morning digging out the ranger, probably get the bill for a broken axle, and he'd never let you or any other kids spend the night on the beach."

David looked crestfallen.

"Sorry," I said. "Was that too much of a reality check this early in the morning?" David stuck out his lower lip and adopted the expression of an unhappy bloodhound. I gave him a hug. "Too much melodrama, too," I teased. "Don't push it."

David laughed and raced ahead to catch up with Belle who was chasing seagulls.

There was little wind. The beach was warmer than it had been for several days. I unzipped my windbreaker and then stripped off my sweatshirt, tying them both around my waist. David and Belle played in the waves, so Max and I headed up the cliff face toward the barn. Cliff face might have been too dramatic a description for the steep hill, but after a sleepless night, my muscles responded as though we scaled a precipice. "An escalator here would be nice," said Max. I didn't have enough spare breath to laugh. I grunted instead.

David caught up with us at the top. "Let's keep our voices down," I said. "We don't know who else is around."

"Surely the police and the sheriff rounded up all the bad guys last night," Max said. "Who could be left?"

We made our way along a dirt path at the side of the barn. I nearly slammed into Max's back when he stopped dead before rounding the corner.

"*Shh!*" he said, raising a finger to his lips and putting Belle on a short leash. I peered over his shoulder and gasped. A mere thirty feet beyond our hiding place, Diego Baker stood speaking with Renée. Our Renée. Our friend. Renée and Diego, the bad guy who the teens had fingered as the ringleader of the smuggling operation only a few hours earlier. Between them was Brian, his face a dreadful gray-green shade. Renée and Diego scowled at him and gripped his arms, holding him captive between them.

What was Brian doing here?

Chapter 26

For repetitive tasks such as vacation packing, keep a master list on your computer to make it easier each time. Adjust the list as you fine tune your needs. Online packing lists are available, but they are often more complex than necessary. Avoid them if you tend to overpack.

From the Notebook of Maggie McDonald
Simplicity Itself Organizing Services

Sunday, June 23, Late morning

I ducked back from the corner of the barn, but I was too late. Renée and Diego had spotted us.

"Max. Maggie," called Renée. "Come on over. We have news."

We sheepishly emerged from our hiding place. Only Belle remained unembarrassed. She pulled on the leash until Max let it go and she bounded toward Renée, sniffing at her pockets for treats and wagging her tail so hard her entire body shimmied.

Diego knelt down, rubbing Belle's chest. "What a good dog. Where've you been all my life, gorgeous? Did you know I'm partial to auburn hair?" He looked up and his face reddened. "I'm a sucker for a golden retriever," he said. "I had one as a kid. It's time for another one."

Belle's endorsement of Renée and Diego's warm doggy greeting disarmed me. Could I have misread the situation? Had Renée and Diego been supporting Brian rather than capturing and threatening him?

"Are you okay, Bri?" I asked. "I thought you'd be home asleep."
Renée stepped forward. "That's my fault, I'm afraid. I stopped by to
ask your advice on some storage cabinets I'm considering for the office.
You weren't around, so I asked Brian if he wanted to come with me to
check out the rumors I'd heard about a big drug raid on Diego's farm."

Diego stood, brushed his hands on his jeans, and then extended his
right toward Max, who shook it firmly. "I've seen you all around," the
farmer said, smiling. "But I don't think we've met. I'm Diego. Diego Baker.
Probably the only farmer in the area who isn't related to Renée. But we're
old friends from school, which after all this time is almost the same thing."

His charming demeanor made me wonder whether Stephen, too, had
got it wrong when he'd told us that the young smugglers had fingered
Diego as the head of the crime ring. Could this affable man who seemed
to be flirting with Renée truly be the ringleader of a deadly local gang?

I tried to smile, but I couldn't fool Renée. We hadn't worked together
long, but it was long enough, apparently, for her to reliably read my face
and my emotions.

"What is it, Maggie?" she asked. "We were just talking about last night.
What excitement, eh? Can you believe it? Smuggling. Back to the days of
the swashbuckling pirates. I knew there was some of it going on around
here, but I didn't expect to find anyone arrested right on my doorstep."

Renée either had stellar acting chops or she was innocent of any criminal
activity. I glanced from her face to Diego's, which was equally guilt-free.

"Did you see anything from your front windows while it was all
going down?" Renée asked. "I heard it took ages for the cops to get there.
Apparently, a local gang was in on it all and set some fires to tie up the
first responders. What a mess. The fire at the apple juice factory got out of
hand quickly in the wind. Several people were badly burned. No fatalities,
thank god, but a lot of people will be out of work for months while the
company takes care of the repairs."

I shook my head, searching for the right words to use to respond to
Renée, but she barreled on. "I heard some local people spotted the activity
on the beach and phoned it in, but the sheriff arrived just in time to arrest
a team that had already been apprehended by some amateur detectives."
She looked at David. "It wasn't you and your brother again, was it? You're
like a superhero team, fighting crime and saving lives."

She paused for a breath and glanced at me again, then Max, then
David. "It *was* you. Unbelievable." She fist-bumped my eldest son. "I did
the right thing when I hired your family, I'll tell you. Tess sure knows
how to pick them."

Diego stepped forward to shake David's hand and thank him. David took a half step back. My confusion must have shown clearly on my face. Diego also seemed surprised.

"What's wrong?" he asked. "Wait. You don't..." He shook his head and stepped backward toward Renée.

"What?" Renée said. "You don't think Diego had anything to do with this smuggling plot, do you?" She laughed. "We were just talking about that. He's so gullible." She glanced from me to Diego. "Tell them." She turned back to me. "He didn't even suspect."

"It seems so obvious, in hindsight," Diego said. "Some guy who said he was from the university approached me. Said I'd won a grant that would foot the bill for hiring former gang members and drug addicts, to help put them on the right path. The plan was that the California Department of Corrections would send me their most promising parolees. Their wages would be paid with the grant money. For me, it was like getting free labor."

He grimaced and shook his head. "I wonder if the situation the university guy described is even legal. It was too good to be true. But I fell for it anyway. Because I wanted to believe it and I was desperate. Without the grant, this year's payroll would have bankrupted me."

Diego's shoulders drooped and he smoothed the ground with his foot. "On some level, I knew it was suspect. The workers who were supposedly funded by the grant had daily meetings in the barn that I wasn't allowed to be a part of. They said they were running a twelve-step program and their get-togethers had to be anonymous."

He clenched his jaw, swallowed hard, and looked up, squinting. "And I fell for it. But about a month ago I noticed that some of newest guys didn't seem to know the first group of people I'd hired under the terms of the grant. They seemed less like *former* gang members and more like current thugs. I wanted to call my original contact to double check the details of the arrangement, but I couldn't find the name and number of the guy who'd set it all up. Now I'm not sure he gave me a card or anything. He said his team would handle all the paperwork."

He kicked at the sandy soil, creating a small cloud of dust. "I'm an idiot. I should have known. Things that seem too good to be true usually are. But I was so busy and, like I said, desperate. And I was afraid to be too confrontational. Ex-cons, you know. If they were bad guys, and I accused them, I was afraid they'd retaliate or try to shut me up. And if they were good guys, they didn't need me second-guessing their activities."

Renée put her hand on his shoulder. "You've always been so gullible, Diego. Always wanting to see the best in everyone. It's one of your best qualities."

Diego reddened and smiled. There was something between the two of them. A blossoming romance? An adolescent attraction rekindled? I couldn't be sure, but amid the turmoil of the last few days, their flirtation was refreshing, innocent, and charming.

I drew my attention back to detangling the details of the smuggling operation. "So, what was going on?" I asked, feigning innocence in an effort to discover how much Renée and Diego knew. "Did anyone get arrested last night?"

Diego nodded. "Two local kids with otherwise promising futures. Smart enough to get scholarships to college. But dumb enough and immature enough to want to make a quick and easy buck."

Max frowned. "What's the justice system like in this county? Will they get decent legal aid? Are there sympathetic judges and a district attorney who can give them a suspended sentence in exchange for a promise to straighten up?"

Renée sighed and brushed invisible dust from her plaid shirt and jeans. "We can only hope. They'll get the wrong kind of education and the wrong kind of job training in jail, that's for sure." She pushed the hair back from her forehead. "Those kids know something about some of the local thugs and their operation though. That information might be a valuable bargaining chip for them. We'll have to see."

"What was the extent of the smuggling operation?" My question was directed at Diego, but I didn't give him a chance to answer before interrogating him further. "Did the sheriff say anything?"

Renée glanced at Diego. She answered for him. "That's another thing we were trying to figure out when you arrived. From what we can piece together, they were using the barn to store contraband they were bringing in from fishing boats with kayaks. They'd pack heroin in regular strawberry boxes and layer the boxes in when they loaded the trucks. One truck would be pure berries, while the other would have both strawberries and heroin. The ordinary truck would go directly to the distributor as usual, but the mixed-load truck made a stop at a storage facility operated by the gang. They'd offload the heroin quickly, and then drive the second truck to catch up with the first one at the distributor."

"Did authorities find the stored heroin?" I asked.

Renée frowned and shook her head. "No. And without it, I'm not sure they have enough evidence. It would just be the kids' word against the adult gang members."

After pretending I knew nothing about the midnight raid, I couldn't figure out a way to smoothly tell Renée that we'd seen the two men from the beach transport packages from the kayak up the hill. That heroin had to be somewhere between the beach and the barn. There weren't that many hiding places unless you counted gopher holes and scrub brush. Any decently-trained drug-sniffing dog could surely have found any contraband stashed along the trail. Was the fact that it was missing an indication that the authorities were holding information back from the public? Or that Diego and Renée were keeping information from us?

David jumped in with a question before I could formulate another one of my own. "But wouldn't the numbers be off? A full truck leaves the field, but after the heroin is separated from the berry boxes, a not-quite-full load is delivered to the distributor. However they pay, by the pound or the box or whatever, one truck was going to be lighter than the other. Unless they had a way of topping off the strawberry boxes?"

Diego's face reddened further, and he pressed his lips together. "You're right. And I should have checked the receipts and the payments. But one of the supposedly ex-gang members with an accounting background volunteered to take care of all the paperwork for me, and I agreed, thinking I was finally getting the hang of delegating. No part of this situation reflects well on me."

Renée touched his shoulder again. "But you didn't know. Do you think the district attorney will charge you? Do you need a lawyer? Maggie's got a good one if you do."

Diego looked increasingly uncomfortable, as though he were scrambling for an excuse to be anywhere but here. "I can't afford a lawyer. I'm barely scraping by as it is. But the sheriff seemed to think that if I gave the forensic accountants full access to all my records, and I told them everything I knew about who was involved, they'd go easy on me." He shook his head. "Cooperating with the investigation will be a hardship, too, though. I'll have to spend time away from the farm, and I'll have to make do with fewer workers now that my 'grant money' has dried up."

Poor Diego looked miserable. I shifted the subject. "But how does this tie into Jake's death? Surely all this smuggling activity didn't play out during the day. And Jake's ultralight had no lights, so he wouldn't have been flying over at night."

Renée, idly stroking Belle's ears, spoke up. "Are we sure that's why he was killed? Maybe all this has nothing to do with what happened to Jake. It could all just be a coincidence."

David shook his head. "Coincidences are unicorns. Our friend Jason, the police chief, says his detectives are more likely to find connections between two seemingly unrelated occurrences than they are to discover a real-life coincidence."

"But the missing memory cards—" I began.

"—could have been misplaced or turned in to the professor who was overseeing Jake's research," Max answered my question before I'd decided how I was going to finish the sentence.

I was stumped. Who *had* killed Jake, and why? We might have been instrumental in busting up a drug ring, but we were no closer to solving our more immediate problem, which was how to resolve the suspicions swirling around David and Brian regarding Jake's death. The best way to do that would be to discover who'd plotted to crash the ultralight. But how? I opened my mouth to ask the question aloud, but Max beat me to it.

"I think this smuggling business has derailed us from our real problem— solving Jake's death. But I have an idea about that. We need to go back and talk to Stephen and Rocket, and we need to do that as soon as possible."

Brian caught a ride back with Renée. I'd considered asking Renée to drive us all back to the resort. Muscles I hadn't used in a long time had stiffened up as we'd stood talking. But she didn't have enough room in her car for all of us, and before I could ask, my phone rang. I glanced at the display. It was Jen Amesti.

"Maggie," Jen said. "I just got off the phone with someone from Jake's department who handles the paperwork for their grants. He says that Kevin Rivers, who owns the organic farm on the hill, wanted to fund research into fungus-resistant strawberries."

"That's generous," I said. "It would help his organic farming efforts but where would he get the money?"

"That's a good question," Jen said. "But I don't think it's the right one. Kevin outlined some interesting conditions he wanted the university to meet before he'd hand over the funds."

I could hear the excitement in Jen's voice.

"Conditions?"

"Rivers told the guy I talked to that he wouldn't hand over the money unless the university promised to cancel Jake's ultralight photography research project. Rivers told him that there had to be any number of other ways for Jake to obtain reliable research data and that the ultralight soaring over his farm was driving him bonkers and disrupting his farm workers. He said he'd do whatever it took to get that flying lawnmower out of the sky."

"So, Rivers might have been motivated to find other ways to stop Jake in case the grant ploy didn't work," I said.

"Exactly," said Jen.

Chapter 27

Stash your phone in a zip-lock bag at the beach to protect the screen and keep it safe from sand, salt, and moisture.

From the Notebook of Maggie McDonald
Simplicity Itself Organizing Services

Sunday, June 23, Early afternoon

On our walk back to the condo, Max outlined his plan to identify all the people who had access to the kinds of tools needed to damage a propeller. He'd narrowed the group down to those who might be able to conceal evidence so well that even the persnickety Jake had overlooked it. "It has to be someone from the airport maintenance facility."

David wasn't so sure. "Farmers must have to mend mechanical equipment all the time," he said. "They must have at least some sort of limited machining capability on site. You never see a tractor up on blocks at a service station."

Max rubbed his chin. "True, but did any of the farmers or the people who worked there also have access to Jake's ultralight? How well did they know Jake? As much as Rivers apparently wanted to shut down Jake's operation, I'm not sure they ever met one another. It's hard to drum up the kind of loathing that leads to murder—especially for someone you've never met."

"But not so difficult, if that person was threatening your smuggling operation," David said. "Maybe Kevin Rivers was more involved than the guys we caught last night let on."

"What do you think happened?" I asked. "Let's look at the whole picture." David stopped walking, chewed his lip, and then continued. "Rivers told the university he wanted Jake's operation shut down because it was annoying. But we don't know whether that was Rivers' *real* motive. Look, no one is going to walk into the research department and say, 'I want to give you a grant in exchange for getting rid of this kid who flies over my fields every day and is about to uncover my smuggling ring.' Right?"

"Good point. But if Rivers thought he'd solved his problem by funding the grant, why go to the trouble of fiddling with Jake's propeller blade?"

David scoffed. "Who am I, the local constable? I don't have *all* the answers."

"What if Rivers was afraid Jake had seen something and suspected the farm was a locus of illegal activity?" I asked. "What if he feared Jake would go to the cops or the sheriff? He could have planned to damage the propeller to delay Jake's next flight until after his guys had cleared out the evidence."

"But then why work so hard to hide the damage?" David said. "Wouldn't that defeat the purpose? If Jake couldn't see the damage, there'd be no reason to delay his flight."

Max shifted the topic so dramatically that I wondered if he'd zoned out of the conversation while he formulated his own theory. "Does Jen have access to Jake's research notes?" He must have spotted the confusion on my face because he quickly fleshed out his idea. "Would Jake have recorded the times and dates that he flew? What if Rivers took advantage of one of these overcast mornings to shift the drugs? He could have assumed the fog would keep Jake grounded and that the gloom would hide his own illegal activities. But an ultralight flies so close to the ground, Jake might be able to get away with operating in limited visibility conditions that would ground more traditional aircraft. Or suppose Jake was squeezing in a flight at twilight and Rivers started moving his packages too early? Could we cross-reference Jake's logs, the weather reports, and sunset?"

David frowned. "You mean conditions were such that Rivers assumed he was safe, moved the drugs, yet Jake spotted him? And Rivers wanted to silence him? You don't need his research notes. All you'd need is the photographs. They're all time- and date-stamped. They may be location-stamped too, unless Jake turned off that function." David whooped and punched his fist in the air. "That's *got* to be why the memory cards have gone missing." He held up his palm and Max gave him a high five.

"If we find the photographs, we'll have our murderer," I said. "But who had access? Jen? Dot and Bill Peterson?" And then I remembered. Jen had told me that Jake rented a rundown old house in the hills with a bunch of other guys. I knew how those households worked. I'd shared an aging Victorian once with six roommates as an impoverished young adult. If Jake's shared living situation operated the way mine had, a wide circle of friends might have copies of the keys or know the secret to unlocking a backdoor without a key. As remote as the house was, the residents probably weren't conscientious about locking up. *Great.* That meant our pool of suspects had widened to include everyone. I groaned and filled David and Max in on my thinking.

Max put his arm around me. "Don't lose heart. We'll solve this. But I want to start by talking to the mechanics again. I want to get Rocket to nose around while I'm keeping the mechanics busy. How 'bout we head to the airport bar for lunch, and you can have a chat with the servers in the restaurant while we're there?"

"Good idea," I said. "Mace, the bartender I spoke to at the restaurant, said that he tends to let students take the more profitable weekend shifts. The younger people might be more clued-in to gossip about the other kids working at the airport like Jake and the mechanics."

Stephen, Rocket, and Munchkin came to the airport but drove separately in Stephen's big black SUV. We'd settled at a table when Stephen joined us, saying that Rocket had gone to check out the mechanics shed and a few other behind-the-scenes operations. "If there's anything shady going on here, Rocket will find it," Stephen said, opening his menu.

* * * *

After downing one of the best burgers I'd ever eaten along with too many onion rings and a local artisanal brew, I felt more prepared for a nap than for serious sleuthing. The bar was too busy and short-staffed for me to grill any of the servers. The boys ordered dessert. I requested coffee. Stephen, Max, and Munchkin left to track down Rocket.

Jen entered just as they were leaving. I waved her over to our table. She eyed my coffee and the death-by-chocolate tortes a server had placed in front of each of the boys. "Looks good," she said and flagged down a waiter carrying an enormous load of plates he'd cleared from the table of more than a dozen elderly men.

"What are you up to today?" I asked Jen after she'd been supplied with coffee and cake. "Any luck tracking down the memory cards?"

Before she could answer, David launched into an explanation of our theory that the time and date stamps on the photos could be incriminating, even if Jake hadn't deliberately documented aspects of the drug scheme.

Jen frowned. "I've looked everywhere and alerted all his friends, and his parents. I was careful at first, telling everyone that I was looking for his camera and stray memory cards because I wanted some photos I'd taken of him." She looked down at her plate and twirled her fork as though she was toying with spaghetti instead of a slab of dark chocolate cake. Her face revealed the mixture of pain and love that the bittersweet memory had conjured. "That story was true. There are some great photos of Jake and me, and I'd hate to think I've lost them."

"But no luck so far?" I asked.

"Not yet."

"Any other leads?"

Before I could stop him, Brian updated Jen on Max's theory that the chief culprit in Jake's death had to have had access to the maintenance shed. Until we were sure, I'd hoped to protect Jen from the pain of learning that one of Jake's friends and co-workers had likely been responsible for his death.

Jen scooted her chair back, with her arms stiffly extended in front of her. "That can't be," she said. "The airport mechanics were Jake's friends. He'd known them forever. I mean, they were always kidding around, telling me that they were going to knock off Jake so they could have me to themselves, but they were *joking*. You know, the way guys do when they really care for one another. There're no secrets there, I'm sure of it."

"But who else could have had access to both Jake's ultralight and the materials required to damage the propeller?" David asked.

Jen's face telegraphed confusion, so Brian updated her on what Max had learned from Howard, the materials scientist—that the propeller blade had been weakened and then disguised to look freshly refurbished.

Jen thought for a moment. "But whoever did that didn't need access to the whole ultralight," she said. "Didn't they tell you? The guys in the shop? Jake had a friend, an old guy, who took care of his propellers for him. Jake had two used ones, and he was meticulous about checking them over. He'd take one in for Mr. Mason to work on in his machine shop in town while Jake operated the plane with the other one. Jake often landed in fields or empty lots, where there was loose gravel that could be kicked up and nick the blades, so he was always checking them." She scooted her chair back in, confident in her assessment of the situation. "I doubt very much anyone could damage those propellers without Jake finding out. He was too careful."

Jen was still fragile. Still grieving. I didn't want to push too hard against her assessment of the situation. But David wasn't nearly so gentle. He pulled out his cell phone and swiped through the photos until he located Howard's images documenting the damaged blade and showed them to Jen. Her face blanched. She gasped and touched the screen. "The only person Jake might have trusted enough with his propellers to risk giving them a cursory look was Mr. Mason. But it can't be him. Why would he want to hurt Jake? Mr. Mason has been friends with the Petersons for decades."

"Does this Mr. Mason have a commercial location?" I asked. "Or is this a side business he operates out of his home or garage? Is he nearby?"

Jen tilted her head and wrinkled her nose. "I can't remember the address. I could give you directions." She tapped and swiped at the screen of her phone, then shook her head. "The guys in the maintenance shed will have Mr. Mason's card, I'm sure. That whole three-block section of Freedom Boulevard is full of auto repair and sheet metal operations, one right after the other. I can't remember the name of Mr. Mason's shop. It's been in the family for generations and still has the original name."

I paid the bill, left a generous tip, and we trooped over to the hangar, looking for Rocket, Stephen, and Max. Several machines were competing for the loudest ear-splitting noise generator award. Our arrival went unnoticed in the din. Max, wearing ear and eye protection and a leather apron, was hunched over one machine that whirred and clunked and spit out sparks. When the machine stopped, he held up the gleaming metal device he'd been polishing and handed it to one of the mechanics for inspection. A tattooed man, still young enough to be struggling with acne, clapped Max on the back and yelled what I thought was *good job*, though it was difficult to hear. Max looked up and waved.

Jen, who had apparently been a frequent visitor to the shop, stopped behind a yellow line painted on the floor that I assumed was a kind of safety barrier. "Hey Joe," she said waving to an older man doing paperwork. "That's Joe Fowler," she whispered to me. "The manager."

Joe smiled, closed the book he was writing in, tucked it into the desk, locked the drawer, and then strode over to greet Jen with a hug. "How ya holdin' up?" he asked her. Munchkin padded after him. Apparently Joe had been charged with keeping the big dog out of trouble and away from the machines.

Jen shrugged and changed the subject. "I'd like you to meet Maggie and David." She lifted her chin in the direction of the door. "Brian's the one leaning against the door on his crutches. They're that guy's family." She pointed to Max.

"Max? He's great..."The rest of Joe's words disappeared as Stephen, covered head to toe in safety gear, started up a machine that seemed to be stamping holes in a sheet of metal. It assaulted our ears with a *clank, whoosh, clank, whoosh* sound. It moved faster than Max did when he split wood using a sledgehammer and steel wedges, but the din was similar.

There was no point in trying to talk until Stephen finished his job, but I watched Max as he meticulously removed his apron and hung it on a hook. He removed ear muffs and safety goggles and placed them in an open cubby, and then came to join us behind the yellow line, accompanied by the younger man with tattoos. His name was stitched over the pocket of his gray work shirt: Zeke.

I smiled and held out my hand. "Good to see you again." Zeke and Max's faces held matching looks of confusion. I came to their rescue. "We met in the airport bar," I reminded the young mechanic. "You were picking up lunch."

Recognition flooded his face and he shook my hand. "Of course. Maggie something, right?"

"My wife, Maggie McDonald," Max said in a protective alpha male tone I seldom heard him use. An excruciating clanging made me cover my ears and saved us from whatever Max had planned for his next move.

Within a few moments, Stephen finished his noisy task and joined us. "Meet Brett," he said, introducing a man who matched Stephen in height and breadth and sported an equally impressive beard dyed an unlikely shade of black. His hair was covered by a grubby ball cap that he made no effort to remove. He shoved his hands in his pockets and nodded to me. He glanced at Jen, blushed, and walked to the far end of the shop, disappearing through an open garage-type door.

Zeke, on the other hand, smiled broadly, stepped forward and introduced himself to each of us. "Today is tour day," he said. "What would you ladies like to see?"

David cleared his throat. Zeke laughed and added, "Young gentlemen too, of course." Belle thumped her tail on the concrete floor, stood, and walked over to nudge Zeke's hand. He stepped away and wiped his palm on his jeans without looking. Belle, nonplussed, moved back to Joe, who bent to pat her again. "Never mind him," Joe said. Belle was willing to be consoled as long as the manager was willing to massage her ears.

Max and Stephen thanked the mechanics for showing them around. I knew better than to ask where Rocket was. I couldn't see him anywhere, which meant he was stealthily investigating some out-of-sight part of the operation. I didn't know whether any of the workers were aware of Rocket's presence, and didn't want to spill the beans if they'd not yet spotted him.

"What can I help you with, Jen?" Zeke asked. "Do you need help with Jake's stuff? I've got my truck if you need a hand moving anything." He looked around the shop. "We sure miss him. I gave all his gear to his mom, though. I hope that was okay."

Jen nodded and swallowed hard. This was the first time she'd been back to the shop since Jake's death. There were a lot of firsts in her future, and each one would be difficult. But she gamely pushed on, doing what needed to be done. "Thanks, Zeke. It's still too soon to move anything, I think. And you'd probably have to check with Jake's parents. They're his official next of kin, not me."

An awkward pause followed. I searched for something appropriate to fill the gap and came up empty. Jen rescued us. "Do you have a card, or know the address of Mr. Mason's shop on Freedom Boulevard?" she asked Joe. "I wanted to pick up any parts Jake left there and pay Mr. Mason for his work. I'll take whatever's there over to his mom's house."

"You wanna grab the card off the board in my office?" Joe asked Zeke, who was already heading toward the office, where Joe's desk was backed by a cork wall covered in promotional calendars, business cards, photos, and scrawled notes. Zeke pulled a card from the wall and rejoined us, handing it to Jen.

* * * *

Back at our cars, out of sight of the shop, Jen handed me the card. "Disregard the listed business hours," she said. "Since his wife died last year, Mr. Mason is almost always there whether the shop is open or not. Please tell him I said hello." Her lips quivered, and her voice broke. "Jake really loved that man. Like an uncle or second father."

"Do you want us to pick up the parts you mentioned? We can drop them off at the. Peterson's house if you want." I offered out of courtesy, but when I heard the words, I winced. We were probably the last people in the world Dot wanted to see. I had no desire to revisit her wrath.

Jen shook her head. "I made up that story about the parts to satisfy Joe's curiosity and keep him from asking too many questions. He always wants to know every detail of what's going on, whether it concerns him and his business or not."

"Too bad he couldn't tell us anything more about who killed Jake," Max said.

"No leads?" I asked.

"Not one," said Stephen. He grinned. "But we got to operate those cool machines."

Rocket appeared behind Stephen, though I hadn't noticed him approaching us. He moved his head in a cryptic signal to Stephen, who nodded. Rocket dropped the cigarette in his hand and extinguished it with the sole of his boot, then picked up the filter and put it in his pocket. As far as I knew, the man didn't smoke. Rocket, I decided, might well be our biggest mystery of all.

A helmeted motorcyclist roared through the parking lot, bending low over the grips of his un-muffled engine. "My poor ears," I said, covering them with my hands. "First those machines, now that. I'll be deaf before the night is out if this continues."

Chapter 28

Large-mouthed plastic cereal containers make great spill-free trash
receptacles for road trips.

From the Notebook of Maggie McDonald
Simplicity Itself Organizing Services

Sunday, June 23, Afternoon

Stephen's black SUV pulled to a stop at the curb about half a block from
Mr. Mason's shop, although there appeared to be parking spaces closer to
the store. He waved our car over, pointing to a parking space behind his.

Max shrugged. "Parking down the road from a targeted business must
be some kind of stealthy special ops procedure."

Brian sighed. "Belle and I will stay in the car. Walking with
crutches is hard work."

I turned to look at him, fearing it might be past time for another pain pill.

Brian smiled. "Chill, Mom. I'm fine. I'll keep my phone camera on and
take pictures of anything that looks like it needs documenting, okay?"

"Leave the windows open so you and Belle don't get too hot." I grabbed
my backpack and was about to open the door when Stephen leaned on
the side of the car and bent to talk to us through my open window. "Why
don't you all stay here," he said. "We won't be a moment. Just need to
ask Mason if he worked on the propellers himself or farmed out the work
to someone else."

"And whether any of Mason's mechanics also work at the airport maintenance shed," Max added.

"I want to meet this Mr. Mason," I said. "I want to hear what he thinks happened and whether he can think of any reason someone might want Jake dead. Jen told me that he was like a second father to Jake." An unattractive wheedling tone entered my voice. I pulled myself together and restated my case firmly. "Step back, Stephen. I'm coming with you."

"I'm with Maggie," said Max. David joined us, as did Munchkin, who dogged Stephen's heels.

"What could possibly go wrong?" I asked Stephen. He rolled his eyes. None of us were displaying our best adult behavior today.

I nudged Max, and pointed to the motorcycle parked out front. It looked remarkably like the one that had burnt rubber peeling out of the airport parking lot. "Yamaha," Max whispered. "Common as dirt."

"Maybe so, but keep an eye out for anyone we've seen at the airport."

Mr. Mason's business was a five-bay garage with an adjacent machine shop. It smelled of oil and hot metal and echoed with the sound of hydraulic equipment and power grinders, but the floors gleamed and tools were stored in orderly racks and cheerful red steel boxes. Rocket led our little group through the door of the first bay and waved to get the attention of one of the mechanics.

"Mason?" he said loudly, although I doubted anyone could hear him over the shop noise. The mechanic pointed toward an office, where an older man rose from his chair and stepped toward the garage. The beginnings of a pot belly strained his belt and a touch of silver highlighted his temples.

I hung back by the garage bay door, watching. Though we all had heard wonderful things about Mr. Mason, I wasn't ready to trust him implicitly. He picked up a tire iron and slapped it into his palm as Stephen and Rocket approached him. My heart rate soared. I tried to convince myself it wasn't a menacing gesture, but I punched 9-1-1 into my phone and my finger hovered over the green call button.

Mr. Mason hit a switch, flicking the lights on and off several times in quick succession, and all the power tools ceased operation. The sudden silence was nearly as hard on my ears as the cacophony that preceded it.

"Mason?" repeated Rocket. The man lifted his chin.

Rocket introduced us all, and then stepped back and turned to Stephen. "He'll tell ya what we need to know," Rocket said. It was the longest sentence I'd ever heard him utter, but it came with the unspoken suggestion that there would be consequences should Mason attempt to withhold information.

I watched the mechanics step back from their work and crane their necks to see around the cars and tool boxes. "Take a break, guys," Mason said. "Ten. No more. Beacon's racer has to be ready by five o'clock."

One member of Mason's staff reached into his shirt pocket for a pack of cigarettes and stepped out through a door in the back of the third bay. The other men seemed reluctant to leave. One held a large wrench and stepped around the car he'd been working on, edging toward us with what looked like fake nonchalance. I glanced at my phone to reassure myself that I could summon help in an instant. Munchkin stayed close to Stephen's side and growled quietly under his breath, making the air around the big dog seem to vibrate.

Stephen cleared his throat and spoke in a soft but clear voice. "We'd like to talk to you about Jake Peterson. I understand he moonlighted here when he wasn't working at any of his other jobs. You machined his propellers." Stephen raised his voice slightly at the end the sentence, turning his statement into a question.

Mr. Mason glanced at the guy holding the wrench and shook his head. I took a half step backward. Something still felt off. In a bad way. Rocket must have sensed it too. He moved into the space between me and the shop owner, making the motion look natural, as though he was handing a note to Stephen. Max took hold of my arm.

"Jake?" Mr. Mason said. "Known him all my life. They don't make 'em any better than him. And that girl of his. Breaks my heart. Those two were the best kind of couple. Independent, but stronger together than they were apart."

"And you worked on his props?" Stephen asked.

"Absolutely. Did 'em myself. Most highly stressed component on any aircraft. Need to withstand tons of force, along with constant flexing and bending. A tiny ding can throw off an entire plane. I taught Jake to go over the rotors before every flight. He didn't trust anyone else to true them up and test them for him."

"So you don't think a propeller failure could have been the cause of Jake's crash?" Stephen sighed and rubbed his hand over his bald head as though pushing back hair he no longer had.

The mechanic with the wrench looked over his shoulder at the rest of the group and stepped closer to Mr. Mason.

"If someone swapped out one of mine with a cheap imitation, maybe," Mason said. "But not if Jake was using one of my props. And there was no way he'd use someone else's."

The mechanic banged his wrench on a pipe. The sound echoed through the shop, along with the sound of running feet, followed by a curse and the clang of metal hitting the ground on the far side of the garage.

Max stepped back and turned, still holding onto my arm and pulling me along with him. "Who's that?" he asked, pointing to another young man who stumbled over a fallen garbage can, started to run toward the motorcycle, and then windmilled his arms for balance as he pivoted and took off down the street. I'd scarcely registered what was happening when Rocket pushed through our group and took chase, gaining rapidly on the boy. Munchkin charged after him. Out of sight, a second crash and a flurry of curses suggested the escape was unsuccessful.

Stephen, with no show of haste, but moving quickly nonetheless, walked to the curb to look down the street. He waved Max and me forward and pointed. "That's some kid you've got," he said.

Brian, leaning on one crutch, pinned the mechanic to the ground while Rocket snapped on handcuffs.

Belle stuck close to Brian's side, but waved her tail enthusiastically, enjoying whatever game she thought her people were playing. Munchkin kept one paw firmly on the boy. The mastiff's endless supply of drool formed a wet spot on the captive's work shirt.

Rocket pulled the boy to his feet and steadied him when he stumbled. It was Zeke, the affable young man from the airport who had offered to help Jen. He held his head down with his shoulders drooped, and didn't speak. Stephen nodded toward me and the jacket pocket that held my phone. "Go ahead and alert the authorities. Now's the time."

I called 9-1-1 and asked the dispatcher to contact Sheriff Nate, who was familiar with the case. Within what seemed like seconds, we heard sirens approaching.

"I'd advise you to hire a good lawyer and keep your mouth shut," Stephen told Zeke. "You're in a lot of trouble."

"I'll tell you anything you want if you keep that dog from eating me," Zeke said, glaring defiantly at Munchkin.

Munchkin and Belle moved closer to Zeke. Their normally active tails remained still.

"It wasn't me," Zeke said. "No way. Rivers wanted him gone. He was working with Ochoa."

"Mom?" Brian pointed the end of his crutch toward a battered black backpack. I moved carefully around our cluster of crime fighters and picked it up, eager to rummage through it before law enforcement arrived and took charge of the evidence. I didn't know what laws might protect

Zeke's belongings from an official search by law enforcement. Luckily, I was a civilian unbound by those statutes. Reaching into the small zippered pocket in the front, I pulled out a plastic zip-lock snack bag and held it up so everyone could see. Inside were a handful of thumb-nail sized plastic memory cards.

"Gotcha," Brian said.

Stephen patted him on the back. "You might want to clear out of here before the police arrive and confuse you with the bad guys."

We piled into the car quickly, and Max pulled away from the curb just before two police cruisers and a sheriff's SUV passed us with lights and sirens. Brian and I peered out the back window as Max drove, pushing Belle to the side so we could see. But anything interesting took place behind the parked cars, out of sight.

I sighed and turned to face forward. "That was more excitement than I needed in one afternoon," I told Max. "But where does it leave us? Does that get Brian and David off the hook? And how does Rivers come into it? I was ready to believe his desire to shut down Jake's operation was a red herring distracting us from the drug operation Ochoa was running out of Diego Baker's barn. Are there two separate criminal activities going on? Are we smack dab in the middle of a gang war?"

Max clenched his teeth and drove.

"Stephen will fill us in later, right?" asked David. "He'll tell us everything. Answer all our questions. Mom? He will, won't he?"

"We'll have to see. I don't know how much the sheriff will tell him nor how much Stephen will be able to pass along to us."

Brian groaned. "We'll see," he repeated. "Do parents know how annoying those words are?"

"We're going to need more evidence against these other suspects if we're going to get the sheriff and the Petersons off our backs." David glanced at the time and date on his phone. "We meet with the district attorney in less than forty-eight hours."

It was my turn to groan. So far, every time I'd thought there was a glimmer at the end of the tunnel, someone unseen had turned off the lights.

I texted Nell on our drive back to the condo, asking if she'd have time to talk strategy prior to our session with the DA. I hoped she'd find a way to use Zeke and the memory cards to get David and Brian off the hook.

Chapter 29

Use bath towels in the car to mop up spills, cradle a sleepy head, or for temperature control. A dark-colored towel on the dashboard can be a great help in managing glare.

From the Notebook of Maggie McDonald
Simplicity Itself Organizing Services

Sunday, June 23, Afternoon

Renée phoned me soon after we got home. "Mind if I come over? Diego has some information I think you could use, but he's not sure he wants to get the police involved."

"Intriguing," I said. After getting off the phone, I put coffee on. Then I sank to a bar stool and leaned my arms on the granite counter. I ached for the comfort of a lined yellow pad and pencil to help organize my thoughts and outline my plans. Max read my mind and handed me a pad along with two pens and a yellow highlighter.

Nell knocked and entered through our unlocked front door, and I figured that at the rate we were going we might as well discard the resort-standard solid wood door and replace it with a revolving unit. So many people were coming and going in our lives that I longed for a quiet, disaster-free weekend with my husband, boys, and devoted dog.

Nell sat next to me at the counter and accepted a cup of coffee from Max, who was pulling an odd assortment of ingredients from the cupboards and fridge. Chocolate chips and carrots? Butter and Jarlsberg cheese? When cookie sheets and a crock pot joined the seemingly random assortment, I relaxed. Cookies and soup were in our future. Max was a man who needed to keep busy. Peeling carrots helped him organize his thoughts in the same way my lined yellow pads aided me.

"What's up?" Nell asked, taking a grateful sip from the steaming mug of coffee. "How can you look so discouraged when you've got coffee like this at your fingertips, and hunky kitchen help like Max here?"

Max grinned, but didn't speak and got on with his work, starting with creaming the butter and sugar for the cookies.

I sat up straighter to avoid the appearance that I was moping. "Our trouble has so many moving parts it's easy to lose track. I'm overwhelmed by the tangled thread of possible explanations for what's going on in this sleepy little resort community. Part of the problem is that there aren't any complete threads. Just as one idea begins to look promising, we follow it to a broken, raveled end, unable to find a connecting piece that explains all and saves Brian and David from interrogation by the district attorney."

"Managing any interviews with law enforcement is my job," Nell reminded me. "And no one is going to badger your boys when I'm around." She glanced at my yellow pad. "If you're making a list, cross that job off of it and fill me in on what happened today. I got an upbeat text from Stephen followed by your dreary one. Something must have gone wrong. Spill."

Nell pulled out her computer and plugged it in, fingers poised over the keyboard. No yellow pads for her. Nell was a card-carrying millennial—or would have been if millennials carried cards.

I'd just finished filling her in on our adventures, including the thrilling capture of Zeke and the memory cards when Renée knocked and entered, followed by Diego. We moved from the counter to the table where there was more room.

The sound of video games came from David's room. "Brian could use a rest," Max said. "I'll tell David to keep it down."

He came back a moment later. "Brian's zonked out on the floor with one hand on the game controller and the other around Belle. David put a pillow under the leg to raise it up a bit, and Brian didn't flinch." Max shook his head. "Healing takes a ton of energy."

Stephen returned and joined us at the table. While we waited for him to speak, a shadow darkened the front window and I heard the door to the apartment next door open and shut. Rocket was back, too.

I looked around the table at my friends, new and old. "This is the problem I was telling Nell about," I said. "Not knowing where to start."

"My news can wait," Stephen said, though I wasn't sure I agreed with him. Diego cleared his throat. "I'll go first," he said. "I'm not sure what to do with my information, or whether it amounts to anything at all. I'd feel silly taking my ideas to the sheriff, but I will if you think it amounts to something."

I leaned forward, and Stephen nodded. Diego took a deep breath and jumped in. "You all know that Kevin Rivers and I are butting heads over our farms. He's gone organic and thinks that I'm poisoning his crops. I'm not, but I think I know what he's getting at."

Diego stopped and swallowed hard. "We both use helpful insects like ladybugs, bees, and lacewings to control aphids and mites that damage the berries. Anything I can do to limit how much pesticide I use saves me money. We used to control costs by chipping in to hire a crop duster that could spray pesticides over both our fields at once. Rivers went organic, and that was the end of that. My costs have gone up, but so have my pest problems."

"You didn't want to go organic when Rivers did?" I doodled on my pad.

Diego bit his lip and rubbed his hands together. "It wasn't a matter of what I wanted. It was a matter of what I could afford. The process of shifting to organic production takes years—years in which your yields go down, but you still have to sell your crop at non-organic prices. I couldn't swing it."

I made a note to check on possible grants to help Diego.

"So what happened?" Stephen asked.

"Nothing much, at first, but we got into a disagreement over who owns that barn and the land it sits on. It's gotten ugly. My deed says the barn belongs to me, but Rivers brought out a surveyor who says it's built on his farm. It's got a dirt floor, so Rivers asked me not to store pesticides in there in case they leach into his soil. I agreed, but I forgot to alert my supplier. He delivered my chemicals to the barn the same way he always had."

"What happened?" Max placed a plate of warm cookies on the table. The fragrance lured David from his room, and we had a moment of silent appreciation of the stress-busting properties of chocolate and refined carbohydrates.

"I moved the canisters, of course," Diego said. "But all hell broke loose. The sheriff came out. Rivers was shouting, glaring at me whenever I went near the barn. And then my pest problems began. Especially in the portion of the field closest to Rivers."

"You think his organic fields were infested, and the bugs were creeping over onto your land?" Stephen asked.

"That's just it. I checked. One night I snuck out and took samples from his field. He had a bit of an insect problem, but it was nothing like mine."

"But how do bugs know where the property line is?" I asked.

"They don't. So you'd expect to find a similar population of pests on either side of the line. But I didn't."

"Hypothesis?" asked Max, prepping another tray of cookies for the oven.

"I think Rivers was seeding my field with bugs." Diego grimaced. "That hurt, you know. We've been friends since grade school, growing up on our dad's neighboring farms. We've had problems before, but have always been able to work things out. But in the last year, it's been like the tiniest thing gets blown all out of proportion."

"Like?" Max asked.

"Like outside the grocery store last week. I'd just parked my car when Rivers was coming out with his cart. He lifted a paper sack and the bottom fell out. A jar of spaghetti sauce broke along with a milk jug, and I jumped out of the way. Rivers glared at me like it was all my fault. I offered to help, and he yelled at me to keep away."

"Has he always had an anger problem?" Stephen asked. "Could be stress or a drug issue."

"Like I said, he's been my best friend since childhood. Makes me feel like he's possessed by a demon."

"Maybe he is." Stephen tapped a pencil on the table top. "Maybe he is."

"Anyway," Diego said. "When Rivers says I've been poisoning his crop, he may have something. I *have* been putting down more pesticide on those infected rows, trying to keep the infestation from spreading."

"Anything else?" Stephen asked.

Diego shook his head. "Like I said, I don't know what it all amounts to. I'm not doing anything to hurt Kevin's operation. And I don't want the sheriff to have any more evidence against me than he already has about that drug operation. I mean, it's mostly true to say that I allowed myself to be taken advantage of by those crooks, but I did have my suspicions."

"It's possible that Kevin Rivers also had a part in the drug smuggling." Stephen bounced the eraser end of his pencil on the table. "The gang could have taken advantage of the rift between you, hoping it would keep you from comparing notes with one another."

"Are crooks that subtle?" I asked.

"I'm not sure. But I've got other news I'll spill in exchange for that last cookie." Stephen raised his eyebrows and glanced at the plate.

"Take it," Max said. "I've got a fresh dozen coming out in thirty seconds."

Stephen pulled a piece of paper from the inside chest pocket of his jacket and unfolded it. He pulled his reading glasses from another pocket and put them on, looking more like a beloved prep-school history teacher than a retired marine. "I got the report back on that plastic packet you gave me, Maggie."

I scooted my chair forward.

"It's kapok," Stephen said.

"Kapok? Like in old life jackets?"

"Exactly."

I frowned. "I was so sure that dreadful condo was connected to all this drug running in some way. I felt better blaming bad guys for the mess than I did fearing that some sweet old lady's life got beyond her control."

"Not so fast," said Stephen. "Don't rule out the bad guys just yet. There were traces of heroin in the kapok package you gave me. The composition of the drug was similar to what we found in the barn."

Renée gasped and her face blanched. She covered her mouth with her hand. "Mrs. Nesbitt was a drug kingpin?"

Stephen adjusted his glasses and consulted the report. "The lab tech who worked on this made a few calls. It's true that there is a small market for recycled kapok, but they usually use clean remnants from manufacturing operations rather than trying to recover the material from old lifejackets. I suspect that Mrs. Nesbitt was taken advantage of by the drug runners, just as you were, Diego."

Diego, who'd chosen that moment to reach for a new cookie, pulled his hand back and looked sheepishly into his coffee mug.

"What are you thinking, Stephen?" I asked. "How was Mrs. Nesbitt involved, and why?"

"I think it's like the strawberries," he said.

My forehead wrinkled. "How, exactly, are strawberries like moldy old kapok?

"Camouflage," Stephen said. "Someone from the gang came twice a month to bring supplies to Mrs. Nesbit and take away packages of kapok. They concealed their heroin in shipments of the fluffy batting to fool anyone who stopped them and tried to look through the crates."

"But if everything was covered with plastic, how did the heroin get mixed into the kapok?" I asked.

"It was only a trace amount. Likely, the gang members handling Mrs. Nesbitt's groceries and kapok supplies were also handling the heroin shipments. Microscopic bits of the drug were transferred from the illegal packets to the innocent ones—enough to be detectable by modern lab instruments."

"But Mrs. Nesbitt was so proud of her conservation efforts," Renée said. "I hope she never finds out that none of her kapok went into making those berms to soak up oil from spills."

"It's possible that some of her recovered material went into those berms," Stephen said. "The lab guy I talked to couldn't rule it out. Any lie or effort to conceal an illegal activity works best when most of the lie is true. Like when all of Diego's strawberries went on to be processed and distributed normally after the heroin was delivered."

Diego's tense shoulders relaxed. "For Mrs. Nesbitt's sake, let's assume they used every ounce of kapok she collected."

Renée raised her coffee mug. "From your lips to God's ears," she said. "She'll never hear otherwise from me."

Everyone else at the table lifted their mugs, except David who lifted his half-eaten cookie. Belle and Munchkin thumped their tails.

Max, his eyes streaming, scraped chopped onions into a sizzling sauté pan and turned on the overhead fan. "Was there any connection between Zeke and Mrs. Nesbitt? I've lost track of who connects to which crimes."

I leaned forward to speak, but Renée beat me to it. "Her grandson. He's the boy I thought was being so helpful, bringing her groceries and taking out her garbage."

"He must also be the guy I saw with his pickup truck. He looked a little squirrelly at the time, but I just assumed he was cleaning out Mrs. Nesbitt's condo." I fiddled with my coffee cup. "At the time, I thought maybe he was a moonlighting employee of yours, Renée, doing some after-hours maintenance."

She laughed. "I wish. The association rules say we can only handle emergency repairs on weekends and the evenings. This place is primarily a resort, and no one wants to listen to hammers and drills on vacation."

"So, back to tomorrow's meeting," I said. "Does the fact that Zeke and the gang were up to no good prove that David and Brian are innocent?"

Nell looked up from her keyboard on which her fingers had continued to click throughout the conversation. "At the very least it will buy us some time as they investigate further. There's no way a judge will arraign your kids when there's so much evidence pointing to others. Means, motive, and opportunity are old-fashioned criteria in the modern world of DNA evidence. They're not relied upon nearly as often in real life as they are in television investigations, but the only time your boys came in contact with Jake is when they were trying to save him. And they did save him. Long enough and well enough that the doctors at the hospital whisked him into the operating room and continued working on him."

"You're saying that if we'd wanted Jake dead, we would have killed him at the scene?" David asked.

"Absolutely," Nell said. "Why wait and hope he died from his injuries later? And if you'd been as inept as Mrs. Peterson accused you of being, you would have hastened Jake's demise, rather than forestalling it. I had investigators talk to the first responders and the medical team. Every single person they interviewed praised the work you boys did. Not one of them saw any sign that you hurt Jake while trying to save him."

David leaned back in his chair. I grinned at him, bursting with pride. "Should I wake up Brian and tell him?" he asked.

I nodded. "Good news shouldn't wait. Even if he goes right back to sleep, he'll rest so much better without the Petersons' accusations hanging over him."

David disappeared down the hallway, and we heard mumbling followed by a loud whoop and the slap of the boys high-fiving one another. Max and I stepped into the hall and the open doorway. "Proud of you both," Max said. "Hey Bri, do you think a chocolate chip cookie, warm from the oven, is enough to celebrate this news?"

Brian scrambled to grab his crutches and join us in the dining room.

* * * *

Stephen, Diego, Renée, and Nell were deep in a conversation when we bubbled back into the kitchen, high on the news that the boys had been exonerated. I eavesdropped as I nibbled on what I promised myself was my last cookie.

"Tonight?" Diego asked.

Stephen nodded. "Yes, so keep all your guys far away from the barn. Make it a poker night. Treat them to the movies. Make sure you all have alibis. This operation could go south in a hurry. It isn't anything you want to get anywhere near."

"What's going down?" asked David, sounding like a character in a caper movie.

Stephen glanced at me and then at Max, who nodded. With that approval, Stephen continued. "The sheriff has set up a joint sting operation with federal drug enforcement officers. They're staking out the beach, the trail, and the barn tonight, hoping to seize more of the contraband."

"Surely they're not stupid enough to bring more drugs in now," I said. "Not when they've already been detected."

Stephen shrugged. "My thinking was the same as yours, but the DEA guys think it's worth a try. Apparently the demand for heroin is sky high here on the coast, and stepped up enforcement efforts on the border mean the supply is limited. The cartel will make a fortune on whatever they can bring in right now and greed trumps all. They've got quite the high-tech set up with night vision and heat detection equipment. The DEA guys are going to have to work hard to remain undiscovered until they're ready to nab the bad guys."

"Can we watch?" asked the boys.

Part of me wanted to echo their eager request to watch the sting unfold, but the mother in me answered quickly. "Absolutely not."

But Renée jumped in. "I've got an idea," she said.

Chapter 30

The most useful skill for families or individuals to nurture while traveling is remaining flexible and well-rested. Keep your sense of humor, expect the unexpected, and don't be afraid to change your plans.

From the Notebook of Maggie McDonald
Simplicity Itself Organizing Services

Sunday, June 23, Late afternoon and evening

Renée had keys to the gate barring vehicle access to an old fire road now used mostly by hikers. It zigzagged up a steep hill behind the Heron Beach condo complex. When we checked it out before hand, it seemed like a perfect spot from which to spy on the sting. At the top, an old water storage tank would hide our car from anyone glancing our way from the beach or strawberry fields to the northeast. From our vantage point in front of the water tank we had a great view of the curving shoreline from Santa Cruz to Monterey and of the patchwork fields of the Pajaro Valley, including Diego's strawberry field where it adjoined the property belonging to Kevin Rivers.

We'd be close enough to observe as the DEA sting unfolded, but far enough to be out of harm's way. In theory, least.

Close to the time we'd normally have been wrapping things up and getting ready for bed, we drove up the hill with the car lights off, navigating by the light of the moon and an incredible array of stars that never appeared so clearly in Silicon Valley. The sound of the waves and the peace of the heavens could easily have lulled us into forgetting the law enforcement agents who might well be putting their lives on the line as the evening unfolded. Max, an amateur astronomer, guided us through the constellations.

"That's Corona Borealis," he told us, pointing upwards. "Representing the crown of Ariadne who helped Theseus defeat the Minotaur."

"*Shh,*" whispered Brian. "Look."

Lights flashed on the bay out near the horizon. A spotlight blinked a response from the field. I held my breath as a spotlight swept the beach. One false move on the part of the person wielding the light, and we'd all be illuminated. We crouched down, silent.

Almost immediately, a small kayak beached on the sand. The paddler hopped out and tugged a tow line to pull the craft beyond the waves' reach. Headlights from four ranger trucks snapped on, along with sirens and flashing lights. Silhouetted, the kayaker looked toward his craft and behind him, and then put up his hands.

Our heads swiveled as DEA headlights lit up the fields above the beach. Task force members in clumsy black tactical gear converged on the barn. Helicopter rotors forced us to cover our heads and narrow our eyes against the flying sand and dust. The helicopter's searchlight created monster shadows, heightening the drama.

"I feel like I've landed in an action movie," Max whispered, although there was no longer any need for silence amid the cacophony of sirens, loudspeakers, and, of course, the helicopter. If there were gunshots, we didn't hear them.

Within minutes, it was over, at least for tonight. The helicopter left, taking several hand-cuffed prisoners with it. Teams of officers remained behind to preserve the scene and secure evidence.

"Is that it?" Brian asked.

I stood, brushing sand from my eyes and jeans, taking stock. I counted several times to make sure everyone was safe, and began handing out water bottles.

"Now's when the real work begins," said Nell. "Interrogators get the bad guys to flip on their bosses so they can shut down the supply lines."

"But what happened?" asked David, after swishing his mouth with water. "Did they catch the right people? Did anyone admit to killing Jake?"

Max clapped him on the shoulder. "You're right. We saw it all play out, but we're going to need someone closer to the scene to explain it all. It may take weeks. Or months."

I looked around our dusty group. Eyes red from dust and lack of sleep stared back, reflecting the disappointment I felt. "The chopper swooped in. The bad guys are in hand cuffs. If this actually were a movie, we'd cut to the law enforcement dudes reading everyone their rights. Then the summation and the credits."

I caught Stephen's eye. He smiled and looked sheepish. "We aren't the only ones who feel let down in a moment like this one," he said. "I guarantee you those DEA agents wish real-life legal battles played out as quickly as they do in fantasy."

* * * *

Despite Max's prediction of a frustrating delay, the sheriff called Stephen the following afternoon. Stephen filled us in. "None of this information is for public consumption," he warned us. "The sheriff was uncharacteristically forthcoming, but if any of us spill these details, their whole case could fall apart." He waited a few moments. Apparently satisfied that we all understood the need for secrecy, he summed up the news.

According to the sheriff's report, a large number of low-level gang members were in custody. Many of them were eager to provide evidence against the cartels in exchange for lenient charges and suspended sentences.

Zeke had admitted to tampering with Jake's propeller, but insisted his intent was to ground Jake's aircraft, not kill him. He'd been motivated by the fact that the more time Jake spent at Mr. Mason's garage, the more time he spent in Zeke's company. And where Jake went, Jen went. Zeke had fallen hopelessly in love with Jen. The two had talked while Jake and Mr. Mason conferred over the refurbished propellers.

Zeke said he stole the memory cards from Jake at the behest of Kevin Rivers, who'd wanted to cripple Jake's research project and stop his intrusive flyovers. The farmer also sought evidence that might prove his neighbor was contaminating his organic operation with nonorganic pesticides.

Jake's photographs, along with extensive soil and crop samples, would help exonerate Diego Baker from accusations of crop tampering, but many of the images, along with their time, date, and location stamps, also were expected to provide critical information to the team prosecuting members of the local gang and the cartel.

As Stephen had suspected, Kevin's anger-management problem was rooted in a drug habit. Kevin had accepted heroin in payment for his role in hiding gang operations on his land.

* * * *

Three months later, the first trials began. Kevin pleaded guilty. His testimony, coupled with a court-ordered stint in rehab, earned him probation and a suspended sentence, providing he stayed out of trouble for five years. Kevin and Diego mended fences. During Kevin's stay in rehab, Diego would farm his fields. Diego, with help from both Kevin and a grant from the US Department of Agriculture, would be converting his fields to an organic operation.

After all the major players in the drug scheme were behind bars, Stephen met with some of the youths who'd inherited leadership positions in the decimated local gang. Stephen introduced the new leaders to a non-profit operation in Los Angeles which worked to fund alternative opportunities for gang members. Local leaders gave slim odds on the likelihood of the gang pursuing a legitimate and sustainable business model, but Stephen had won over the sheriff with his evidence of the New York City gang members who now operated a thriving venture in the design, manufacture, and sale of edgy street fashion.

The rest of the summer played out much more as we'd originally expected. I spent my mornings working in the office with Renée, and my afternoons with the kids.

Brian's leg healed quickly and his cast was removed after eight weeks. Swimming and walking in sand provided a challenging but effective physical therapy routine.

The Petersons apologized for their accusations against the boys and sent them flowers, which they appreciated less than the certificates for surf lessons enclosed in a thank-you note. In a few lines, the couple praised the boys for helping Jake, saying it comforted them to know their son wasn't alone during what must have been the most fearsome moments of his life.

The sheriff later told us Mrs. Peterson had admitted to sending the text I'd received threatening the boys. We chalked her odd and alarming behavior up to extreme grief and didn't press charges.

Jake's parents patched up their relationship with Jen, though she decided to accept the graduate school position she'd been offered at UCLA. "I'll never forget Jake," she told us over lunch at the Giant Artichoke. "But I need to grieve privately. Here in town everyone cares. They all watch me, fearing I'll fall apart. At UCLA, I can tell people about Jake or keep him to myself. It will be my choice and that's comforting."

"Whatever works for you is the right thing to do," I told her, wishing her luck with her studies and reminding her to stay in touch.

Renée hired a hazardous materials company to clean Mrs. Nesbitt's condo, but footed the bill herself rather than burden the old lady with the cost or responsibility for her neglected home.

"That gang was operating right under my nose," Renée said. "I allowed them to take advantage of Mrs. Nesbitt. Paying for renovations is the least I can do."

Renée's life had changed the most in the short time we'd been at Heron Beach. She'd rekindled an old romance with Diego, who loved the three children Renée was caring for. When my new friend finally had time to tell me the whole story, it broke my heart. It also made me realize how lucky the kids were to grow up in the close-knit neighborhood that Renée called home.

We were creating a new filing system when she finally told the story, applying bold stickers to brightly colored folders in open shelving. Renée and anyone who worked for her would be able to tell at a glance if a file was out of place. Maybe because the work was repetitive and soothing, or possibly because we'd become close friends, Renée opened up, telling me that her new foster children were American citizens, born in the United States to legal residents who'd let their green cards expire when money grew tight.

Federal Immigration and Customs Enforcement officers had detained the children's father when he was taking them to day care before starting work at a local firm as an engineer. He'd failed to update the company when his legal status changed.

After separating the children from their father, ICE had called the mother and arranged to drop off the three kids, but when they came to the house, they detained and eventually deported her.

Alerted by the commotion, neighbors had stepped in, backed up by the local police. At that point in the story, Renée burst into tears and left for the day. Later in the week, she was able to complete the narrative. When she was finally able to reach the children's mother, who was staying with family in Mexico, Renée learned her former neighbor had been diagnosed with metastatic breast cancer with a poor prognosis. The children's father was lost in federal bureaucracy, and despite attempts by various local agencies and non-profits, no one knew where he was nor when he might be returned to Mexico or released.

The mother begged Renée to adopt the children. Renée agreed, encouraged by Diego. Nell was facilitating the paperwork on a pro bono basis. As soon as the adoption was final, Renée planned to get passports for all of them. Diego and Renée hoped to take the twins and the baby to Mexico to visit their mother after the last strawberries were harvested, and again at Christmas time. I hoped the cancer would hold off at least until they could all say good bye.

By the time I had all the details, we'd finished the filing and killed a boatload of tissues.

As the drama played out behind the scenes, Brian and David still had time to entertain their friends for summer weekends filled with teenaged chatter, beach bonfires, and body surfing. Max joined us as often as he could between projects that required his immediate attention.

Renée and I prepared proposals for her board of directors and secured funding to rebuild the offices with modern amenities for the benefit of resort staff and guests. We'd found a company to install portable buildings out of which Renée's team would operate while their new facility was built. Their temporary digs had a footprint similar to the more permanent design.

I worked with a local contractor to design custom storage Renée could use in the portables, but that would slot right into the permanent offices as soon as they were finished.

The NTSB's preliminary report came out on Jake's crash, ruling it an accident caused by a faulty propeller. Though we all believed Zeke had tampered with it deliberately, the nation's best labs and scientists couldn't come up with enough proof to charge the mechanic with a crime. It was impossible, given current technology, to prove that Zeke intended to kill Jake, or even to connect the damage he'd inflicted with the cause of the crash. According to experts consulted by Nell and Forrest, a good defense lawyer would argue that Zeke knew nothing about aviation or aeronautics, despite his apprenticeship in the maintenance shed at the airport.

Given Jake's history of frequent propeller damage and repairs, it was impossible to say whether some other problem had hobbled the propeller and caused the crash. Zeke moved out of state to avoid censure from the local community.

Ranger Charlie Adams was promoted to a position in the northernmost part of the state. Before he left, he successfully lobbied for the funding his team needed to prevent a recurrence of the light staffing that had allowed the smuggling operation to thrive. No longer would bad guys be able to tie up his staff with false alarms or fake fires that kept all his personnel off the beach and allowed them to pursue illegal activities unmonitored.

While Renée got most of the budget increases she'd requested, the board held off on approving her personnel requests. In the meantime, we'd created a plan to contract out much of the work until she compiled statistics proving it could be done more efficiently with onsite staff.

As for us, Brian's physical therapy efforts made it possible for him to keep his position as trumpet section leader in the marching band, though he gave up his place on the cross-country team. David would juggle both activities, along with a heavy load of advanced placement classes as he began his college search and application process.

Throughout the summer, we reveled in the wonders of the Monterey Bay Marine Sanctuary, entertained by the sea otters, harbor porpoises, whales, seals, and sea lions we could spy on while sipping breakfast coffee. We bought strawberries and organic vegetables at the farmer's market in town on Friday evenings, knowing they'd been picked only hours earlier.

Max and I supported each other as our boys matured faster than we could keep pace. We did our best and tried to take our lives one day at a time, without fearing the rapid approach of our empty-nest years.

Whatever the future had in store for us as a couple or as a family, we promised to march into it together, accompanied by our beloved Belle, our cats Watson and Holmes, and our friends in both Orchard View and Heron Beach.

Maggie's Homemade Anti-Skunk Shampoo

1 quart of 3% Hydrogen peroxide
1/2 cup of baking soda
1 teaspoon of liquid soap

Combine ingredients to make a shampoo. Large dogs may require a triple batch. Rub vigorously. Repeat as necessary.
Rinse well.

Note: Hydrogen peroxide is often thought of as a bleaching agent. Online instructions for lightening hair recommend applying a peroxide and soda mixture and letting it sit for more than an hour. Shampooing Belle's fur with this mixture, I left it on for a moment or two, and could detect no change in the color after I'd rinsed it out well.

Sneak Peek

If you enjoyed *Cliff Hanger*, be sure not to miss Mary Feliz's

Professional organizer Maggie McDonald manages to balance a fastidious career with friends, family, and a spunky Golden Retriever. But add a fiery murder mystery to the mix, and Maggie wonders if she's finally found a mess even she can't tidy up . . .

With a devastating wildfire spreading to Silicon Valley, Maggie preps her family for a rapid evacuation. The heat rises when firefighters discover the body of her best friend Tess Olmos's athletic husband—whose untimely death was anything but accidental. And as Tess agonizes over the whereabouts of her spouse's drop-dead gorgeous running mate, she becomes the prime suspect in what's shaping up to become a double murder case. Determined to set the record straight, Maggie sorts through clues in an investigation more dangerous than the flames approaching her home. But when her own loved ones are threatened, can she catch the meticulous killer before everything falls apart?

**Keep reading for a special look!
A Lyrical Underground e-book on sale now.**

Chapter 1

A crisis is a terrible time to develop an emergency plan. Be prepared.

From the Notebook of Maggie McDonald
Simplicity Itself Organizing Services

Sunday, August 6, 8:00 a.m.

I told the kids it was a drill. I told myself it was a drill. But I wasn't fooling anyone, especially not the cats.

Late summer in California is fire season, and the potential consequences had never been more apparent, nor closer to home. Air gray and thick with smoke and unburned particulates was so dry it hurt to breathe. My compulsive refreshing of the Cal Fire website throughout the night revealed that the cause was an illegal campfire abandoned on the coastal side of the Santa Cruz Mountains. Thirty-six hours later, it now encompassed miles of state- and county-owned hiking areas and threatened to jump the ridge and barrel down on the South Bay, Orchard View, and our family home.

This morning, a dry wind originating in the Central Valley had driven the firestorm back across land it had already transformed to charred desert. Firefighters hoped it would burn itself out due to lack of fuel, but I knew anything could happen at any time, and I needed my family to be ready.

Like everyone else in flammable California, we work year-round to keep vegetation from growing too close to our house. Wide stone and concrete verandas surround our hundred-year-old Craftsman house on three sides, while our paved driveway and parking area protect the east-facing walls. A plowed firebreak separates our barn and field from the summer-dry creek that borders our land.

"Do you want these in the car, Mom?" Brian, now thirteen, would one day tower over me. For now, I pretended that perfecting my posture and straightening my spine would maximize my five-foot six-inches and preserve my position as the taller one. Brian held an empty cat carrier in each hand.

"Leave them here in the kitchen for now. Leave the crate doors open."

"David," I called to my fifteen-year-old, who was now unquestionably the tallest in the family. To the chagrin of my husband, Max, David had recently gained the few inches he required to realize that Max's luxuriant walnut-colored curls were thinning. "Make sure to leave room on the back seat for the animals and two passengers."

"Two?" David entered the kitchen from the top of the basement stairs.

"Ideally, we'll take both cars. But I want to be prepared for anything." I tilted my head toward the view outside the kitchen windows. A plume of smoke filled the sky on the far side of the ridge to the west. "If that blaze shifts direction and marches this way, we'll need to clear out fast, no matter what. If one of the cars breaks down, I want us all to be able to jump into the other one."

"We could strap Brian to the roof." David's eyes twinkled as he nudged his younger brother.

I rolled my eyes, but a smile escaped when I saw that both of my thrill-seeking boys were intrigued by the idea. I turned my attention back to packing up snacks, water, and our perishable food. Our initial plan, should we be forced to evacuate, was to camp out in the living room of my dearest friend, Tess Olmos, whose son, Teddy, was fourteen and a buddy of both Brian and David.

Tess's house was a great Plan A, but I'm a belt-and-suspenders kind of gal and I needed a backup strategy. We packed as though we might resort to Plan B and end up in a shelter for a day or two. As a professional organizer, it's part of my job to help people anticipate emergencies. It's my superpower and my business. I sighed and pushed my wavy light-brown hair back from my forehead. Using my skills to streamline the lives of friends and strangers was a snap compared to getting my own family in line.

I heard a scuffle on the kitchen tiles, looked up, and burst out laughing. All three of our animals, Belle, our boisterous golden retriever, and Holmes and Watson, our marmalade-colored cats, assisted Max as he loaded their food, travel dishes, water, and kitty litter into a plastic bin. Watson's head was buried in a bag of cat kibble, while Belle nudged Max's arm with her snout. She knocked Max's steady hands out of alignment as he poured dog chow from a ten-pound bag into a one-gallon screw-top container. Dried nuggets skittered across the floor. Belle scrambled to help by gobbling up each morsel as quickly as possible. Holmes, Watson's more reserved brother, batted at a tidbit that had bounced to a stop at his feet.

"When you're done with that, hon, can you help the boys gather up the electronics? It's too soon to put them in the cars, but I'd like them all down here charging up and ready to go."

"Yes, ma'am," Max said, saluting without looking up from his task.

"Too many orders? Too bossy?" Under stress, I tended to bark out instructions without thinking about how they might be received by the folks around me—even the people I loved the most.

My phone rang, saving Max from responding. I pulled it from my pocket and glanced at the screen as I answered. "Hey, Tess," I said. "We're nearly there. Did Patrick show up?"

The day before, Tess had told me that Patrick hadn't responded to her phone calls. She'd wanted to let him know we might be camping out at their house for a few days to get out of the path of the potential firestorm. She'd speculated that he'd gone on an extended run or become caught up in a project at work. A devoted engineer, he often vanished into the thicket of a thorny technical problem and lost track of time, especially on weekends. But Patrick had been out of touch longer than usual, and I knew Tess was worried.

"That's just it." Tess's voice caught, and I could hear her take a deep breath.

"What's wrong? What's happened? Do you want us to make alternative plans? If it's not convenient—"

"No. No. No. It's not that. It's..."

"It's what? You're scaring me. Spill."

"It's Patrick. The police think they've found him."

"The police?" The words I was using and the strained tone of my voice must have worried Max. He looked up and furrowed his brow.

"Does she need help?" he asked. "Take off if you need to. The boys and I can finish up and meet you in half an hour."

I flapped my hand at Max, urging him to stop talking so I could hear Tess, who was, uncharacteristically, having trouble completing a sentence. She sighed.

"Oh, Maggie. The sheriff's office just called. Around dawn this morning, they found a man up off the old Pacific Gas and Electric maintenance road. It looks like he fell. Patrick runs there all the time. They...they think it's Patrick."

"Is he hurt? Where is he now? Do you need a ride to the hospital? Is he conscious? Why don't they just ask him who he is?"

"He's dead." Tess's voice broke with a sob. "I mean, the guy they found is dead. It's not Patrick, but they think it's him."

I couldn't think of a thing to say, and Tess didn't give me time.

"Can you get down here, Maggie? Can Max and the boys stay with Teddy? They want me to identify the body, and..." Tess coughed and soldiered on. "I mean, they want me to confirm that it's not my Patrick so they can figure out who he really is, poor guy." Tess struggled to get her voice, tears, and breathing under control. In her grief, she sounded as if she'd just finished a marathon. Breathless and exhausted.

"Of course. Whatever you need. We'll be right—"

Tess didn't let me finish. "I don't think I can drive safely, Maggie. It's in Santa Clara. The medical examiner's office." She sniffed. "This is so stupid. I keep bursting into tears. But it's ridiculous. Of course it's not Patrick. He's at work. Only he's not answering his phone. The battery is dead, I'm sure. You know how he is."

I did know Patrick. Keeping his phone charged wasn't high on his priority list. But my skin rippled with goose bumps and I shivered. Whatever we discovered at the medical examiner's office, I suspected the lives of Tess and her son, Teddy, would never be the same again.

Meet the Author

Photo Credit: Kathleen Dylan

Mary Feliz writes the Maggie McDonald Mysteries featuring a Silicon Valley professional organizer and her sidekick golden retriever. She's worked for Fortune 500 firms and mom and pop enterprises, competed in whale boat races and done synchronized swimming. She attends organizing conferences in her character's stead, but Maggie's skills leave her in the dust.

A certified California Naturalist, Mary lives near the Monterey Bay National Marine Sanctuary and enjoys sharing her enthusiasm for the area's rich natural diversity.

Visit Mary online at MaryFeliz.com, or follow her on Twitter @ MaryFelizAuthor.

Address to Die For

For professional organizer Maggie McDonald, moving her family into a new home should be the perfect organizational challenge. But murder was definitely not on the to-do list . . .

Maggie McDonald has a penchant for order that isn't confined to her clients' closets, kitchens, and sock drawers. As she lays out her plan to transfer her family to the hundred-year-old house her husband, Max, has inherited in the hills above Silicon Valley, she has every expectation for their new life to fall neatly into place. But as the family bounces up the driveway of their new home, she's shocked to discover the house's dilapidated condition. When her husband finds the caretaker face-down in their new basement, it's the detectives who end up moving in. What a mess! While the investigation unravels and the family camps out in a barn, a killer remains at large—exactly the sort of loose end Maggie can't help but clean up . . .

Scheduled to Death

Professional organizer Maggie McDonald has a knack for cleaning up other people's messes. So when the fiancée of her latest client turns up dead, it's up to her to sort through the untidy list of suspects and identify the real killer.

Maggie McDonald is hoping to raise the profile of her new Orchard View organizing business via her first high-profile client. Professor Lincoln Sinclair may be up for a Nobel Prize, but he's hopeless when it comes to organizing anything other than his thoughts. For an academic, he's also amassed more than his share of enemies. When Sinclair's fiancée is found dead on the floor of his home laboratory—electrocuted in a puddle of water—Maggie takes on the added task of finding the woman's murderer. To do so, she'll have to outmaneuver the suspicious, obnoxious police investigator she's nicknamed "Detective Awful" before a shadowy figure can check off the first item on their personal to-do list—Kill Maggie McDonald.

Dead Storage

As a professional organizer, Maggie McDonald brings order to messy situations. But when a good friend becomes a murder suspect, surviving the chaos is one tall task . . .

Despite a looming deadline, Maggie thinks she has what it takes to help friends Jason and Stephen unclutter their large Victorian in time for its scheduled renovation. But before she can fill a single bin with unused junk, Jason leaves for Texas on an emergency business trip, Stephen's injured mastiff limps home—and Stephen himself lands in jail for murder. Someone killed the owner of a local Chinese restaurant and stuffed him in the freezer. Stephen, caught at the crime scene covered in blood, is the number one suspect. Now Maggie must devise a strategy to sort through secrets and set him free—before she's tossed into permanent storage next . . .